"I'm not trying to save you."

"No? Then what are you doing?"

He met her steady gaze. "Trying to make you mine and me yours."

She stared at him for a long moment before her eyes softened. "Trent, please try to understand. I can't spend every day wondering if today is the day I lose you. I have no one who needs anything from me. I'm free to do and go where I want, and that's exactly what I should be doing. My pictures could be a hit in the city. I could make more money than I've ever dreamed of."

"And you think money will make you happy. It never made anyone happy. You know that."

She put down her menu and looked past him toward the bar, her expression unreadable.

He studied her beautiful profile. "I'd never hurt you, Izzy. I know you don't need me protecting you or caring for you, but Robbie..."

"Would've wanted you to." She met his gaze, tears glinting in her eyes. "And maybe part of me wants that, too, but I'm scared, Trent. Really, really scared."

Dear Reader,

So happy to welcome you back to Templeton Cove! *Saved by the Firefighter* is book six in the series, but all the stories can be read as stand-alone books. I've always wanted to write a story with a firefighting hero, but the right tale didn't come along until now. Trent Palmer and the heroine in the story, Izzy Cooper, are two new characters to the Cove, and they were a joy to write.

After Izzy loses her brother in an explosion at the local garage, she blames Trent for not coming to his rescue soon enough. Even though her brother was already dead on the fire crew's arrival, Izzy needs to blame someone, and in Trent, her friend and past lover, she has a safe place to direct her anger and grief.

As willing as Trent is to shoulder the blame if that's what Izzy needs from him, he isn't so happy to sit by and watch the woman he loves morph into someone he hardly recognizes. As he coaxes Izzy back into life and toward the people who care and love her, the trust begins to build...but the obstacles keeping them apart escalate.

Their story is one of overcoming grief and learning to love and live again. I hope you enjoy meeting these two wonderful people in my favorite seaside town, Templeton Cove.

Happy reading,

Rachel

Twitter: @RachelBrimble
Facebook: Rachel Brimble

RACHEL BRIMBLE

Saved by the Firefighter

Recycling programs
for this product may
not exist in your area.

ISBN-13: 978-0-373-61011-2

Saved by the Firefighter

This edition published by arrangement with Harlequin Books S.A.

For questions and comments about the quality of this book, please contact us at CustomerService@Harlequin.com.

Printed in U.S.A.

Rachel Brimble lives with her husband, two teenage daughters and chocolate Labrador in a small town near the famous city of Bath, England. She writes mainstream romance and romantic suspense for Harlequin Superromance and Victorian romance for Kensington.

Agented both in the US and the UK, Rachel is currently working on book seven of the Templeton Cove Stories as well as the first in what she hopes will be an ongoing Edwardian saga.

When she isn't writing, you'll find Rachel reading, knitting or walking the beautiful English countryside.

Links:

www.RachelBrimble.com
Twitter: @RachelBrimble
Facebook: Rachel Brimble

Books by Rachel Brimble

HARLEQUIN SUPERROMANCE

Templeton Cove Stories

Her Hometown Redemption
Christmas at the Cove
What Belongs to Her
A Man Like Him
Finding Justice

Other titles by this author available in ebook format.

For Mum & Dad—who are so supportive of my dreams. Thank you for making me feel as though every book I write is something huge to celebrate. I'm proud to be yours!

CHAPTER ONE

Three months earlier

IZZY SLOWLY OPENED her eyes and languidly stretched, inhaling the scent of sandalwood and man. Turning her head, she stared at Trent's dark brown, sleep-ruffled hair as he dozed peacefully beside her. She smiled and waited for the regret to set in…but instead only happiness flowed through her.

She'd done it.

She'd finally invited Templeton Cove's hunkiest firefighter into her bed.

After months of self-protection, weeks of carefully executed sanity, she'd let down her defenses and given in to the man any sane woman on the planet would want to wake up next to. Would this morning bring a new beginning…or would they slip back into their casual friendship once more?

Her smile dissolved. A friend with benefits was most definitely not on her agenda. Her morals and need for order put paid to that sort of nonsensical relationship.

She couldn't guarantee Trent would feel the same way.

He was a firefighter. A man who thrived on the thrill of risking his life every day; a man who needed to save people. Templeton considered Trent a hero. Someone who lived and breathed his job. One part of a team relied upon by the Cove's residents to keep them as safe as much as they relied on their police force to do the same.

Izzy turned her gaze to the ceiling. Her life was the antithesis of Trent's. She was methodical. Careful. About everything. Trent lived his life as though every moment was his last.

He shifted and murmured something intelligible. Izzy glanced at him just as his eyes flickered open. His bright green gaze met hers and he smiled sleepily. "Hey."

Izzy forced a smile, her stomach tightening just at the sexy sight of him. "Hey."

He reached his hand across her naked abdomen and tugged her closer, brushing a kiss over her ear, inching lower to kiss her jaw. He inhaled. "How come you still smell like flowers first thing in the morning?"

She grinned. "I didn't realize I smelled like flowers any time."

"You do. Always."

As he moved his hand higher to gently stroke the underside of her breast, her body heated, and all thoughts of making it clear to him that their relationship couldn't be a casual thing faltered.

The frenzied, almost illicit surrender of just a few hours before was replaced with gentleness. A slow, exquisite exploration of each other's bodies. Izzy stared into his eyes, secretly hoping he saw her and no one else. That she was special to him.

Her reward was better than she could have imagined or hoped for. His usually intense, concentrated gaze was soft, trusting and full of only her. She had no choice but to respond, her body turning pliant under his gentle caresses as her heart inched closer to love than like. Surrendering, she moved her hands over his back, higher to his shoulders until her fingers were in his hair and their kisses intensified.

She made love to Trent with every part of her. Held him. Touched him. Loved him because whatever happened next between them… her eyes smarted with tears, it felt so right to be with him. Always.

IZZY BLINKED AND the memory vanished.

She took a deep breath and clutched her

newest portfolio of photographs to her chest as she walked from the developing lab at the back of her photography studio into the front open-plan office. Spreading out the shots on the surface of her huge workstation, she battled the unjust resentment she felt toward the family who'd paid for them. Mother, father, toddler son and his baby sister all smiled at the camera, their eyes shining with love and happiness. She squeezed her eyes shut, anger and frustration making her tremble.

Nine weeks had passed since Robbie was killed in an explosion at the garage, but the pain still resided in her heart as mercilessly as it had the day it happened. She was nothing but a shell, inside and out.

She had no brother and two parents who spent months at a time traveling the Mediterranean as they worked as singers on a cruise ship. And now she was entirely alone. Maybe she should have tried harder to reconcile with her parents, apologized for pushing them away. They had tried so hard to comfort and be there for her, but there was nothing Izzy wanted other than her brother. She swallowed. And now separation from her mum and dad had eased a little of the fear of loving them too deeply.

Opening her eyes, she snatched up the photographs and reached beneath the workstation for an envelope. She slid the shots inside, her hands trembling. Kate, her best friend, continued to accuse Izzy of changing beyond recognition. She'd even suggested counseling. Izzy swallowed against the lump of humiliation as it rose in her throat.

Doesn't Kate know how strong I am? That I'll deal with my grief any way I see fit, and right now that is work, work and more work.

The security alarm chimed. Someone had stepped inside the studio. Exhaling a heavy breath, Izzy pulled back her shoulders, lifted her head and forced a smile.

"Hi, how can I..." Her heart stopped. Trent Palmer stood just inside the door. "Why are you here?"

His dark green gaze bored relentlessly into hers, his strong jaw set as he reached behind him and shut the door. "I came by to see how you're doing."

Traitorous attraction skittered over the surface of her skin before Izzy turned and strode toward the corner she used for staging portrait shots. The fluffy bunnies, huge furry dice and toys she'd used to relax a toddler earlier now felt macabre.

She spun around, clutching a teddy bear. "The same as I was doing yesterday and the day before. I told you I don't want to see you.

I don't *ever* want to see you. Why do you keep coming back?"

He came closer, his gaze locked on hers. "You have to talk to me. I was Robbie's friend. There was nothing—"

"You could do. Fine. I get it, but why do you feel the need to keep coming in here and checking up on me? What do you want me to do? Dance in the street? Kick up my heels at the fairground? God, just leave me alone."

"There's a beach party tonight. I want you to come with me."

She stared. Why him? Why would a man she really liked—a damn firefighter—have to pursue her like she was someone worth pursuing? "No."

He looked at the equipment covering the desk alongside him. He lifted and replaced a camera, the hunch of his wide shoulders indicating his discomfort. Izzy hated that she drew no satisfaction from that...only sadness.

He turned. "I want you to come and show your face to the people who care about you. Kate said—"

"Kate had no right to say anything to you." She lifted her chin. "I'm fine."

"Then come to the beach."

"No."

He crossed his arms. "Why not? What good

is it doing you, hiding away in here twenty-four-seven?"

"I'm not hiding." *Liar.* "My work is better than it's ever been. I have lots to keep me busy, and I don't need you or a damn beach party to make me feel better."

"This isn't who you are, Iz. You've always worked, always been ambitious, but everyone is used to you taking pictures while you play as well as work. Where have you gone? Don't you think Robbie would've wanted you to step out into the sunlight now and then?"

The sound of her brother's name on Trent's lips brought the sting of tears to her eyes. "Don't talk to me about Robbie. He would want me to do whatever I wanted, and right now the last thing I want to do is talk to you." She turned her back to him and tossed the bear into a plastic crate of other props. She sighed. "Please, Trent. Just get out of here."

"You know as well as I do that Robbie wanted us together. He actively encouraged it."

"Yeah, he did and look how that turned out."

His jaw tightened. "Are you saying it was no good? That we were no good? God, Iz, Robbie would've loved knowing we finally got together."

Loss wrapped around her heart, making it ache. "Maybe, but he would've also seen we were a bad idea together too."

Hurt flashed in his eyes, before he exhaled heavily. "Look, you might not want to talk to me, but there's someone else we have to think about."

She planted her hands on her hips, her body humming with irritation and the urge to grip him by his stupidly large biceps and march him out of her studio. Didn't he realize he was invading her only place of peace? "Who?"

"Maya Jackson. We have to do this calendar, Iz. We promised. If we don't set up the shoot soon, it won't be ready for Christmas. That little girl, her family and Kate are relying on you...us...to do this."

She tipped her head back and glared at the ceiling. There was no way she'd let down Maya, suffering so acutely with leukemia, any more than she would continue a relationship with the firefighter who'd failed to respond quick enough to save her brother. No matter how the results of the ensuing investigation had confirmed that it was a falling beam that killed Robbie at the garage, she had to blame someone or she'd go insane.

The safest person to blame was strong, reliable Trent. A man she'd grown to deeply care for and admire during the four years before Robbie died. A man who knew her and her brother. Knew her home and her life…and who still wanted to know her.

He didn't deserve her derision; he didn't deserve everything she threw at him, yet time and again he became her target. She had to keep his interest at bay. Better still—stop it altogether.

She dropped her chin. "Fine. I'll call Kate and set up a meeting. I don't see how that has any bearing on my going to a beach party. I'll call you when you need to be involved with the calendar, okay?"

"No, it's not okay. I wanted you before the explosion and I want you now. Why are you shutting me out like this? What good is it doing you?"

"For your information, I'm doing just fine. Just forget about us. We aren't right for each other."

"Why? Because I'm a firefighter?"

The disbelief in his tone hitched her stretched nerves tighter. "You're too different. I've told you this before. I want more than you'll ever be able to give me."

"Like what?" His gaze burned with frustration. "You don't want a man who can care for you, look after you and treat you how you deserve?"

She closed her eyes. She wanted all of those

things. So much. "You really don't understand what I'm saying, do you?"

"No."

"Because it's you, Trent." Izzy opened her eyes, her heart aching. "Before Robbie died, I was reluctant to date you because half the female population wants to sleep with you. Now that Robbie's gone, I would never, *ever* go out with a firefighter. Whether he was you or not."

The silence stretched. Izzy fought not to squirm under his appraisal, fought not to reach forward for one blessed kiss from a man any woman would be a fool not to want. *Well, better a fool than a grieving girlfriend.*

His eyes darkened with determination. "I'm not giving up on you, Iz. You can fight me as much as you want. I won't give up. If we're nothing else, I hope we're still friends."

"For God's sake, what is it you want from me?" Her eyes filled with tears. "I didn't ask you to look after me. Why do you feel you have the right to keep hassling me?"

"Hassling you? I'm not hassling you, I'm caring about you. You accused me of hassling you before Robbie died… Nothing's changed."

"Nothing's… How dare you? Everything's changed." Her cheeks burned hot as her traitorous tears slipped to her cheeks. She swiped at them with trembling fingers. "*Everything.*

If you can't see that, then I have less to say to you than I thought."

He briefly closed his eyes. "I didn't mean that the way it came out."

"No? Then if you can't think before you speak, why would I want to spend time with someone that insensitive?"

"Iz, please. Just come to the beach party tonight and I promise if you don't have a good time, or at least relax awhile, I won't bother you again." He raised his hands in surrender. "I'll respect whatever it is you're doing on your own and leave you be."

"On my own. Something you, Kate and every other person with a family alive and well will never understand." As soon as the words were out of her mouth, she regretted them. She'd revealed every ounce of her vulnerability. She crossed her arms and dragged her gaze from the humiliating sympathy in his expression to look toward the window behind him. "Is Kate going? Is this invite some way to get her and me talking again?" She looked at him. "I just told you I'll call her and get things in motion with the calendar."

"I don't know if she'll be there or not." He stepped toward her and then stopped as though he changed his mind. He shoved his hand into his dark hair and held it there. "Doesn't the fact that you two aren't talking show you something is seriously wrong? You need people around you who care. Work doesn't do what a hug can."

She frowned. "A hug? You think a hug is all it will take to get rid of this pain?"

"No, but it will go a damn sight further than making another bundle of money will. Just take a break."

Izzy glared. She'd made more money in the last few weeks than she ever thought possible. Her phone was ringing nonstop with assignments. It seemed the photography world, and collectors, relished pictures leaning more toward the dark than the dazzling. It was true the money had done nothing to alleviate her grief, but the work provided her with something to stop her thinking about her dead brother.

He cleared his throat. "You need something to take your mind off Robbie."

She blinked. "I have that."

"Let me guess…work."

Asshole.

Their gazes locked until Izzy weakened under the weight of his glare. She spun away from him and headed to her desk. "Fine. I'll come to the party." She met his relieved gaze and ignored the way her heart lifted to see that her agreement had banished his rare and unwelcome anger. "I'll go to the beach and I'll eat, drink and be merry if you think that will fix this, but believe me, nothing will scratch the surface of what I'm feeling. Nothing. You've got what you come here for, so just go."

He strolled toward her and came around the desk, standing so close she was forced to tip her head back to meet his eyes. Her heart picked up speed as she resisted the urge to inhale the musky, male scent of him. "What?"

He leaned down and brushed his lips over her cheek. "I'll see you later."

Her body paralyzed, yet her heart beat out of control as he turned and walked toward the door.

Only when the studio door swung shut behind him did Izzy drop into her chair and finally cry. She wanted to hit him. Hurt him. Inflict some of her physical pain onto Trent's wide incapable shoulders and see what the hell he would do about it.

Tears rolled down her cheeks like water releasing from a dam, yet all she could think of was how it would feel to have Trent hold her. Now. At this moment when the pain came and hurt so damn much.

CHAPTER TWO

TRENT TIPPED HIS beer bottle to his lips and icy-cold lager slipped down his parched throat. Dance music thumped from the speakers and a hundred or so semiclad people yelled, screamed and danced on the sand. What had he been thinking asking Izzy here? This was the very last place she should be. Why hadn't he insisted on cooking for her at his place? A glass of wine, some of that classical music she liked…

"You're an idiot," he murmured. "A class-A idiot."

"I couldn't agree more, but since I'm here, you can start by getting the first of many glasses of wine I intend to have tonight."

Relief swept through him and Trent smiled. Izzy. She came. He slowly turned and the smart comeback he had in mind froze on his tongue. Holy crap. She'd twisted her long blond hair to the side in some sort of fancy plait, the tip brushing her right breast. Her eyelids softly shimmered, the lashes thick and dark, making her blue eyes bigger than ever.

Trent blinked. "You look…you look…"

"Underweight according to Kate. I know." She lifted her shoulders. "Losing a brother can do that to a girl. How about that wine?"

He swallowed against the dryness in his throat and he was relieved when he opened his mouth and words actually emerged. "I admit, I'd be more than happy to see some more meat on your bones, but I was actually going to say you look amazing."

Their gazes locked for a second before she looked to the beach behind him. "Thanks."

He took her hand and pride washed through him when she didn't pull away as he'd expected. "Let's get you that drink."

People stared as they passed on their way to the makeshift bar and Trent stiffened his shoulders. As much as he'd loved living in Templeton Cove these past four years, there were still times when a guy couldn't be blamed for wanting the anonymity of a city.

He tightened his grip on Izzy's hand. When her fingers clenched his in response, it was all too clear she felt the heat of the town's curiosity too. He stopped. "Do you want to get out of here?"

Her eyes darkened with determination. "And why would I want to do that?"

"Come on, Iz. You know why. If I had known people were going to—"

"Stare? Pity me? Then that's too bad, because I've thought of little else since you stormed into my studio and gave me no choice but to come tonight." She eased her hand from his and lifted it in a nonchalant wave. "Well, I did as the big alpha male commanded and I'm here. I want to dance and get drunk. Now, you either stay and look after me, or I'll find someone else equally as capable."

She brushed past him and he stepped back, his gaze falling to her perfect ass in a short black skirt. Hope rose inside him and he smiled. Whether Izzy realized it or not, she was already showing signs of her old self. Long may it continue. He was more than happy to deal with whatever she had in mind to throw at him—he was strong enough, liked her enough to take her punches. He was a patient man and would wait for her to come to the conclusion that they were great together, just as he'd thought she had done three months before.

He sidled up to her at the bar, where the barman filled a large glass with white wine. The guy's gaze slid back and forth between the V of Izzy's shirt and the glass he filled. Trent cleared his throat. "And a bottle of beer when you're ready, my friend."

The barman lifted his gaze. "Be right with you."

Trent narrowed his eyes as the guy moved to the fridges behind him.

"What's your problem, Firefighter Trent?" Izzy laughed. "You think he's edging in on your territory or something?"

Rare heat hit Trent's face. Worse, it matched the heat of the protectiveness roaring behind his rib cage. "'Course not, but you being hit on wasn't part of the deal tonight."

"Part of the deal?" Izzy grinned and sipped her wine. "The deal tonight will be whatever I choose it to be."

He tossed a glare at the barman. "Is that so?"

Her fingers touched his chin, turning his face to hers. The spot where her fingers lingered simmered with a frisson of electricity. He met her gaze and fought the urge to kiss her. "What?"

"Once you have your drink, we're going to dance."

Trent shook his head, his gaze hovering on her mouth. "I don't dance."

"You do tonight." She picked up her glass and left the bar.

She walked across the small breadth of

decking and down the sand-covered steps onto the beach. Why couldn't it be any other girl in the entire world who haunted his dreams and made him want to fix her life in every way? Why Robbie's sister? Why the woman who blamed him for an unthinkable tragedy, detested him and would undoubtedly rip his heart from his chest once she found the worst possible way to do it?

He clenched his jaw. Deep inside, he sensed Izzy would be incapable of cruelty no matter how much she might want to humiliate him. Her kindness and false sense of bravado were the things that struck at his very core since he first laid eyes on her. From the moment she'd walked into the Coast bar to join her brother for a late-night drink, Trent had wanted to know who she was. The discovery that Izzy was the sister of the first guy he'd befriended in Templeton had been an obstacle he was determined to overcome.

It had taken him almost four years to have the honor of kissing and touching such a beautiful and wonderful woman. Then Robbie was killed and Trent hadn't for one moment considered the strength of Izzy's resistance to having anything more to do with him.

"That's six pounds, twenty, mate."

The barman's voice sliced through Trent's

reverie and he turned, sliding his hand into his back pocket for his wallet. Saying nothing, his eyes still on the barman's. The guy had clearly decided Izzy was a free agent from the way his cool stare met Trent's.

Trent slid a ten-pound note from his wallet and held it out. "Keep the change."

The barman nodded, his face somber as he reached for the money. "I'll put it in the charity box."

"You do that, and for the record, that girl I'm with, she's out of bounds."

The barman smiled. "I didn't get the impression she considers herself yours, mate."

"One, I'm not your mate and, two, she's had a rough time of it lately and doesn't need guys hitting on her left, right and center."

The barman took the note from Trent's fingers and raised his eyebrows. "Fair enough. Might be a good idea if you took your own advice, if that's the case."

He walked away and Trent glared at the barman's retreating back as he picked up his beer. He took a hefty slug and turned to the beach, his gaze immediately picking out Izzy as she stood alone, jigging lightly to an R&B track, her almost-empty glass swaying back and forth in her hand.

He headed in her direction. Even if he could

never get her to accept that Robbie had died before the fire service's arrival on the scene, he would do anything to make her genuinely smile again. He'd make that happen, even if he was eventually forced to admit defeat and surrender her to another man. If someone else—apart from the cocky barman—could hold her in his arms and make her smile, it would be enough for him to let her go.

Yeah, you keep telling yourself that.

He moved beside her and she turned, her eyebrows raised. "Finished your face-off with the bar staff?"

He took another drink. "Yep."

"Good." She reached up, took the bottle from his hand and placed it beside her glass on an upturned crate beside her. She took his hand. "Now we dance."

"I told you I don't dance."

He tugged her back and she stopped short. "What?"

His gaze drew like a tracker beam to her sweet, kissable mouth. "You'll regret making me do this."

She shrugged. "Maybe I will, maybe I won't."

IZZY REGRETTED HER decision to dance with him the instant Trent's hands touched her waist.

Boom! The sexual tension took off like a damn rocket.

What was wrong with her? For months and months, even before Robbie died, she'd avoided having anything less than two feet of space between her and Trent in the name of self-preservation. She'd watched enough women embarrass themselves by salivating after her brother's best friend to know there was something about Trent that was potent and dangerous.

Then she'd gone and slept with him.

What had she thought would happen after such an amazing night? That one or both of them would walk away, be unaffected by those hours? The truth was, three amazing weeks had followed...and then Robbie was killed and ever since, everything between her and Trent had been different. Irrevocably different.

She would never again open herself up to the risk of falling in love only to have the guy die or walk away.

Yet she'd given in to the childish need to call Trent out, to bluff his advances and now she was suffering the consequences of his magnetism all over again. Once Trent had his entire focus on a woman and she was close enough to smell his scent, she was caught.

Then to have him put his hands on her?

Izzy swallowed her groan as it threatened to erupt, slapped on a smile and raised an eyebrow in an attempt to impersonate a femme fatale who could nonchalantly separate the men from the boys whenever she chose. "Are we going to move? Or just stand here with you looking at me like that?"

He smiled. "Like what?"

"Like you're going to…" Her shaky facade faltered. "Bite me."

He laughed…and goddamn it if she didn't smile. *Really* smile. He met her gaze again and winked. He pulled her closer and, against her better judgment, Izzy didn't move away.

The music slowed and a soul ballad pumped seductively from the speakers like a cruelly planned serenade. He nodded. "Now, this kind of dance I can do. We just need to get real close and shuffle. You can shuffle, right?"

Every inch of her body screamed with suppressed sexual attraction. Her heart beat fast as she fought the heat tingling through her breasts and lower. The man was a walking, talking love machine.

She forced her gaze to stay on his. "Of course I can."

"Good."

He lifted one of her hands to his chest and, with a single tug on the other, eased her close enough a grain of sand couldn't have lodged between them. His heart beat under her palm, as hers pulsed in her ears. The soft teasing in his eyes slowly dissolved until he looked at her with such focused attention her legs grew feeble. Her feet shifted upon the sand of their own accord. He was so tall, broad and wide at this close proximity, she felt fragile in his arms. She looked into his eyes and her stomach flipped over as if she were a fifteen-year-old girl instead of a twenty-nine-year-old woman. Heat burned. Attraction soared. At last, for just a few moments, everything felt right in the world.

She froze.

Everything wasn't right in the world. Despite the slowly gathering peace between her and her parents, they were still thousands of miles away. Robbie was still dead, and the man who held her so close his breath whispered across her lashes had arrived too late at the garage to save her brother's life.

She stepped back and Trent gripped her hand, keeping it pressed to his chest as the determination she knew so well seeped into his gaze.

Izzy closed her eyes as claustrophobia grew. "I need to go."

"Don't do this, Iz."

She opened her eyes.

His gaze held quiet pleading mixed with challenge. “You’re okay. I’ve got you.”

Fear gripped her heart and squeezed. She couldn’t lean on him. She couldn’t lean on anyone without the risk of furthering the pain of loss she continued to battle every single day. She squirmed out of his grasp and he released her. “You’ve got me? God, Trent, have you forgotten Robbie was your best friend? That he’s dead?” She cursed and looked around, before stepping back. “I have to get of here. I want to leave. Right now.”

She whipped off her shoes and ran across the sand toward the steps that led to home and safety. Memories crashed into her mind and coated her throat with the bitter taste of fear.

The explosion that killed her brother had been so loud, so sudden, the first thing that went through Izzy’s mind had been that someone had thrown a petrol bomb through her studio window. She’d gripped her best friend’s arm as they simultaneously dropped to the floor. The floor tiles had vibrated through Izzy’s palms as the echoes of people’s screams filtered through the open studio window.

She’d looked at Kate, her heart racing. “What the hell was that?”

Kate’s eyes had been wide as she visibly

shook. "I don't know, but whatever it was, people are going to need our help." She'd leaped to her feet. "Come on. We have to go out there."

They'd sprinted from the darkroom and into the studio, running toward the picture window at the front.

Bright orange flames had rolled from the entrance of the garage where Izzy's brother worked, blurring Izzy's vision. Thick black smoke spiraled on a plume through the doors, diving and leaping on the summer breeze.

"Robbie..." Izzy had reached blindly for Kate's hand, arm, anything. "Robbie!"

CHAPTER THREE

TRENT CURSED AND took off after Izzy as she bolted onto the promenade.

The idea had been to get her to the party and then concentrate on whatever she needed. He wanted her to relax, smile, have a drink and realize the whole world wasn't a threat to her existence. Hadn't his entire mission tonight been about making her trust him enough to feel safe? That maybe one day she might see him as a man rather than a monster?

He was sick and tired of trying to get her out of his mind by dating other women. Life was too short not to listen to his heart and act on feelings that refused to abate. He clenched his jaw. He'd seen too much death in his career, but it had been Robbie's that made him determined to act on his feelings for Izzy. He wanted her…and deep in his heart, he sensed she wanted him too.

Something had always held her back from him. Something he wanted to hear her explain. Her new reason for not giving them a chance was Robbie's death. If she wasn't attracted to him, didn't like him...regretted the three fantastic weeks they'd spent together...then she only ever had to say that and he'd leave her alone.

She hadn't, and every time she looked at him, her eyes said the exact opposite was going on. She was attracted to him, liked him...but still held herself out of reach.

She'd only gotten as far as the small circle of shops situated on a paved area above the beach. Trent slowed to a walk. She sat on a wrought-iron bench, hunched over with her face in her hands.

He sat beside her and leaned his forearms on his thighs. "Tonight was a bad idea. Sorry."

Slowly, she lowered her hands and turned to face him. The silver tracks of her tears shone beneath the streetlight beside her. "I don't want to go on like this."

It was painful to see her blue eyes so full of anguish, confusion and pain. He tilted his head toward her hand. "May I?"

She nodded. Releasing his held breath, Trent lifted her hand and put it on his thigh, holding it tightly. Despite the warmth of the night, her fingers were like ice. He rubbed them against his jeans to warm her. "I miss him too, Iz. There was nothing I, or any of us, could've done. If for one minute I could've saved him, don't you think I would have?"

"That doesn't make it any easier for me to be around you."

"But it isn't just me, is it?" He kept his voice soft, not wanting to sound accusatory because he wasn't. It was up to Izzy how she dealt with the grief emanating from her, but that didn't make it any easier for him to stand by and let her push him and her friends away. "I'm not trying to tell you what to do, Iz, but if you won't give me a chance to be there for you, can't you at least let Kate back in?"

She slipped her hand from his and stared ahead. "I just need some time, that's all."

"It's been three months. We're just trying to be there for you."

"How much time I need is anyone's guess, but I'm not ready to sit around chatting and laughing as though Robbie's still here."

"No one's asking you—"

"Trent. Please. Just let me do things my way."

Frustration and helplessness rolled through him. "Why can't you give us another chance?"

"It's too complicated."

"Complicated? I've never found anything less complicated."

Her gaze darkened. "Maybe not the first

time around, but it would be different this time. If you don't understand that—"

"I don't, so you need to explain it to me." He hated pushing her, but she needed to say the words clearly before he could accept what was in her heart and mind.

She exhaled a slow breath. "When my parents left…or when I demanded them to…" She shook her head. "They tried so hard to reach me, Trent. Tried to help me through my grief, but in the end none of us were strong enough for the other. Mum and Dad resumed their careers and I was alone. I just don't trust… Not anymore."

"You don't trust that I won't leave you alone too one day?"

Her gaze bored into his until she looked away into the distance. "Maybe. Those few weeks we were together weren't enough to make me believe you'll always be around. I have no one left. I'm not in the right mind to give myself to anyone at the moment, let alone a firefighter. You run into danger every day." She faced him, her eyes filled with determination. "I can't deal with that. I don't *want* to deal with it."

"But what about before Robbie died?"

"There is no *before* Robbie. All I have in

my head is *since* Robbie. How can you not see that?"

He exhaled, lowered his voice in an effort to soften the battle going on inside him. "We were great together. Or did I imagine that? Were you not there with me?"

Her gaze ran over his face, lingered a moment at his mouth before she met his eyes. "I was there. All the way there. That was part of the problem. You're a great guy and I know if things don't work out…or if you get hurt working…" She shook her head. "Right now I'm way too needy for someone like you."

"Needy? You? Iz, you've proven over and over how much you stand on your own two feet. Being with someone doesn't make you needy, it means you're living. Taking risks."

Her eyes shadowed with sadness before she looked away once more. "That's just it. I don't like risks and never will. You're completely the wrong guy for me. You're too…"

Trent tensed as the minuscule shred of hope he had left of being with her snapped and pinged across the pavement in front of them. "Too what?"

She turned and her eyes shone with unshed tears. "Too something. I need to be able to blame you. To blame *someone* for what happened. If I don't, if I accept that Robbie's death was nobody's fault, then all I'm left with is this irrational anger. What if I can only feel anger all the time? Why would you even want to be around someone like that?"

He stared into her eyes, desperate to gently ease her head to his shoulder and let her cry until she had no more tears, but she'd never allow that to happen. She was too independent. Too strong.

"It will get easier." Trent swallowed as memories he kept deeply hidden resurfaced. "You won't believe me right now, but it will."

"Don't say that. I'm sick of people telling me that. How can you, someone who has seen people die, burned and scarred, say this will pass?" She pushed to her feet and looked around as though seeking escape. "I'm going home. Thanks for tonight. At least I got out of the apartment for a while and now know working all the time is exactly what I need to do."

She turned away and Trent let her take a few steps before he released his held breath. "My sister died in a fire when she was twelve. That was the day I knew exactly what I wanted to do for the rest of my life."

She came to an abrupt halt but didn't turn around.

He stared at her turned back and stood. "It's your choice what happens now, Iz. You have some decisions to make, but think very carefully if you still want me and everyone else to stay away. The one thing I can guarantee is that your loss won't get easier if you try to deal with it alone."

Slowly, she faced him. The music from the beach boomed, the screaming and laughter mocking and twisting his heart. He wanted to turn around and tell them to shut up. To stride across the space separating him from Izzy so he could take her in his arms and be the one to get her through her pain.

Her chest rose as she took in a breath. "What?"

"My sister. She died in a fire too."

"I never knew…"

"Because I never told you, Robbie or anyone else in the Cove. I'm telling you now because I know what it's like, Iz. I've felt every single thing you're feeling and I hate that you won't let me be with you."

She stared for a long moment…and then she ran to him.

Trent scooped her into his arms and covered her mouth with his. He kissed her with everything he had. Her lips were soft, her tongue eager and commanding. He held her close and relished the fullness of her breasts pressed against his chest. Her hands moved over his shoulders to the nape of his neck. She clung to him, and for one blessed minute Trent allowed himself to believe someday Izzy Cooper might come to want him as he wanted her.

"Take me home." She stared into his eyes, her body trembling.

"What?"

"Take me home. Make love to me."

His heartbeat quickened and every muscle in his body tensed with desire and need. "This can't be a temporary thing. You have to want me for the long haul."

"Trent, come on. I'm asking you to—"

"I mean it. I care about you too much to—"

"You're rejecting me?" Her cheeks darkened.

"I'm not rejecting—"

"No? Then what was all the times you came to the studio with flowers, food and God knows what else about if it wasn't about getting me back into bed?"

Was she serious? "You think that was about sex?"

"Isn't it always? Goddamn it, Trent. What's the matter with you? Put me down."

As though she were a china doll, he gently eased her to the ground, fighting the need to shake her. "What's the matter with *me*? Jesus Christ, Iz."

"What? You think I've got this all wrong?

We're talking about the great Trent Palmer, aren't we? The brave, handsome firefighter who struts around town with his dark, glossy hair, green eyes and sexy, toe-curling smile. What else am I supposed to think other than you want to have sex with me again? For God's sake, don't treat me like a moron."

He would've have been flattered by her summary of him if her voice hadn't cracked on every syllable. "Iz…"

He reached for her and she held up her hand. "Don't you touch me." She pushed the hair back from her face and snatched up her purse that had somehow landed on the asphalt. "At least we both know where we stand. I just offered you sex and you refused. Now I want you to stop coming around to my apartment, the studio and every other damn place and leave me alone."

He crossed his arms. "I want us to go back to the beginning."

She huffed a laugh and widened her eyes. "And where is that? Once I dated you, things took off between us at eighty miles an hour. Feelings make things complicated. Sex is good. Sex is hot and needy. Wham, bam and out of the apartment with no one getting hurt. But an actual relationship? No way, no how." She closed her eyes. "Go and find one of the other girls hanging off your every word to date, because I'm not one of them."

He clenched his jaw, his previous arousal quashed by his skyrocketing irritation. "I just told you something personal about me for a reason. I don't want people knowing about my sister or my family's loss. I told you because I want you to know I can listen. I understand. If this was all about sex, we would've gotten past that years ago."

She opened her eyes and they flickered with hurt even as she lifted her chin. "If you think what happened to your sister hasn't affected me, you shouldn't even be able to look at me, let alone be with me. Don't you understand I'm saying no for your good as well as mine?" Her eyes flooded with tears. "If anything happened to you…if I can't handle the intimacy between us and end up hurting you…" She raised her hands and shook her head. "This isn't happening. I'm sorry about your sister. I really am, but—"

"When I target you for sex, you'll know it, but right now I want you to have a meal with me, laugh and spend some time."

Trent could've sworn he saw a flash of longing in her eyes before she blinked and it was gone. "You really don't get it, do you? Every day…" She slumped her shoulders and looked deep into his eyes, her gaze soft and spent. "Every day you go into situations that have the potential to kill you." She looked to the ground. "Maybe, deep inside, I know it wasn't your fault Robbie died, but how can you expect me to separate my grief for Robbie from my feelings for you?" She met his eyes. "I can't do this, Trent. Not anymore. I'm sorry."

"Iz, come on. The job—"

"No. No more."

Spinning around, she stormed away.

"Goddamn it." Trent shoved his hand into his hair and held it there.

What now?

IZZY CLUTCHED THE BUNCH of lilies she held a little tighter, her heart thumping with trepidation. Guilt over how she'd treated Kate, her best friend, lay like a lead weight in her chest. Trent's words about her rebuffing people's sympathetic actions and words had kept her awake half the night.

He'd spoken the truth…about a lot of things.

All people wanted to do was help her—especially Kate. It was time Izzy made amends.

Her messed-up feelings about family, trust and forgiveness weren't Kate's…they were Izzy's, and her friend hadn't deserved Izzy's mistreatment of their love and friendship.

Taking a deep breath, she approached Kate's front door and rang the bell.

Swift footsteps sounded from the other side before the door swung open, revealing Kate with her usual wide and welcoming smile. Her curly brown hair was whipped up into a messy knot on top of her head and she wore her uniform of jeans and a shirt, currently dotted with what looked like white paint.

Kate's smile dissolved. "Wow. It's you."

Izzy grimaced and held out the flowers. "For you, with a humungous apology."

"It's a cheap shot, considering lilies are my absolute favorite flowers." Kate took the lilies with a wink, her smile reappearing. "But apology and flowers accepted. Get in here. We have some serious catching up to do."

Izzy stepped inside and grabbed Kate into a bear hug, almost crushing the flowers in the process. "I love you."

"Yeah, yeah, take a ticket and join the queue."

Izzy laughed and, arm in arm, she and Kate walked along the hallway into her bright and sunny kitchen.

Kate walked to the sink. "Grab a chair while I wash this paint off my hands and put these flowers in some water."

"What have you been up to?"

"I'm painting the utility room. Fancied sprucing it up a little."

"It's so great to see you." Izzy glanced toward the open utility room door as she slid onto a seat around the scrubbed pine table. "I've been such a nightmare. I'm sorry."

"Don't be silly. You're grieving and I wish I could do more to help." Kate filled a vase and arranged the flowers in a blur of effortless skill. She glanced over her shoulder, her gaze sympathetic. "My heart breaks for you, Iz. It really does."

"I know and I'm so sorry for pushing you away. I'm not even sure what I was trying to achieve." Izzy sighed. "Someone gave me a talking-to last night and his words cut pretty deep."

Kate frowned. "*His* words? I thought if anyone, it would've been Marian who gave you a talking-to."

"Believe it or not, it wasn't our town matriarch. And I shouldn't have rejected your support…or anyone else's for that matter. I'm slowly clawing my way back and so glad you still want me around."

"Of course I do." Kate brought the flowers to the table and positioned them in the center. "So, who was it that broke through that stubborn facade of yours if it wasn't Marian?"

Heat immediately rose in Izzy's cheeks. She slid her gaze from her friend's to the table and drew invisible circles on its surface with her finger. "None other than firefighter Trent."

"Really? Well, well, well..."

"What does that mean?" Izzy frowned and met Kate's eyes, which sparkled with an almost demonic glee. "And why are you looking at me like that?"

"It means I love the guy and so should you."

"Love Trent?" Izzy huffed a laugh, fighting the softening in her heart since she'd learned of his sister's death and accepting that he must have gone through the same heartbreaking pain as her. "The man has more than enough admirers. He certainly doesn't need any more."

"Yeah, okay, you keep telling yourself Trent isn't worth your attention. We'll see how that pans out, shall we?"

"He practically forced me to go to the beach party last night."

Kate sat and leaned forward on her elbows, her brown eyes wide with interest. "Forced you? I can't see Trent forcing anyone to do anything."

"Yeah, well, he forced me and I regret giving in. It did me no good at all."

"No? Not even considering that he got you to come here bearing flowers and an apology?"

Izzy grimaced. "Well, okay, yes, that did me good."

"Glad to hear it. So this is it? No more pushing people away? You're going to accept all the love and condolences half the town has been trying to offer you over the last three months?"

"Yes. Everyone's except Trent's."

"I don't understand why you won't give the guy another chance. You finally got together before Robbie died and I've never seen you so happy. Isn't it worth trying again? Trent likes you, Iz. He always has as far as I can tell."

"Just leave it, Kate. Please."

"Robbie's gone and the one person who's tried the hardest, over and over, to be there for you, you have basically kicked in the teeth."

"Not the one person. I've crawled back to you with my tail between my legs, haven't I?"

"Maybe, but I don't have the equipment to provide you with the happiness Trent can, do I?" Kate winked.

Izzy sniffed. "Don't bother going along that route. I offered him sex last night and he refused me. Do you know how humiliating that is? Trent could've had me and he didn't take me. Fact."

Kate's eyes widened. "You offered him sex?"

"Yes. Temporary insanity, I guess."

"You do know why he turned you down,

right? The man wants a full-on relationship with you. Do you know how different that makes him than the fifty other guys who could be there for you?" Shaking her head, Kate stood and walked to the wine rack. She selected a bottle of red and grabbed two glasses from the cupboard. "Trent Palmer turning you down is huge. I honestly believe he has a serious thing for you." She carried the wine and glasses to the table and unscrewed the bottle. "More important, I think you have a serious thing for him too."

"I do not."

"You're lying."

"Are you going to pour that wine or not?"

Kate filled the glasses and nudged one toward Izzy. "There, careful you don't choke on it."

Izzy narrowed her gaze and took a hefty gulp. "Cheers."

Kate grinned and sat, lifting her glass to her lips. "I say you call Trent right now and ask him out. He's probably beaten himself black and blue by now for not taking you up on your offer. He'll be putty in your hands."

"Trent would never be putty in anyone's hands. Anyway, he's dangerous."

"Dangerous?"

"Yes." Izzy took another sip of wine, her

stomach knotting with trepidation of her oncoming admission. “He makes me weak. He makes me want things that are stupid.”

“What things? Fun? Romance? Great sex?”

“He doesn’t want sex. Remember?”

Kate sniffed. “Of course he wants sex. *All* men want sex.”

“Not Trent.”

“Oh, come on, Iz. He wants you to want him *all* the time. He’s not doing anything different than you or I would under the same circumstances. He respects you.”

“I don’t think so.”

Kate rolled her eyes. “Before Robbie died, did you ever offer Trent a one-night stand? No. You went on a date. No sex. You went on a second date. No sex. Then a third date…” She winked. “And maybe some sex. Or was it the fourth?”

Izzy narrowed her eyes.

Kate laughed. “Whatever. All I know is Trent’s being damn smart and going straight after your heart. He’s an intelligent man.”

“That’s ridiculous.”

Kate grinned. “And true.”

Panic thundered through Izzy’s body. How long could she keep denying her true feelings for Trent? Feelings that had been there for so long she'd eventually given in and opened herself up to potential heartbreak.

Trent lived his life at such a faster pace than she did. She would never be able to keep up. What was the point in risking the loss of their friendship on top of a broken heart? She drew in a shaky breath. "Maybe Trent's refusing sex because he thinks he's a bad lay. Let's just focus on that thought and forget everything else you just said."

Kate quirked an eyebrow. "I saw you after you and him got down and dirty, remember? No woman walks around looking like you did after a bad lay."

Izzy rolled her eyes. "Can we just change the subject?"

"Fine."

"What about this calendar and Maya Jackson? How are things going with the preparations for the charity?"

"Ooh, I've got something to show you." Kate stood and rushed from the kitchen, her bare feet slapping against the hardwood flooring in the hallway. "Be just a second."

Izzy stared after her and took another fortifying sip of wine. Whenever Kate was excited, further trouble lingered on the horizon. Izzy's friend's footsteps sounded overhead before Kate came thundering downstairs and into the kitchen.

She stuck a business card in front of Izzy's face. "You need to ring this guy. He's an agent."

Izzy put down her wine and took the card. She lifted an eyebrow. "Francis Sanford. He sounds like a member of the aristocracy."

"He's Richard Crawley's agent."

Izzy frowned. "Who?"

Kate rolled her eyes. "Richard Crawley. *The* hottest game show host right now. Better than that, Templeton is his hometown. I called his office and they directed me to his agent. They want to meet you."

"Why? What do I want with a game show host? What do *you* want with a game show host?"

"Richard Crawley is good-looking, smiley and happy. I've spent the last fortnight looking for a front man or woman for the calendar. If I could get someone in the media to back our campaign…"

"All the better for Maya."

"Exactly. Richard Crawley was my breakthrough. He wants to meet you before he agrees to help out, but he's the biggest name I've managed to nail down. If we get him on the cover with Templeton's finest firefighters, it's a done deal. Maya will be on her way across the pond for her treatment." She winked. "Of course, it would be even better if you could convince him to lose his shirt midshoot."

Izzy laughed. "Right. Now I see where we're going."

"So you'll call his agent and set something up?"

"Sure." Izzy shifted forward and slid the card into the back pocket of her jeans. "Anything for Maya. You know that."

Kate released a breath. "Good. So…back to Trent. Are you going to make me completely happy and call him too?"

Izzy groaned and snatched up her wine. "It's a bad idea."

"But one you need to act on anyway."

"No, I don't."

"Yes, you do. You *have* to. You and Trent are meant to be. I know it."

Izzy frowned, the determination in her friend's eyes making her uneasy. "No one knows that, including you. I'm not calling him."

Kate dropped her shoulders. "Fine. Then will you at least start focusing on the future? Stop looking back. Robbie's gone and Lord only knows when your mum and dad will decide they're too old to be touring the world on a cruise ship. Can't you just start accepting what an amazing woman, friend and photographer you are? You have the potential to be a huge name. Please, just focus on that."

Izzy exhaled. Try as she might, she had a hard time believing anything Kate so vehemently believed of her. "I'm trying, okay?"

"Good. Then try harder."

CHAPTER FOUR

TRENT BURST THROUGH the Coast Inn doors ahead of his firefighting colleagues. He strode tall and proud through the bar, having earlier saved a family of four from a burning building. Satisfaction heated his blood, and need gathered strength for an ice-cold beer, a few games of pool and some great tunes coming from the TV rigged above the table.

Despite a shower, change of clothes and a passing hour, the lingering smell of smoke still coated the inside of his nostrils and parched his throat. He strode toward the bar and Dave, the Coast's landlord and owner, came toward him, only to be intercepted by his wife, Vanessa. "I've got the boys covered, my darling," she said. "Why don't you go and see what the family of four at table eight would like to eat?"

Trent tried and failed to hide his smile as Dave rolled his eyes behind Vanessa's back but obeyed her order anyway.

Trent met Vanessa's sparkling gaze and

laughed. "Not sure Dave appreciated you serving us rather than him."

She shrugged. "Too bad. What woman in her right mind would choose a visiting family of four over three strapping and, I must say, extremely gorgeous firefighters? I might be the wrong side of forty, but that doesn't mean a lady can't enjoy the view. Now, what can I get you?"

Sam and Will came to the bar on either side of him and Trent looked at his friends. "Beer, lads?"

They nodded.

"Then we'll have a pitcher of your finest lager, please, Vanessa."

"Coming right up. Where will I find you?"

Trent nodded toward the pool table in the far corner. "It looks like our usual spot is free so we'll be there for the duration."

"I'll bring it straight over."

Laughing at her blatant appraisal of him, Will and Sam before she busied herself at the pump, Trent turned. "Pool, gentlemen?"

Sam Paterson and Will Kent led the way toward the table. Pumped and ready for a good night with the men he relied on to have his back both in and out of work, Trent fought back as Izzy slid into his mind. Not tonight.

He would not think about her after such a successful day.

Thinking about Izzy—wanting her—only served to ruin his good mood whenever he had occasion to enjoy one. She'd made it painfully clear she would never consider dating him as long as he continued to fight fires.

The fact that she'd dismissed his motivation for becoming a firefighter cut him deeper than her refusal to see he might live for years. His sister had died. Didn't she see he understood her pain? Her anger? Her fear that things would never be the same again?

He refused to believe there wasn't a deep want inside her waiting to break free and live a little. He understood her fear and need for control. She'd found it hard to talk to anyone when Robbie died, pushing away her parents until they'd sailed away from their daughter's anger. Then it was Trent she pushed away, then Kate and so many others.

His pain over losing his kid sister, Aimee, when she'd been in his care wasn't so far away from Izzy's pain of losing Robbie. Her carefully guarded control wasn't so different than his either. He stared blindly toward the TV. Nothing was guaranteed in this world, and when you suffered losing a sibling, the lack of guarantee struck far too close to home.

He should make time this week to go home and check on his parents in Kingsley. It had been a month or so since he showed his face, and they'd be as worried about him as he was about them. His family's need to look out for one another, to be there for one another was what Trent waited for Izzy to understand. Death could bring people closer. It didn't have to separate them.

Guilt pressed down on him. Time and again, he went home when things got tough knowing his parents would be there with wise words and reassurance to bolster him.

Izzy didn't have a family in the traditional sense…but she did have people who cared for her. Deeply.

"And there he goes."

Will's voice from across the pool table snapped Trent's focus to his friends. "You talking to me?"

Will shook his head. "What's with you, man? I've been trying to get your attention for the last couple of minutes. Thought I was going to have to resort to dancing the fandango on the pool table."

"Now, there's something I don't want to see." Trent smiled. "Ever."

Vanessa broke the conversation by placing a pitcher of lager and three glasses on the low table beside Will. She wiggled her eyebrows at him. "I wouldn't mind seeing that."

Will grinned. "You do know Dave's over there giving me the evil eye right now? I'd rather keep my manhood intact, so I'll have to pass."

Vanessa threw a hasty glance over her shoulder toward the bar. "You know Dave, he wants me happy above everything else."

Trent laughed. "Sure he does, but there's happy and there's *happy*."

Vanessa smiled and tapped Trent's chin. "And Dave keeps me plenty happy as you know. Nothing wrong with ruffling his feathers now and then." Her gaze turned sober. "In fact, there would be nothing wrong if a woman gave your feathers a proper ruffle one of these days. When am I going to see you and Izzy Cooper in this bar together, huh? It's about time you patched things up and got on with that special something you two had."

Trent's good mood ebbed into obscurity. "If Izzy's got anything to do with it, that ship has sailed. Permanently."

Vanessa's gaze turned sympathetic, which was so much less appealing than her earlier flirtation. "She's scared of letting herself feel anything after Robbie died. We all know that, but you two are perfect together. I know it and so does everyone else in town. Don't give up on her, okay?"

Before he could respond, Vanessa walked away, calling out hellos to everyone in her usual bubbly and welcoming way. The crash and thump of balls being tossed onto the table turned Trent's attention. It seemed half the town sensed Izzy was meant to be with him. Yet what was he supposed to do when she kept refusing him? He liked her a lot—but there was no way he'd beg. It was time he focused on getting on with his life while saving others. Period.

He filled the three glasses with lager and joined Will and Sam at the table. Each of his friends took a drink and Trent held his aloft. "Here's to another successful day's work, boys. Long may it continue."

They raised their glasses in a toast before each taking a hefty slug of beer. Trent sighed. As long as he had an ice-cold beer and his colleagues fit, well and alive, he'd get through. He had to, because there was no way he would ever break his promise to God, or his sister, that he would fight fire for the rest of his life… however long that might be.

Will racked the balls and selected a cue from the selection hung on the wall. As he chalked the end, his gaze locked on Trent. The scrutinizing look his friend gave him alerted Trent to more unwanted advice.

He took another mouthful of his drink and licked the froth from his lip. "Something to say to me, Will?"

Will put the chalk on the table as Sam leaned down in between them and took the first shot. "I have, as a matter of fact."

The assessing, "know it all" look in Will's eyes caused Trent's irritation to unfurl and obliterate the remnants of his previous good mood. "Well, spit it out. It seems I'm the topic of conversation in here tonight."

"We didn't like the way you tackled the blaze earlier. You weren't focused on the rest of us."

"What are you talking about?" Trent snapped his glare between Will and Sam as he rose from the table. He crossed his arms over his pool cue, his defenses high. "Have you guys been talking about me or something?"

Sam nodded. "You need to get your shit together."

"I need…" Trent laughed. "I have got my shit together. Didn't I get two kids out of a second-floor window this afternoon? Did I dream that?"

"You went into that house ahead of the chief's call. You went in there without looking back to see where the rest of us were. You were on a mission, Trent. Trouble is, I'm starting to wonder if your mission has more to do with you than it does the job."

Trent tightened his fingers around his cue. "Are you serious?"

"Deadly serious."

Will stepped between Trent and Sam and placed his hands on each of their shoulders. "Look, just take it down a notch." He looked at Trent. "What we're trying to say is, you're not yourself and over the past few months, you seem to be getting worse. What's going on?"

Grief and adrenaline blended into a potent mix inside him. If his best friends didn't understand what losing Robbie…and Izzy…had done to him, then who would?

Trent shrugged Will's hand from his shoulder and laid down his cue. Lifting his glass, he drained his beer and put the glass on the table. He looked at his friends. "You really don't get it, do you? I've lost people. Not just people who mean something to me, but people who mean something to others too. It's starting to feel like a regular occurrence. I have to do more. Step up my game. Stop thinking so much and get in there and save them. What if I could've gotten to Robbie quicker if I hadn't waited for the all-clear?"

"That's bullshit and you know it." Will's cheeks darkened as his angry gaze bore into Trent's. "Robbie was dead on arrival. That falling beam killed him. It wasn't even the damn fire."

"Yeah? Well, you try explaining that to his sister. You see how well Izzy takes that summary of the situation, because I sure as hell can hardly bear to look in her eyes and see her pain."

Will swiped his hand over his face and slumped his shoulders. "Then let her go, man, and maybe you'll accept we can't save every single person from a fire. If you don't accept that, this job is going to screw you up. Sam and me aren't going to stand by and let that happen. Do you hear me?"

Trent looked from Will to Sam, his heart pumping and his mind racing. Were they right? Was his need to be there for Izzy, to care and protect her, messing with his ability to do his job properly?

The music grew louder and the walls came in closer as the smell and smile of one out-of-reach woman slammed into him. "What I feel for Izzy is no one's business. Not even yours. If I let you down, if you get hurt on my watch, if I fail in any way when I could have won, then come back at me again. In the meantime, if I have your back, if I'm saving lives, do me a favor and keep your opinions to yourself."

Trent shouldered through the dense crowd as he made his way to the bar's double doors and into the fresh evening air. He breathed deep and blinked against the stinging in his eyes as he looked to the star-spangled sky.

If Izzy was so wrong for him, then why did he want to run to her right now rather than get his ass back home where it belonged?

IZZY STEPPED FROM the cab and paid the fare through the window. She turned and stared at the front office window of Sanford & Co. Having spent the last couple of days researching Richard Crawley, she'd learned there was good money to be made in early-evening entertainment. The guy owned a Ferrari as well as a fifty-foot yacht. She doubted either had a softening effect on Crawley's inflated ego.

Clearing her throat, she tugged on the hem of her fitted white shirt and smoothed it over the hips of her black skinny jeans before pushing open the door of the agency. The pride she'd felt at finally dragging herself out of Templeton for a few hours faltered as insecurity threatened its return.

Kate might have been right that it was time for Izzy to get out of town for a while, but was

Kate right when she'd said Izzy could cope with the visit to a big-city agency? Now she was here, nerves leaped like jumping beans in her stomach.

She breathed deep against her rising panic.

She could do this. She could get Richard Crawley to front the calendar. She would do it for Maya.

Lifting her chin, her ballet flats brushing over the beige carpet tiles, she approached the young woman sitting behind the reception desk.

"Hi. Welcome to Sanford and Co. Can I help you?"

Izzy cleared her throat. "Um, yes. I have an appointment with Mr. Sanford and Richard Crawley. I'm Izzy Cooper."

"Of course. Nice to meet you. They're in Mr. Sanford's office waiting for you. Would you like tea? Coffee? Juice?"

"A coffee would be great, thank you."

"Latte? Cappuccino? Black? Cream? Mocha?"

Izzy stared. "A latte would be great. Thanks."

"Fabulous." The receptionist came around the desk and held out her hand toward a closed door at the back of the office. "They're just through here. If you'd like to follow me."

Clutching her portfolio a little tighter, Izzy felt her hand turn clammy. It was just another assignment. No big deal. She was a damn good photographer and she'd met celebrities before. No doubt Richard Crawley would be just the same as any other. All she needed to do was make him feel as though he was the most important aspect of her plans and everything would go swimmingly.

The receptionist knocked on the door and pushed it open. "Mr. Sanford, I have Izzy Cooper here for you."

"Ah, send her in. Send her in."

She turned and smiled at Izzy, easing the door wider. "Ms. Cooper."

"Thank you." Izzy stepped into the room.

Richard Crawley, and the man she assumed was Mr. Sanford, rose from their chairs in a plush seating area at the far end of the office. They came toward her and Izzy forced her feet forward as Mr. Sanford held out his hand. "Francis Sanford. Nice to meet you."

Izzy took his hand and smiled. "You too."

He shook her hand and touched the base of her spine lightly with the other, turning her toward Richard Crawley. "Let me introduce you to Mr. Richard Crawley."

She met the eyes of the TV host and ex-Templeton resident. With his dark hair and even darker eyes, square jaw and strong build, it would be hard to deny his good looks.

Izzy blushed under his friendly gaze and held out her hand, relieved it was steady. "Nice to meet you, Mr. Crawley."

"You too. I like your work. And please, call me Richard." His dark eyes sparkled as they bored into hers, his equally dark tan accentuated under the glare of sunlight through the large window beside them. "You're a phenomenal photographer. I'm delighted with this chance to work with you."

Izzy dipped her head, a little of her self-consciousness deteriorating in the face of his kindly stare and infectious smile. "Thank you."

He nodded and gestured toward a black leather sofa. "Would you like to sit down?"

Izzy eased her hand from his and walked around the low coffee table to sit in an armchair. The men asked for more coffee from the receptionist and returned to the sofa beside her.

Richard Crawley lounged back, crossing his legs so his ankle rested casually on the opposite knee. "So, from what I've heard, it's been a while since you've taken any work past the mundane bread-and-butter stuff."

Mundane bread and butter stuff? I love my work. All of it. Her smile faltered. "Excuse me?"

He looked apologetic. "I mean, it seemed

to me you were quite in demand around the Southwest until a few months ago—"

"I still am."

"Yet you haven't accepted any work that's taken you from Templeton in months."

Izzy swallowed, hating the unwelcome observation. She'd barely left the studio since Robbie died, let alone ventured out of the Cove. "Can I ask how you know that?"

He smiled. "I did a little research…as I'm sure you have too."

Busted. She coughed. "Well, I hope my being here shows that I am ready to step out again. I've had other things going on." She held his gaze, annoyance straightening her spine. "Personal things."

He stared for a moment longer before raising his hand. "I'm sorry. I didn't mean to pry. I just assumed someone with your talent would want to stretch her wings a little, that's all."

Izzy curled her hands around her portfolio in her lap. "The Cove's a great town, Mr. Crawley. I love it there."

Mr. Sanford shifted in his seat. "Shall we talk about the project?"

With an infinite amount of effort, Izzy dragged her gaze from Richard Crawley's, her spine so rigid, she concentrated on not making any sudden movements for fear of it snapping clean in half. She smiled at Mr. Sanford, ignoring Crawley's stare as it bored into her temple. "I've brought a few examples of my work along with some ideas for what I have in mind for the firefighters' calendar. These are purely suggestions, so anything either of you don't like, I'm more than happy to discuss and rethink with you. The guys at the fire station are happy for me to proceed as I see fit, so really it's a case of whatever you and—" she faced Crawley "—and you, are happy to do."

He uncrossed his legs and leaned forward, his gaze on her photo examples. "I'm convinced whatever you have in mind will be great. I'm at your command." He met her gaze. "Honestly. I've admired pretty much everything you've done from your shots of the Cove, land and seascapes, to celebrities, everything."

Izzy's shaky confidence itched for renewal under his seemingly genuine admiration. "I'm flattered. Thank you."

"I mean it. I'm really looking forward to working with you. Maybe we could discuss the possibility of shooting the entire calendar in the Cove. What do you think?"

Surprised and pleased, Izzy steadfastly pushed away the notion that shooting in Templeton was borne from cowardice. "That would be great."

The office door opened and the receptionist came in with their coffees. She laid the tray on the table in front of them. "Would there be anything else, Mr. Sanford?"

"No, that's great. Thank you, Tiffany."

She nodded and walked from the room, softly closing the door.

Izzy picked up her latte and took a sip. When she raised her eyes, she saw Crawley carefully watching her. She frowned. "Mr. Crawley?"

"Richard, please." His gaze turned somber. "I was sorry to learn you recently lost your brother."

The switch from her professional to personal life slammed Izzy's defenses back into place. She cleared her throat. "Thank you. I miss Robbie every day, but I didn't come here to talk about my brother."

A faint blush stained Crawley's cheeks and he briefly closed his eyes before opening them again. "I apologize."

Swallowing hard, Izzy turned to Mr. Sanford. "I assume you're happy if we decide to shoot the calendar entirely on location at Templeton?"

Mr. Sanford nodded, his gaze darting between Izzy and Crawley. "Of course. I'll leave the order of things to you and Richard. In fact, why don't we set up a meeting in the Cove as soon as possible? I understand Kate Harrington would ideally like the calendar to be shot by the middle of September so we have the finished product ready for sale at Christmas?"

Izzy nodded. "That's right."

Sanford looked to Crawley. "Your schedule is pretty free for the rest of the month. Would you be okay to spend a few days in Templeton next week? How about you, Miss Cooper? Would next week be okay with you?"

Izzy fought back her sudden panic. She could fit anything in at any time. She worked twelve-hour days whenever she needed to. More than that, this shoot was all for a little girl lying in a hospital bed, her parents praying for a miracle to save their daughter. If she, Richard Crawley and Templeton's firefighters could play a part in making that miracle come true, next week would be perfect.

She nodded. "Absolutely."

Sanford faced Richard Crawley. "Richard?"

His gaze met Izzy's rather than his agent's and she struggled not to fidget under the celebrity's blatant study. He looked almost remorseful as he ran his gaze over her hair, lower to her eyes. He smiled warmly. "Next week would be great. It's been too long since I've been to

Templeton. Is there anywhere in particular you suggest I stay, Miss Cooper?"

Izzy softened. The guy looked genuinely sorry for mentioning Robbie and wanted them to start over. She smiled back. "Considering your celebrity status, I would recommend you stay at the Christie Hotel. It's one of the best in Templeton and you can trust in their service and discretion."

His shoulders relaxed beneath his smart black jacket and crisp white shirt. "The Christie it is, then."

Mr. Sanford stood and Izzy turned to face him.

He held out his hand. "Well, that's settled. I'll be in touch as soon as we have Richard booked into the hotel so you'll know when to expect him."

"Great." She shook his hand and then held her hand out to Richard Crawley. "I look forward to working with you."

His gaze burned with a whisper of flirtation as his fingers curled around hers. "And I you."

Cursing the sudden warmth at her cheeks, Izzy slid her hand from Crawley's as Mr. Sanford held his hand out toward the door. Izzy gratefully walked toward it. As the agent reached for the door to open it, he stopped. "When I read about the explosion that killed your brother and was then approached by Ms. Harrington for Richard's help, I was onboard immediately. I'm confident the extra emotion you'll bring to the shoot will be invaluable."

Izzy stilled. "The emotion?"

He flitted his gaze from her to Crawley, and back again. "What I mean to say is, we, Mr. Crawley and I, believe having a local photographer, shooting a local celebrity, will really reunite the community after such a devastating tragedy. It will bring people together, knowing even celebrities as big as—"

"It doesn't take something like my brother's death to bring Templeton together, Mr. Sanford. Everything brings us together. You and Mr. Crawley need to be absolutely clear on that. Otherwise the people of Templeton will think celebrities have zero morality when it comes to promotion and making money. It will be up to you and Mr. Crawley to prove differently."

"I think you misunderstand—"

Richard Crawley raised his hand silencing his agent. "Miss Cooper, Francis doesn't speak for me. I've admired you...your work... for a long time and very much look forward to working with you to help raise money for Maya Jackson. That desire has nothing to do with your loss. We apologize."

Torn between Richard's clear sincerity and his agent's ignorance, Izzy drew in a strengthening breath before nodding. "Then I'll wait for your call."

She strode from the room, nodded at the receptionist and continued to walk to the glass front door. Holding her breath, she rounded the corner toward the taxi stand. She opened the passenger door of the cab in front and gratefully slid into the seat. "Templeton Cove, please. The photography studio on Nelson Street."

He nodded and turned the ignition.

Izzy shifted back in her seat and sighed. The sooner she got home to the safety of the Cove, the better. City life crawled with leeches… some clearly more blood-sucking than others.

CHAPTER FIVE

TRENT STROLLED OUT of the fire station, his body aching from cleaning and polishing the trucks all day. Thankfully, the shift had been entirely uneventful. No fires. No accidents. No cats stuck in trees. The Cove's firefighters had enjoyed a day of peace, and now all he had planned for the night was to sit in front of the TV with a take-out dinner and a couple of beers.

He walked along the promenade lining Cowden Beach and smiled to see two teams of teenage lads playing a game of soccer on the sand, the goalposts made up of their discarded jackets. Trent wandered over to the iron railing and leaned his forearms on top to watch the boys play, remembering his own time doing the exact same thing in a park not too far from Templeton Cove.

As soon as he could afford it, he'd moved out of parents' home, leaving them behind… along with the tortured memories of Aimee. Little did he know that no matter how far he ran, his sister's ghost would follow. As often as he tried to visit his mum and dad, Aimee permeated every room of their family home and his anguish sometimes felt as raw as if the fire had happened yesterday.

The shout of a scored goal jolted Trent from his unwanted memories. He straightened from the railing to head to the fish and chip shop when he spotted Izzy standing on the tumble of rocks at the far side of the beach. Hunkered down, she held her camera to her face with the lens turned to the sea. He followed her line of sight to where she photographed.

The day had been unseasonably gray and the ocean showed its disproval. Waves churned, the sea dark and moody. Now that he'd seen her, the ocean echoed the torment inside him. Should he try to talk to her? Or leave her to work?

She lowered the camera and let it hang on the strap around her neck as she stared into the distance. Even from this far away, the high set of her shoulders and her immobilized stance showed her misery. The need to comfort her lurched in Trent's chest.

As if she sensed him watching her, she slowly faced him.

He pulled back his shoulders and met her gaze.

She stood still awhile longer before she lifted

the camera to her face and aimed the lens directly at him. He fought the need to smile or pull a face to make her laugh, as he would have before Robbie died. Helplessness writhed inside him. What did she want from him in that moment? He had no idea. Not anymore.

Once upon a time, he'd thought Robbie, being Izzy's brother, had been the obstacle keeping him and Izzy apart, but it hadn't taken long for Robbie to give Trent the go-ahead to ask out his sister. Little did Trent know how much of a flirt Izzy thought him, rebuking his advances at every turn. Yet now it wasn't other women keeping Izzy from him, but his firefighting.

How was he supposed to make her understand how Aimee's death brought forth a need so ingrained and painful inside him that he didn't know what else to do with his life but fight what killed his sister? Could he ever give up that fight? He very much doubted it.

She carefully climbed down the rocks, one hand steadying her as she made her slow descent. Trent waited, needing to know she was safe on the sand before he could leave.

He wanted to protect his family and loved ones—to never fail someone again as he'd failed his baby sister. In Izzy, he saw his future. Why her, he wasn't sure he could ever explain, but she mattered. Deeply.

Yet with every day that passed, she slipped further away from him and he wished it didn't hurt so much.

He briefly closed his eyes before opening them again, ready to walk on. Walk away. He glanced in her direction one last time as she leaped from the final rock, her hand protectively clasped around the camera at her breasts. Looking up, she held up a finger toward him as though asking him to wait for her. Surprise turned to pathetic relief as she jogged across the sand, her long blond hair swinging back and forth in its ponytail. As she got closer, the more Trent tensed.

It had been over a week since he saw her. The beach party was a bigger disaster than he could ever have anticipated.

She came up the steps toward him, tucking some fallen hair behind her ear. He noted the way she tried to give him a smile, but it didn't quite meet her eyes. "Hi."

He pushed his hands into the pockets of his work trousers. "Hi."

Slightly out of breath, she exhaled through pursed lips. "I think I owe you an apology."

She might as well have said she loved him. The pleasure that jolted through him probably wouldn't have been any less powerful. He dragged his gaze from hers to look blindly toward a spot over her shoulder. "For what?"

"For the way I spoke to you at the beach last week." She sighed. "Won't you at least look at me? You know apologizing doesn't exactly come as second nature to me."

He turned. The trepidation and pleading in her gaze teemed with the blush at her cheeks, tugging at his chest. "I get it, Iz. It's fine."

"What do you get?"

"You need to blame me for Robbie's death. You'll only ever look at me and see a firefighter now. The man who couldn't save your brother. You'll never see just *me.* A guy who really likes you."

The shouts from the teenagers on the beach, the passing traffic and the odd screech of a seagull punctured the silence. She closed her eyes. "I'm sorry."

Guilt pressed down on him. The last thing he wanted was to add to her pain. He touched a finger to her chin. "Hey." He winked. "I can't be irresistible to every woman in the Cove, can I?" Her smile was slow in coming, but when it did, the sight of it pushed the air from Trent's lungs. "Apology accepted, okay?"

She nodded. "Okay."

He glanced toward the row of shops on the

opposite side of the road. "I was going to grab some fish and chips. Do you want to join me?"

Hesitation flashed in her eyes before she nodded. "Okay. Could we take them back to my studio? I want to show you something."

"Sure."

They walked side by side and Trent fought the need to take her hand, instead fisting his fingers in his pockets.

Twenty minutes later, Trent walked into Izzy's studio behind her, their wrapped fish and chips in his hands along with two cans of soda. "Do you have plates or shall we eat these straight from the paper?"

"From the paper, of course." She raised an eyebrow as she shut the door. "You disappoint me. I'll go as far as providing knives and forks, but that's it."

He laughed and stared at her denim-clad ass as she threw the lock in place and checked the sign was turned to Closed. Anticipation churned with the rumbling in his stomach. Her wanting to be alone—and undisturbed—with him could only be a good thing.

He inwardly berated himself as he carried their food over to her workstation. She pushed aside some papers and then walked over to the corner of the room, where she plucked a plaid blanket from the floor. "I used this for a shoot earlier, so it needs washing anyway. It can be our makeshift tablecloth."

"Sounds like a plan."

She lifted the blanket and covered half of the enormous worktop before pulling two stools to either side. He slid onto one as she walked to the kitchen at the back of the studio. As sounds of a drawer opening, cutlery clattering and then the drawer slamming shut filtered through the open door, Trent tried to figure out the best way to play out the next minutes, or maybe hours, he'd spend with her.

His friends' warnings about his distraction on the job poked at his conscience, along with the way everyone but Izzy believed they were meant for one another. He couldn't keep pushing her. For his own self-preservation, he had to back off and be the friend she needed.

The soft scent of her perfume floated across the room as she emerged from the kitchen. Awareness lifted the hairs on his arms as Trent concentrated on unwrapping their meal. The aroma of fresh, battered fish and fried chips filled the studio and they both gave an appreciative, unified sigh.

They laughed and Trent's gut wrenched at the fleeting sight of undisguised joy in her eyes. She plucked up a chip. "So, how was your day?" She popped the chip into her mouth. "Anything interesting happen?"

"Nope. It was one of the quiet days firefighters are grateful for."

"Really?" Her bright blue eyes scrutinized him as though she suspected him of lying. "Do you really mean that? You're grateful for the quiet days?"

His appetite wavered as the feeling he was being tested pressed down on him. "Of course. We don't relish the idea of running into a burning building or rescuing people trapped inside a mangled car. It comes with the job…and I hope you understand now why I took the job."

The skin at her neck moved as she swallowed. "Your sister."

"Yes. Aimee." Trent cut into his fish and lifted a chunk into his mouth, trying to act normal despite the sudden and oppressive silence.

She coughed. "It's kind of sad the biggest thing we have in common is that we've both lost a sibling." Her gaze shadowed. "Aren't you angry? Don't you want to lash out at anyone and everyone all the time?"

He picked up his soda can and drank, carefully watching her over the top as he considered his next words. He lowered the can. "The anger is normal and I promise it will pass."

"I find that hard to believe. I'm always angry. Really, really angry."

"I know you are."

Her eyes glazed with unshed tears. "I don't want to be this way, but I have no idea what to do if I'm not angry. Does that make me crazy?"

"No, it makes you human. Anger is a normal stage of grief, Iz. Don't give yourself a hard time about it, but at the same time, don't choose to stay in the anger either. You have to fight it or the grief will win."

"And you fought back by signing up to be a firefighter?"

"In a way, yes. I wanted to do something to vent my frustration. What better way than fighting the thing that killed Aimee?"

She stared at him, her eyes sad, before she nodded and looked back to her food.

When it seemed she wasn't going to say anything else, Trent shifted his gaze to the studio walls. The difference in the images on display was as devastating as Izzy's grief. Cowden Beach, the sea dark, waves crashing, its sands empty of people. He continued to scan the walls, disappointment and helplessness twisting inside. Where were her previous images? The ones full of light, color, romance and fun.

It was clear to see that the images Izzy saw

through the lens lately were heartbreakingly different than when Robbie had been alive.

"You need to change your focus." He ate another bit of fish and purposely continued to stare around the room. "You've decided to show Templeton in a completely different light than you ever have before." He looked at her bowed head as she pushed her food around on the paper. She'd barely eaten any chips, her battered fish untouched. "Is this how you feel?"

She lifted her head, her cold gaze showing she was once again trying to shut him out. "I look through my lens and photograph what I see. I can't help what's there."

"That's not true and you know it." He put down his fork. "Your work has never been about what's in front of you. You can make anything look beautiful. No, mesmerizing, heart-wrenching, yet hopeful. Do you know why? Because that's who you are. Inside."

Color tinged her cheeks. "Who I *was*. Not who am I anymore."

"It's a choice, Iz. You can be happy again if that's what you want to be. Believe me, you might have to force it sometimes, but happiness is out there. You just have to be willing to open up to it."

"And I guess you're going to say my happiness could be you? It's you who will make me happy?"

He swallowed. Apparently, she thought he was that arrogant. "No, not necessarily."

"I want to be happy, but it's going to take time." Her voice softened. "I know you understand...now I know about Aimee."

"But?"

"But what?" She focused on her food and put another chip into her mouth.

"There's a but in there somewhere. You aren't just avoiding me. You're avoiding life or having fun, and that has nothing to do with me being a firefighter. You need to force yourself to get out there. Eventually, it won't feel as hard as it does right now."

"I'm trying." She gave a wry smile. "I even ventured out of the Cove last week and met with the celebrity Kate wants to front the calendar. He arrives tomorrow." She ate another chip, took a drink of her soda. "I just hope he doesn't arrive with an entourage, expecting me to wait on him and them hand and foot."

The change in subject was obvious, but he wouldn't push her. "Who is he?"

"Richard Crawley."

Trent stopped, a chip midway to his mouth. "The game show host? Wow, Kate's outdone herself once again. I always got the impression the guy was too far up his own ass to give a crap about anyone else. Kid or no kid."

She smiled softly. "Well, whether or not that's true, only time will tell. All I know is he seems okay as far as celebrities go. Whether he'll go for Kate's idea of stripping off for the calendar remains to be seen."

"If she convinced me and the rest of the crew to do it, I'm sure she'll convince a celebrity who lives for the limelight."

"I suppose so."

The dejection had returned once more to her tone, and Trent gazed around the studio walls a second time. "You know, I heard a rumor there's a gallery opening in Templeton in the new year. It would be pretty fantastic if you could get your pictures exhibited there."

"A gallery? Here in the Cove?"

He met her gaze. "Marian told me."

"Well, if Marian told you…"

"Exactly. Nothing passes her without being sanctioned and verified. You should go into the bakery and speak to her. She'll tell you all about it."

"I don't know if I'm interested, to be honest."

Concern flooded through Trent, heavier and darker than before. "News of a gallery opening in Templeton would've had you flying off that seat and making plans before Robbie died." He reached for her hand where it lay on the work-top and squeezed her fingers. "This could be the next step for you. Who knows what opportunities having your work shown in a gallery could do for your career? Jay Garrett's financing the whole thing as far as I know. Bringing in someone who knows what they're doing to run the place."

Skepticism darkened her gaze. "And what does Jay Garrett know about art?"

"He's Templeton's richest resident. What does it matter what he knows? As long as he believes in it…in you…that's all that matters. Having said that…" He took a deep breath and braced himself for the onslaught that was sure to follow. "I don't think these pictures are going to sell to the tourists, rich or poor, who come to Templeton, do you?"

"Jeez, who died and made you art critic of the year?" She squeezed her eyes shut. "I can't believe I just said that. I didn't mean to talk about dying when—"

"Hey. It's all right." Trent stood, came around the workstation and took her hands. "Why don't you speak to Jay? Having something new to focus on will help. Believe me."

She nodded. "Okay. I'll think about it."

"Good." He ran his gaze over her face. "Let

me help you through this, Iz. I'm here for you. Even if it's only as a friend if that's what you want."

She slipped her hands from his and put them in her lap. "Friendship is all I can handle. Anything else is too much right now."

"Fine, I'll back off, but promise me you'll think about the gallery. Your work is too good not to be seen and noticed. Too good to stay in this studio and the homes of the locals. You've got talent, Iz. Use it to get you out of this dark place you're in before it's too late."

"I will. I promise."

He pushed his hands into his pockets, relieved he'd broken partway through her defenses. "So, what was it you wanted to show me?"

She closed her eyes and huffed a laugh before opening them again. "I wanted your opinion on my latest collection."

"Your latest collect..." He grimaced. "And that will be the pictures I just basically told you I hated, right?"

She smiled. "Right."

IZZY TOOK A DEEP BREATH as she approached the opulent Christie Hotel and walked through the revolving door into its spectacular lobby. This place was the very best in town and she could only dream of affording to stay a single night—Richard Crawley had booked his stay for the whole week.

She smoothed her hands over her hips and hoped the long navy skirt, teamed with a sheer white blouse and camisole beneath, was suitable enough for dinner in such a fancy place. Time and again, her fingers had hovered over her phone while she considered canceling, but after receiving a sharp talking-to from Kate, there was no way Izzy would risk Richard Crawley walking away from helping raising funds for little Maya Jackson.

So here Izzy was. Late by fifteen minutes, but here all the same.

For the second time in a week, she'd stepped out of her comfort zone and into an arena that felt as dangerous as a gladiator fight at a Roman amphitheater.

Her high heels clicked on the marble floor as she walked toward the restaurant doors. The place was the epitome of 1930s glamour with gilded mirrors and huge, resplendent flower displays in every corner and atop every plinth. The chandeliers shone, sending rays of light to prism on every reflective and spotless surface.

A uniformed member of the staff opened the restaurant doors as she approached, directing her to a sign that asked guests to wait to be seated. Glancing around the bustling room, Izzy fought the need to turn around and flee before Richard Crawley, or anyone else, saw her. Bursts of conversation and laughter bounced from the walls while a pianist played on a white baby grand in the far corner. What was she doing here?

Her mouth dried and her hands turned clammy.

"Good evening, miss. Have you a table booked with us this evening?"

Izzy jumped and turned to the young, black-suited maître d'. "Um, yes, I'm here to meet with Richard Crawley. I'm a little late, I'm afraid."

"Ah yes. Mr. Crawley is at your table. If you'd like to follow me?"

Izzy forced her shoulders back, fighting her nerves and insecurity. She'd had hundreds of meetings with moneyed businessmen and visiting tourists happy to spend their holiday savings on her paintings. This meeting with Richard Crawley would be no different. He was here to talk about Maya and the calendar. Not Izzy's life. Not Robbie.

Business she could do.

Richard rose to his feet as she approached, his smile wide and his dark brown eyes shining as warmly as they had the first time they met. "Miss Cooper." He held out his hand. "It's great to see you again."

Izzy smiled and relaxed her shoulders. It was easy to see his appeal and why he was so successful at his job. His face was open, kind and, she was reluctant to admit, trustworthy. She took his hand. "Thank you. You too."

He gestured to the chair on the other side of the small table. "Have a seat. What would you like to drink?"

She turned to the maître d'. "A glass of Sauvignon Blanc would be lovely, thank you."

He nodded. "Of course. Suzie will be your waitress for this evening. I'll ask her to bring your wine and the menus. Enjoy your evening."

He walked away and Izzy lifted her gaze to Richard.

He shifted back into his seat. "So, how are you?"

"Good. You?"

"Very well." He smiled and glanced around the restaurant. "Feels kind of surreal to be back in the town I grew up, but kind of nice too."

Izzy relaxed further and placed her clutch purse at her feet. "How long ago did you live here?"

"A good ten years ago now. My parents moved to the city for my father's job. It's strange how I've never been back since."

"Were you happy here?"

"For a while, but I was barely into my teens before I was itching to get out and spread my wings. Small towns suit some people, but definitely not me."

As silly as it was, his dismissal of small towns and Templeton rankled, but Izzy forced a smile. "Well, for me, the Cove is most definitely where I belong."

He raised an eyebrow. "Never say never. Things change…people change."

Uncomfortable with the knowing tone in his voice despite being aware of the huge changes to her personality lately, Izzy cleared her throat and laced her hands on the table. "Shall we talk about the calendar?"

His gaze lingered on hers before he leaned forward, mirroring her posture. "Sure. How's it going?"

"Really well. I spoke with Kate earlier and she's drawn up a schedule of when each of the volunteer firefighters will be available. It's now just a case of me deciding what to feature for each month. For the cover, we thought it would be a great shot to have you and the firefighters together."

"Sounds good…" He grimaced. "As long as they're not all built and buff and I end up looking like a stick between them."

Izzy laughed. Richard Crawley was at least six feet tall, and the width of his chest gave the impression that the gym wasn't exactly non-existent in his schedule. "I'm pretty confident you'll give them a run for their money."

He lifted an eyebrow, his eyes glinting with flirtation. "Glad to hear you say so."

Her cheeks heated and she turned from his gaze as a waitress approached carrying Izzy's wine on a tray in one hand and two leather-bound menus in the other. She placed the menus in front them and the drink in front of Izzy. The young girl smiled. "Your wine, Miss Cooper." She looked at Izzy and Richard in turn. "I'll be back to take your order shortly."

Reaching for her glass, Izzy took a fortifying sip and fought the nerves that jumped into her stomach. Richard was handsome, charming and effortlessly charismatic. The combination made her nervous when she would so rather be at home wrapped in a blanket and watching an old movie, or else working at the studio.

He opened his menu. "Shall we go for starters as well as mains?"

Richard scanned the menu, his brow slightly furrowed and his concentration somber. She needed to stop thinking about her need to be home alone and get fully on board with the project or risk letting Kate down, not to mention Maya.

Mustering her confidence, Izzy looked at the menu. “Well, as I’m at the Christie and haven’t had the chance to step inside the place before, I think we should take full advantage.”

He laughed. “I agree. The bill’s on me, so I want you to have whatever you’d like.”

“Oh, I didn’t mean for you to pay—”

“I want to. Please. I’m an old-fashioned kind of guy and like to treat a lady to dinner…if that’s okay with you?”

How could she refuse when his tone was so friendly and gentle? This wasn’t a date. It was a business meeting and the man was being polite and attentive. “Thank you.”

“You’re welcome. Now, what will it be?”

The evening passed with a steady stream of conversation about everything from the calendar, to their childhoods, to Richard’s time in Templeton as a young boy to his current work as a TV presenter.

Their starters were delicious, but it was only as they came toward the end of their mains that Izzy realized just how much she had relaxed. Her plate clean, she set down her knife and fork and sighed. “That was amazing. Thank you for inviting me here tonight. I’ve really enjoyed it.”

"Good." He smiled. "I couldn't help worrying I'd never see you again after my and Francis's insensitive words about your brother. I can only apologize and promise it won't happen again."

Izzy held his apologetic gaze as insecurity threatened once more. For an hour or so, she'd been in someone's company who'd made her forget about Robbie. Richard had made her smile, even if laughter had been a step too challenging. Now the guilt over how she'd enjoyed herself and might be able to move on one day came back heavy and unwanted, making her want to flee from the restaurant.

She picked up her glass and drained the remainder of her wine. "Of course you'd see me again. The only reason we're here is Maya. Nothing is about you or me...and certainly not my brother."

"I couldn't agree more. What happens outside of the calendar is no one else's business."

Izzy frowned. "Outside of the calendar?"

"Yes." He put down his knife and fork and touched his napkin to his mouth, a slight blush coloring his cheeks. "I was hoping you might show me around town while I'm here. I'm sure Templeton must've changed since I was a teenager. I'd rather have your company than see things alone. What do you think?"

Indecision battled. Her mind turned to Trent and his unwavering insistence to be there for her…to be *with* her. Yet she'd made no promises to him. Had protected herself from his yearnings for both their sakes. When Trent had kissed her at the beach, her entire world tipped on its axis—his sexual need matched her dormant desires with dangerous ferocity. She couldn't be with Trent and guarantee the safety of her heart, but to spend some time with Richard, an easy, amicable, friendly man who would be in the Cove for barely a week? That could mean a few hours of release and enjoyment without any complication or risk of further pain.

"Okay, why not?" The concurrence slipped from her tongue before she could stop it. "I'll happily show you around."

He exhaled and grinned so widely, Izzy automatically returned his smile. He picked up his wine and drained the glass. "How about we meet at Marian's Bakery for breakfast in the morning?"

Izzy raised her eyebrows. "You want to go to Marian's?"

He frowned. "Is there a problem with Marian's?"

"No, but as much as I love her baking, I should

imagine the Christie's breakfast will stretch further than Marian's delicious croissants."

"Maybe, but I'd love to meet her. I hear she's quite the character."

"Of course. You wouldn't have met her."

"It seems we moved away from the Cove before George Cohen brought his mystery woman back to the Cove. All I remember is my mum being told the gossip surrounding their quick and unexpected marriage. From what I've been told by the staff here, Marian has quite the reputation. It would be nice to make her acquaintance."

Izzy smiled, enjoying Richard's blessed ignorance of Marian's inevitable curiosity. "I'll make the introductions. But be warned, she has the uncanny ability to see straight into people's hearts, so I hope you're not hiding any deep, dark secrets. She has no qualms about exposing people's failings, even if it's only to the person himself."

"Thanks for the warning." He smiled. "But I'm sure she'll agree I'm just a normal guy."

"Hmm, leading an extraordinary life as a household name." Izzy glanced around the restaurant and caught the curious and openly gawping gazes shooting in their direction. *Maybe it will be me who needs protecting from Marian rather than you.*

Nerves knotted her stomach when she considered what people might think about her and Richard spending time together. Templeton was not a place of anonymity, and as much as she didn't want anyone jumping to the wrong conclusions about them, she wanted to enjoy Richard's company.

She faced Richard and put her napkin on the table. "How about I meet you there around nine? We'll have breakfast and then maybe scout out some locations for the shoot. I have quite a few ideas already, but I'd be happy to share them with you."

"Great."

"Well, it's time for me to get home. Thank you for such a nice evening."

She stood and Richard pushed to his feet, holding out his hand. "Tomorrow, then."

"Tomorrow." She took his hand and he gently pulled her forward and pressed a quick kiss to her cheek.

Izzy smiled. "Thanks for dinner."

He nodded and she walked out of the restaurant with the weight of people's stares at her back, and the acute awareness that Richard was most likely watching her too. Uncertainty rolled through her as she played the evening through in her mind. It had gone a lot better than she'd expected and she couldn't deny that

Richard's pleasant and interesting company had taken her by surprise.

Maybe she had no romantic interest in the man, but Trent was right. It was time she participated in life again.

She continued forward until she was outside onto the street. Breathing in the fresh night air, Izzy headed for home, steadfastly pushing away the inexplicable feeling she was betraying Trent by seeing Richard. She wasn't. She would never do anything to hurt Trent. Which was why spending time with someone she wasn't in the least bit attracted to could only be a good thing.

CHAPTER SIX

MARIAN'S BONNIEST BAKERY was the perpetual beehive of activity it always was every morning. Trent scowled out the window toward the promenade as suited workers, joggers and romancing couples made their way across the planked walkway. He waited in line for coffee, the same as he did every Tuesday and Friday.

He, Will and Sam all had their designated days for coffee collection, and when he turned toward the open door, he cursed that today was his.

Izzy wore her long blond hair loose and lovely. It hung like sheets of gold over the shoulders of her short-sleeve white knit sweater. Skinny blue jeans and knee-high boots completed her seemingly effortless perfection. He narrowed his gaze. There was something different about her today. Something he hadn't seen in far too long. She looked relaxed, more at ease than she had in weeks. She'd even decided the day was good enough to warrant the pink lipstick he hadn't seen on her lips for months.

She turned toward the guy coming in behind her as he leaned over her to say something close to her ear. Trent's gut knotted when she dipped her head, her smile partially concealed by her golden curtain of hair as it grazed her face.

Who the hell was this guy?

Then he remembered.

Richard bloody Crawley.

Trent clenched his jaw and faced front. He didn't want to be here. Not now. Not when some TV celebrity had managed to make Izzy smile like that. God, she looked almost shy. Izzy shy? The notion was laughable. It could only mean one thing. She liked Crawley. A lot. He'd managed to peel back a little of her protective barrier in a matter of days, something that Trent hadn't managed in months.

Trent inwardly cursed. How had he gotten it so wrong?

Now, with Richard Crawley so openly flirting with her, Trent acknowledged his stupidity. Was it any wonder Izzy had told him she didn't want him when she offered herself to him and he rejected her?

"What can I get you, sweetheart?"

Trent started and lifted his scowl to Marian

as she stood behind the bakery counter. Her smile vanished. "Well, that's a look I don't see on your face every day. What's got you so riled up this morning? Or don't I want to know?"

"You always want to know." Trent risked another glance behind him. Izzy spoke so intently with Crawley, their conversation so interesting, that they seemed entirely unaware of anyone else. He faced Marian. "Can I have our usual coffees, please? To go."

The older woman's shrewd gaze lingered over his shoulder before she snapped her focus back to Trent, her brown eyes shining with amusement. "Got yourself a little competition, I see."

Trent shrugged. "Competition, my ass."

Marian gave her renowned and, too loud, burst of laughter. "Hey, if that man can make Izzy smile like that, you should be happy for her."

"I am."

"Sure you are." She scribbled down his order on a piece of paper and handed it to the barista behind her. "He looks kind of familiar. Do I know him?"

"Not unless you spend your days watching game shows."

Marian frowned and peered past Trent's

shoulder a second time. Her eyes widened. "Is that—"

"Yep. Richard Flashing Teeth, Fake Tan Crawley."

"Well, he's not to my taste, but he does have that cheeky chappy kind of look about him."

"Cheek..." Trent turned just as Crawley brushed some fallen hair from Izzy's brow. He scowled. "Cheeky is not what I see going on with that guy at all."

Marian lifted an eyebrow. "No? What do you see?"

"I see..." He glared at her twinkling eyes and tormenting grin. "Never mind."

The barista came forward with his coffees pushed into a take-away tray and Trent handed Marian a ten-pound note. "Put the change in Maya's collection tin."

"Sure thing. And, Trent? Let Izzy find her own way. Trust me, that girl's got more sense in her little finger than most women her age have in their entire bodies. She'll find her way through her grief and see what's right. You just need to give her some breathing space."

"I give her plenty of breathing space."

"Really?"

"Yes. Really."

"Then prove it and stop fretting over some TV presenter showing her a good time while he's in town. She'll come back to you when she's good and ready. For the time being, concentrate on your own life, rather than hers." She turned to her next customer, her smile wide and her and Trent's conversation clearly over. "Good morning, lovely. What can I get you?"

Trent inhaled and turned from the counter. There was no other way to leave the bakery than to walk straight past Izzy and Crawley, which meant Trent had two choices. Either throw himself through Marian's plate-glass window or, the less gutless option, actually speak to the guy.

Slowly strolling toward the exit, Trent smiled and nodded hello to a few people before Izzy reached out and gripped his forearm. "Trent, hey. I've got someone here I'd like you to meet." She turned to Crawley, her hand slipping from Trent's arm toward the presenter. "Richard Crawley, meet my good friend Trent Palmer. He's one of the volunteer firefighters for the shoot."

The pride that rang in Izzy's voice should've gone some way toward hammering out the mammoth-size dent in Trent's ego, but instead, all that echoed in his head was the word *friend*. Shaking it off, he held out his hand to Crawley. "Nice to meet you." Firm, but not hard enough to break the guy's fingers, they shook and parted hands. Trent held up the coffees. "I'd better go. The guys can't function on sea air alone. See you around."

He glanced at Izzy, and her blue eyes narrowed as she stared at him.

He stepped toward the door.

"Trent?"

He briefly closed his eyes before turning to Izzy. "What?"

Her gaze burned with annoyance. "Richard's staying in the Cove for a few days and was hoping to meet you and the other firefighters I'll be shooting for the calendar. Would it be okay if I brought Richard to the station sometime today? Or maybe tomorrow?"

Irritation vibrated through every muscle in Trent's body as he glanced at Crawley. The knowing smirk on the guy's face made Trent grip the coffee tray tighter. He shifted his gaze to Izzy. "I'll check with the chief and call you."

He turned toward the door.

"Trent..."

"I said I'll call you, Iz." He opened the door without looking back.

The door closed on her answer...if she answered him at all. He strode along the high street, every muscle in his body wired with tension as he battled the jealousy burning inside his gut. He had no right to feel so possessive over Izzy. Marian was right. He needed to focus on his own life rather than Izzy's. He needed to move on.

So what if she got on well with Crawley? It didn't mean they were destined to end up in bed together. So he made her smile, made her look more relaxed than she had seemed in weeks…motivated her to wear a little lipstick. It was no big deal.

Trent stomped closer to the station.

So what if she considered him a *friend*? Her once-upon-a-time lover. Her damn nemesis that happened to fight fire for a living. What did it matter that the evening they'd spent in her studio talking and laughing had given him futile hope they had turned a corner toward a reunion?

His misinterpretation was his own doing. It had nothing to do with Izzy.

So what was he going to do next? What would be his first step in moving forward?

He turned into the station courtyard and glanced up at the guys' mess room above the garage. All he needed was either right here at work or else waiting in a nearby town with their arms wide open and ready for a visit from their son. Maybe he should forget Izzy, forget all women for a while, and figure out what he wanted from his own life instead of worrying about everyone else he cared for.

Trent shook his head and entered the station. Yeah, like that was the easiest goal in the universe. How was he supposed to stop caring about his parents? His colleagues? His friends and Izzy? They were who made him the kind of man he was, who made him get up in the morning and want to be the best he could be for all of them.

To live for himself, to do what he wanted now and then…that kind of selfishness was what led to the worst event of his entire life and it was a path he'd be hard pushed to ever tread again. He had Aimee's memory to remind him of what happened whenever he thought about himself. She was right there, in his head, every single day.

AS IZZY WALKED along Templeton's main street, she dialed Trent's number. Every time she'd phoned him for the last two days, the call had gone straight to voice mail. She took a breath, ready to leave, yet another message asking him to call her back when he picked up.

"Hi."

Izzy frowned. His tone was cold enough to halt any worry about the world's ice cap thawing. "At last. Anyone would think you've been avoiding me."

"Nope. Busy."

She stopped, ignoring the tuts and moans of the people forced to unexpectedly walk around her. "Too busy to answer my fifteen calls to you over the last two days?"

"What can I do for you, Iz?"

Hurt twisted her heart. She'd thought things between them were better now, but it seemed something she'd done had upset him. Again.

"Have I done something wrong?"

He exhaled. "No."

"Then why are you being so distant?"

"I'm busy with work. That's all. What's up?"

Not wanting their conversation to evolve into another argument, Izzy took a deep breath. "I was wondering if you'd managed to speak to your chief about bringing Richard by the station for a visit. I've come up with the idea of having the cover shot with him in the center, you guys standing around him and the station in back. It would be nice to show him around the place a little first. What do you think?"

"Does it really matter what I think?"

Irritation simmered beneath the surface of Izzy's skin. "What's with you?"

"Nothing."

"You sound incredibly annoyed for nothing."

His released breath rasped down the line. "Ignore me. It's a great idea."

"Really?" She smiled. "You'll show us around?"

"Yes."

"Thank you."

"You're welcome. I'll speak to the chief and call you back."

"Great." Izzy walked from the middle of the pavement to lean against a wall in between the toy shop and a discount store, still concerned by Trent's aloofness. "Trent?"

"Yeah?"

"You'd tell me if something was bothering you, wouldn't you? We're still friends, I hope. You sound so fed—"

"I'm not having the easiest time seeing you with a guy you barely know, smiling and relaxing like you're having the best time you've had in months, but that's my problem, not yours. I'll call you when I've spoken to the chief."

Annoyance rippled through her. This was the last conversation she wanted to have with him. He was the one man she knew above all others who held on to his self-control and kept a level temper, even when chaos reigned all around him.

She closed her eyes and pushed her fingers at the headache starting at her temple. "There's nothing going on between me and

Richard apart from the calendar. I don't know why seeing me with him bothers you. We're doing this for Maya, remember?"

"Fine, I'm sorry. It's just..."

She opened her eyes. "Just what?"

"It pisses me off that Crawley makes you smile in a way I haven't managed in months, but I'll deal with it. For the record, I know I should be happy you're smiling and I'm trying, okay?"

Izzy relaxed her shoulders and smiled, a little amused by the jealousy in his voice. "I'm smiling now."

"Great. So you like it when I act like a six-year-old?"

"No, I like it when you realize you're being an idiot."

"Ouch. Guess I deserve that. Forget I said anything, okay? I'll clear your visit with the chief. Bring Crawley by about six, although there's no guarantee we won't be called out while you're here."

Izzy closed her eyes again, not wanting to think about Trent being called out to a fire at any time of the day or night. "I understand."

"Good. I'll see you then."

The line went dead.

Izzy opened her eyes and ended the call before staring blindly ahead. Trent's distance and the horrible emptiness it created in her proved he was a big part of why she called Templeton home. Space was what she'd wanted, and Trent had given it to her, but the brief coldness in his voice was something she'd never heard from him before and it had shaken her.

She needed to accept that she didn't know him as well as she thought. She always thought him so strong and untouchable. Strong and in control...which is probably why she continued to push him away, assuming he'd get over her eventually. But how could anyone be strong all the time? He also had feelings and an innate sense of loyalty and honor.

A man, she hadn't known until recently, that had a sister...a sister he'd lost in a fire.

The deaths of their siblings should bring them closer, not force them apart, and she only had herself to blame. How could he still want her when she floundered through each day, trying her best to fit into a new life without her brother when he'd managed so well without Aimee?

He never let Izzy down or looked at her as though she was anything less than perfect. She couldn't bear for him to see her so weak.

It was time to stand up and be counted by her own actions and decisions.

Pushing away from the wall, she had started

to walk toward her studio when one of the shops across the street caught her eye. She stilled.

A sign had been pasted to the whitewashed windows.

Garrett's Art Gallery is scheduled to open in the New Year.

Izzy pressed her hand to her stomach. Trent had urged her to speak to Jay about the gallery. Maybe this was the chance she'd been waiting for to prove she could keep living without Robbie. Even though her work was gaining more and more interest, having a permanent display at an art gallery would mean an immediate elevation as far as she, and most likely, the press, were concerned. To have it continually shown in a gallery that was bound to be successful, bearing in mind Jay's entrepreneurial track record, could open doors she'd never considered before. Who was to say he wouldn't do all he could to use his money and influence to promote her work in a way she couldn't afford herself right now? Excitement churned in her stomach. She had to at least try to impress Jay; had to try and move forward in her career if she couldn't in her heart.

Checking that the road was clear, she hurried across the street. Beneath the sign pasted in the window was another.

For Any Inquiries, Please Contact Jay Garrett's Office on…

Izzy took out her phone and entered the number into her contacts. Happiness was a choice. Wasn't that what Trent told her? She smiled before dialing Kate's number. "Hey, it's me."

"Hey, you. Hold on just a second, will you?"

Izzy waited as Kate's muffled voice spoke to someone else before she came back to the phone. "Sorry about that. I was just talking to Maya Jackson's mum. Maya's started to respond well to treatment at the hospital, but we need to get moving on the calendar. I don't want it to be my fault that the money isn't there for her to fly across to the States should she need to."

Guilt pressed down on Izzy. She'd been busy thinking about a next career move while Kate had been speaking to the mother of a critically ill child. "We'll be ready, don't worry. That's good news that Maya seems to be improving a little."

"It is. So, what's up?"

"Are you free around six? I'm meeting with the firefighters at the station. It would be good if you're there to remind them just how good the cause is before I ask them to bare their chests for, hopefully, thousands of people."

Kate laughed. "Sure. You don't need to ask me twice to spend time with a group of firefighters. How are things with you and Trent?"

"Up to a few minutes ago, I would've said better, but it seems I've annoyed him big-time."

"What? How?"

"Richard Crawley. He's here. In town."

"He's here? Why didn't I know about this?"

"Probably because he's been keeping a pretty low profile. Anyway, I've been taking care of him so you didn't have anything extra to worry about."

"Taking care of him? What does that mean? I hope you didn't tell Trent you *were taking care of him*. That would've been the same as you sticking a red-hot poker in his eye."

Izzy grimaced. "I didn't tell him anything, but he's seen Richard and me together and he's clearly not happy about it."

"And what has Trent seen exactly?"

"Me doing my bit for Maya. I've been out for dinner with Richard, smiled and nodded in all the right places. You don't want to be blamed for the money not being there for Maya, and neither do I. We have to keep Richard Crawley sweet, right? And he's a safer bet than me spending time with Trent right now."

"But there must be more to it than that if Trent is pissed."

Izzy closed her eyes. Wasn't she enjoying Richard's company because he flirted with her, made her feel better about herself and she was under no personal obligation to him? That he was someone safe to have fun with without risk to her feelings?

"Iz?"

Izzy walked along the street. "There's nothing going on. The guy's a bit of a ladies' man, but he clearly fancies himself more than anyone else. Which is exactly the way I want it. I'll see you at the station at six, okay?"

"Sure. See you then."

Izzy cut the call and then dialed Richard Crawley's number.

"Hey, Izzy."

"Hi. I just wanted to check if you're free at six. I've managed to get us a free pass to visit the fire station. I thought it would be a good idea to introduce you to some of the guys and have a look around."

"Sounds good. Why don't you meet me at the hotel? We could have a drink first."

With Trent's jealous tone ringing in her ears, Izzy shook her head. "I can't. There's something I need to do first. Why don't we meet at the station?"

"No problem. I remember where the station is, and like you predicted, the residents have barely blinked an eye at my being here, so I should make it there in one piece."

"We're a small town, Richard." The guy's ego was way too big. "As much as I'm sure people are excited you're here, they won't fall over themselves to show it. Well, most of them won't anyway."

"Fair enough. I've enjoyed the time we've been able to spend together, though."

Izzy frowned. It was time to draw a line. She didn't mind showing him around, but she shouldn't be hiding behind the safety of Richard's short stay. She needed to halt any indication she was interested in him in any way past Maya. "Okay, so I'll see you at the station shortly then."

"See you then."

She ended the call and headed for home, wanting to get back so she could speak to Jay Garrett. Depending on how the call went, she would then get out of her new uniform of jeans and shirts and get back the flair that had carried her through the tough times when Robbie was alive.

It was time to show Templeton Cove she might be down, but she wasn't out.

She'd dress up a little and enjoy the tour of the station. It would be good for her and Trent to spend some time together without all the pain and anger that surrounded her every thought, action and deed. A falling beam killed Robbie, not Trent. Despite her bitterness, he'd never been anything less than honest with her. Believed in her and her work.

It was time she showed him how much she appreciated it.

CHAPTER SEVEN

FIGHTING THE TEMPTATION to change the dress and heels she wore, Izzy studied her reflection in her bedroom mirror one last time. She was moving forward. Nerves clenched in her stomach and she looked longingly toward her discarded jeans on the bed before quickly turning back to the mirror. No. It was time.

She snatched up her purse from the dresser and walked into the living room. Picking up her phone, she ignored the trembling in her hands and dialed Jay Garrett's office number—or at least one of his office numbers. It was well known throughout the Cove just how many offices Jay had scattered through England and, possibly, beyond. The number pasted to the empty gallery window had been for his parent company situated on the outskirts of Templeton. The place he spent more and more time since he and his wife, the town's detective inspector, had their first baby. A little girl they'd named Sarah, after a close, mutual friend of theirs who had been found murdered near Jay's home a few years back.

A tragedy that had shaken the Cove, as well as the Garretts, to its core.

"Good afternoon, Garrett Holdings. How may I help you?"

Izzy shook off the macabre memory. "Hi, I'm calling about the new gallery in town. Is it possible I can schedule an appointment to meet with Mr. Garrett?"

"Can you tell me a little more about your inquiry?"

Izzy strode about her living room. She needed to draw on every ounce of confidence if she had any chance of securing a meeting with someone as busy as Jay. "My name is Izzy Cooper and I have a small photography studio on Nelson Street. My work is starting to gain some recognition and I wondered if Mr. Garrett might be interested in exhibiting some of my pictures when the gallery opens."

"Can I ask the type of photography you specialize in?"

"Mostly land and seascape images. Although I very often do private portrait work and will also be shooting a charity calendar we hope will raise funds for a little girl needing medical treatment in the US. My work can be quite eclectic, so I can't really specify a particular area any more than that, I'm afraid."

"I see, and do you have a portfolio?"

"Yes."

"Okay, well, if I can take some contact details, I'll pass them on to Mr. Garrett. He will either call you himself or pass a message to me. In which case, I will call you back."

"Great." Izzy gave the woman her phone number and email. "Do you have any idea when you or Mr. Garrett is likely to get back to me?"

"We'll be in touch as soon as possible."

"Okay. Thank you. Goodbye."

Izzy ended the call and collapsed onto her sofa, tapping the phone against her bottom lip as her heartbeat slowly returned to normal. She'd made initial contact and for the first time in a long while, excitement rippled through her.

Smiling, she pushed to her feet. It was nearing five thirty. She really ought to be at the station to greet Richard, rather than have him turn up alone to meet Trent. She had no idea what sort of reception he'd give the TV host after their strained meeting at Marian's.

Grabbing her keys and purse from the kitchen counter, she was about to slip her phone into her bag when it rang. She stared at the display. It couldn't be.

She accepted the call. "Hello. Izzy Cooper speaking."

"Ms. Cooper, this is Jay Garrett. How are you?"

Izzy froze, clenching the phone tighter. "Mr. Garrett. I'm fine. How are you?"

"All the better for hearing from you. Please. Call me Jay. I can't tell you how pleased I am you're interested in the gallery. I had every intention of getting in contact with you next month."

"You did? I didn't even know you were aware of my work. Your enthusiasm is flattering. Thank you."

"Well, Izzy…can I call you Izzy?"

"Of course."

"My wife has been a fan of your work for a year or more. In fact, we have a couple of your shots hanging in our home."

Izzy found herself smiling with pride. "That's wonderful."

"I understand you'd like me to consider exhibiting your work at the gallery?"

"Yes. I have some great ideas for future work—"

"What if I said I'd like you to work even closer with the gallery?"

She frowned. “I don’t understand.”

Jay Garrett was a businessman above all else, and Izzy fought her natural defenses as they closed in on her. Why did anything new frighten her so much these days?

He cleared his throat. “How would you feel about managing the gallery? My experience goes as far as looking at a picture, photograph, whatever, and knowing whether or not I like it. I assume, as an artist, you have a much better idea of what’s quality and what you think will appeal to the residents and masses of visitors who come to the Cove each year. I have an extremely busy life now that I’m a dad, and as much as I wanted to snap up the gallery when it went on sale, I have no wish to run it.”

“You want me to run it?” Izzy froze. “But I don’t have any experience. Plus, I want to continue to work on my own photography as much as possible.”

“Of course, but you told my assistant that you take portrait work on top of your own desired projects. Can I assume the portraits are done to supplement your income?”

“Well, yes. It helps pay my way while waiting for my big break that I’m sure will come one of these days. Or, at least, I hope so.”

“And that’s why I’m proposing a decent salary to manage the gallery, plus the promise of the majority of the exhibition space for your own work. I will scout out possible talent alongside you, but it will be your decision which artists we back and when. On top of that, I'm happy to keep the gallery open on a part-time basis, excluding the busy summer months, which will leave you extra time to work on your photography. What do you think?"

Izzy's mind raced. With a regular salary and more time to work on her own projects, her instinct was to yell her acceptance down the phone, right there and then. She hesitated. She had to think this through. What did she really know about running a gallery? She merely photographed what she loved, and the results were as mixed as her emotions.

She slowly paced the room. "I'll need to consider everything you've said very carefully."

"Absolutely. I don't expect an answer straightaway. The gallery won't be open until February, or maybe even March, next year. Think about what I've proposed, how you envision the gallery to look and prosper in the future. Any ideas of artists you have in mind to exhibit alongside your own work would be great too. I know this could be a brilliant venture between us. With you at the helm, it will work."

Izzy smiled as her excitement grew. Jay's

enthusiasm was infectious and there was no doubting the man's instinct for what worked and didn't work in business. She took a breath. "Okay, let me think it over and I'll get back to you with a decision shortly."

"Perfect. It's been great talking to you. Speak soon."

"Speak soon. 'Bye."

Izzy ended the call and let out a scream before dancing a jig and heading out the door. Today has just gotten a whole lot better and she couldn't wait to tell Trent.

THE CLOSER THE HANDS on his watch got to six, the more agitated Trent became. He deserved a medal for convincing the chief that Richard Crawley coming to the station was a good idea. If it wasn't for Maya Jackson, Trent wouldn't spend a minute with the too-smiley, too-cocky, too white-teethed TV presenter for a million bucks, let alone however long a tour of the station was going to take.

How could he be nice to the guy who currently had Izzy's attention day in, day out? As much as he hated the jealousy seeping through him, Trent was powerless to stop it. He wanted Izzy and she didn't want him.

The truth was hard to accept, no matter how much he told himself it was for the best.

The barrage of laughter and fire station rowdiness came to an abrupt stop. He hadn't joined in the usual station ribbing and camaraderie with any amount of enthusiasm for the last forty-eight hours, but experience told him something was afoot.

Pushing away from the truck he'd been checking over, Trent turned toward the entrance.

Izzy.

His traitorous heart lodged like a rock in the center of his chest.

He glanced at the crew.

As though joined by a rope, each of his colleagues turned from staring at Izzy to stare at Trent. Identical expressions of pure male-orientated ecstasy was etched on each of their stupid faces.

As though she was his, unmerited pride knotted Trent's gut.

She looked fantastic.

Trent took the seemingly frozen moment to take in the entire, sexy and very pleasing sight of her. Her dress fit like a second skin: pristine white with huge colored flowers splashed all over it. She looked amazing.

His gaze wandered lower.

The occasional blue of the dress matched

the pair of heels on her feet, higher and sexier than he'd seen her wear in a long, long while.

Down, boy. She's not here for you...

Despite her face being in silhouette from the blazing sunshine behind her, and her eyes concealed by sunglasses, Trent sensed her nerves and hesitation. He had to get her away from the overpowering surge of testosterone she was undoubtedly drowning in.

"Hey, Izzy. Over here." He raised his hand and strolled toward her, his colleagues' stares burning holes in his back.

She didn't relax her shoulders and she didn't walk any farther into the station. Instead, she stood stock-still and waited for him to come to her.

He stopped in front of her. "Hey."

She slowly removed her sunglasses and tipped her head back to look at him. "Hey."

Their eyes locked and his attraction soared. She looked different. Softer. Trent glanced over his shoulder. Although the guys made a valiant effort of not paying attention by attempting to clean the truck or sweep a broom around the station floor, they were the worst actors known to man.

He touched her elbow. "Let's get away from this lot, shall we?"

She nodded and he steered her away from the front of the station toward a low wall that ran around a circle of lawn outside. "Do you want to sit down?"

She shook her head and then cast her gaze along the street. "We haven't got long. Kate and Richard..." She faced him. "Crawley will be here soon."

He inhaled. "Yeah. I know. Can't wait."

"This is for Maya, Trent. You know I wouldn't have agreed to do this calendar for any other reason." She looked to the ground for a moment before lifting her gaze to his, her blue eyes soft. "You and I both know how hard Kate works to raise money for any and every cause. It can only be a good thing for Maya to have a recognizable face involved. Kate's on a mission for this little girl."

"The woman is on a one-woman mission with life. Lord help the guy she marries."

"Absolutely."

They laughed before their smiles dissolved and the silence stretched. Trent shoved his hands into his pockets to stop from touching her or brushing the fallen hair from her eyes.

She looked at him. "Before I went to the city to meet with Richard and his agent, it had been too long before I'd been anywhere outside Templeton. I'm glad I went. It's given me perspective. Some of the old me back."

Unable to fight the need any longer, he rubbed his hand up and down her upper arm, surprised and relieved when she didn't pull away. "That's good. Really good."

A blush darkened her cheeks, and her gaze lingered at his mouth before she looked up, closing one eye against the glare of the sun. "Do you want to have dinner with me tonight?"

Surprise jolted through him, quickly followed by alien uncertainty. "You've changed your mind?"

"It's more a case of trying to move past all the anger I'm holding on to. I'm not sure we'll work things out so that we're together, but I know I don't want to lose you completely."

Euphoria battled with caution. "You seemed so cornered when we last spoke. As much as I want to be there for you, I don't want you to feel obligated to spend time with me."

"I don't. I want to."

He drew his gaze over her face. "Are you sure?"

"Yes."

"Because I didn't tell you about Aimee so you'd—"

"I want to, Trent. This isn't about your sister.

It's not entirely about Robbie either. It's about us. Both of us moving forward." She took his hand. "Although I'd like you to tell me more about your sister and what happened whenever you're ready."

Relief whispered through him and he smiled. "Then tell me when and where and I'll be there."

"Are you free tonight?" A faint blush colored her cheeks. "Tomorrow?"

Trent couldn't remember a time she looked more beautiful. "I'm on duty tonight, but tomorrow would be great. What time shall I pick you up?"

"Why don't I meet you at the Coast Inn at around seven?" She eased her hand from his. "There's something I want to do tomorrow, so I'll be busy all day."

He lifted an eyebrow. "The Coast? We can do better than the local bar surely?"

"One step at a time, okay? The Coast's about as far as I can stretch right now."

Idiot.

He briefly closed his eyes. "Right. Sorry." He winked. "The Coast it is, then."

"Great. I'll just wander down the street to see if Richard's on his way."

"Sure. See you in a minute."

She nodded before turning and walking away.

Trent frowned as frustration coursed through him. God, what he would have given to kiss her.

She halted and his heart beat a little faster. *Come back to me, Iz. Come back and kiss me...*

She turned and strode confidently toward him, only stopping when she was inches away. She lifted herself onto her toes and brushed her lips over his. "I'm looking forward to our first date."

She walked a few steps backward, her smile wider than the sun, before turning around and walking from the front of the station onto the street.

Trent released his held breath. "Holy Mother of God, am I in trouble."

He had barely made it from the station yard into the kitchen when Will sauntered in, a goofy smile splitting his face as Crawley, Izzy and Kate walked in behind him.

Will opened his arms to Trent and the rest of the guys dotted around the room. "Gentlemen, this is Richard Crawley." He turned to the presenter. "Mr. Crawley, let me present Templeton's finest team of firefighters, shortly to become temporary models."

The guys laughed and made their way toward Crawley, their hands outstretched in greeting. Annoyance curled through Trent's gut and he turned from Crawley…only to meet Izzy's steady gaze.

There was no mistaking the concern in her eyes, or her worry, as she trapped her bottom lip between her teeth.

He forced a smile and walked toward her, putting his arm around her shoulder. "Stop worrying. I'll be a good boy. Promise."

She looked into his eyes as though accessing his inner thoughts. "Promise?"

"Promise." He dragged his gaze from hers toward Kate and the guys as they huddled in a group around Crawley. The guy seemed to be in his element as admiration and questions were fired at him from every direction. "As long as he doesn't as much as look at you."

"Trent…"

He laughed and squeezed her closer. "I'm joking. Watch this."

Mustering every ounce of self-control, Trent reluctantly pulled his arm from Izzy's shoulder and strolled toward his colleagues and Crawley. He held out his hand. "Mr. Crawley. Nice to see you again."

Crawley's gaze locked on Trent's as he took his hand. "Trent, right?"

Tension rose, testosterone seeming to fill the

room as Trent shook and released Crawley's hand. "Right."

Crawley looked past Trent in Izzy's direction, and Trent turned to follow his gaze. Izzy stood watching them, her arms folded. The delight in her eyes moments before had been replaced with hard, no-nonsense business.

Trent glanced at Crawley and caught the wink he tipped Izzy. Swallowing the urge to swing at the guy, Trent took a deep breath and threw his arm around Crawley's shoulders. "So, Richard, has Kate convinced you to strip to the waist like the rest of us?"

As the chatter and banter erupted once more, with Kate playing referee in the center, Trent slid his gaze toward Izzy. She slowly walked toward the circle, her eyes locked on Trent's. He could've bet a hundred pounds that her mouth twitched with a smile as her blue gaze shone with pride.

His heart kicked. One way or another, he would marry Izzy Cooper or die trying.

CHAPTER EIGHT

IZZY TOUCHED HER HAND to her car door just as Richard Crawley strode into the private parking lot of her apartment building.

He raised his hand in greeting.

She returned his wave, surprised and curious. She was pretty certain she hadn't told him where she lived. What was he doing here?

Once he reached her, he leaned against the side of her car, his posture relaxed and easy… a man used to doing what he wanted, when he wanted. "Hi."

Izzy slid her sunglasses atop her head. "This is a surprise. I thought you planned to spend the day working on your upcoming show."

"I worked on it for most of last night, so I thought I'd come and find you this morning."

"I see." She looked toward the security booth at the entrance of the gated apartments. "And I guess Mitch was so bowled over by your celebrity status that he let you walk in here without calling up to my apartment for my say so first?"

He smiled. “Something like that.”

She lifted an eyebrow, insistent on an explanation to ease her wariness. Celebrity or no celebrity, obnoxiousness annoyed her.

He laughed. “What? I merely told him you were expecting me and then when we saw you by your car, he clearly couldn’t see a problem with me meeting you outside. I’m sure if I wanted access to your apartment, he would have called you first.” His smile faltered. “I didn’t mean to make you uncomfortable.”

Izzy fought her distrust. “You haven’t made me uncomfortable, but I do wonder how you got my address.”

“I asked someone in town.”

“Who?”

He lifted his eyebrows. “Does it matter? Look, I’m sorry. The last thing I want is to upset you.”

“Forget it.” She jangled her keys. “I need to get going. I’m going across town to see someone about the new gallery opening there in the New Year. The owner might be interested in exhibiting my work.”

“Of course he is. He’d be mad not to.” His gaze roamed over her hair and face. “I’ve followed your work for a while. It’s fantastic. Truly.”

“You’ve seen my latest shots on the website?”

"Yes and I love the change in outlook, colors and perception compared to your previous work."

Trent's reaction to her darker pictures seeped into her mind. It couldn't have been more different than Richard's, and she had no idea how she felt about that. Good or bad, the pictures reflected her sadness. "Well, thank you, but lately my work has taken a more…darker edge. I'm not sure what the gallery owner's take will be on them, but it has to be worth a shot."

He tilted his head toward the portfolio she had clutched to her chest. "Are these new pictures? Ones that aren't on your website?"

"Yes, I'm still not sure—"

"May I?"

Insecurity threatened her earlier confidence that Trent was wrong and her images were different, yes, but they held a certain depth and sorrow she hoped would appeal and be understood by the hundreds of people who'd lost loved ones.

What if Richard, TV host extraordinaire, seemingly unerring optimist, saw the images up close and agreed with what Trent's tone had implied, that they were depressing, morose and self-pitying?

Of course, Trent hadn't actually said those words, but still…

Drawing in a breath, Izzy pulled the portfolio from under her arm and carried it to the hood of her car. She opened it and Richard came close to her side. Close enough for her to inhale the fresh scent of soap and lime. She stepped back, her unease returning. From his body language, he acted as though they were dating. Which they weren't and never would be.

He leaned over the portfolio and slowly turned the pages, studying each image for a few excruciating seconds before moving on to the next.

Izzy embraced the nerves that swooped and dove in her stomach; savoring the courage it had taken to show, through her art, the internal storm she now battled daily. She wasn't ashamed to show the world Robbie's death had changed her into a sadder, lonelier, more cautious person even if others, Kate and Trent for instance, refused to believe it to be true.

"These are…" Richard shook his head and flipped back a few pages to restudy some of the images. "Amazing. Extraordinary, in fact."

"You really think so?" Izzy released her held breath as the relief of his approval washed through her. "I really hope Jay Garrett is as impressed as you seem to be."

"That's who owns the gallery?"

"Yes."

"I remember the family. They were pretty well off as I remember." He straightened and looked deep into her eyes. "Jay's the son?"

She nodded.

"Well, if he's anything like I remember his father to be, Jay's no fool. I'm sure he'll love them."

She smiled. "Thank you."

"You know if Jay says no and you start to believe your work should be exhibited on a much larger scale than what Templeton has to offer…"

"Yes?"

He turned back to the portfolio, turned the pages back and forth again, his eyes narrowed. After a few moments, he closed the book and faced her, his dark brown eyes somber. "I'd really love to invest in you…in your career."

Izzy frowned. "How?"

"I spend my money wisely, Izzy. I'm ashamed to say your earlier skepticism about mine and Francis's attitudes at the agency was warranted. As soon as I knew you were shooting this calendar for Maya, I saw it as a fated opportunity to meet you."

She stepped back and folded her arms. "Because?"

"Because I part-own a gallery in the city.

I'd really like to arrange an exhibition for you there. I loved your previous work and love this new work even more." He gently touched her elbow. "If you'd allow it, we could showcase your pictures in a kind of timeline, before and after bereavement."

She did want her work to be seen, but… "That would be using Robbie's death in a way that's wrong. Exploitation of my personal tragedy isn't something I can even begin to contemplate. My brother was—"

"Everything to you. I get that and so will the hundreds of people who see your pictures. I promise you. Everything you're going through will be truly understood."

Wasn't this the reaction, the realization, she'd secretly wanted from Trent the moment she invited him into her studio to see the images? Instead, he'd been disappointed, had wanted the old her back. A woman who had gone forever. She'd hidden her hurt that Trent didn't understand what she was trying to say through her work under a laugh.

She hadn't the courage to tell him how her work gave her an outlet she couldn't find through conversation. No matter with whom she might be speaking.

Richard cleared his throat. "Of course, for the exhibition to truly be a success, it would mean you leaving Templeton. At least, for a while. Do you have any commitments here that would stop that from happening?"

"Well, no. Not really." She swallowed as trepidation about moving away from the safety of the Cove and the people here threatened her inner ambition. "I'm very busy, but there's nothing I wouldn't be able to postpone with some prior warning. But—"

"I know the Cove means a lot to you, but I'm giving you a way out that will benefit your career enormously." He eased her arms from her chest and squeezed her hands, his gaze kind and considerate. "Francis would be more than happy to represent you, I'm sure. You'd be agented. Who knows what doors that could open for you? Plus, there will be promotion, TV and radio appearances and that's *before* the exhibition. After? Who knows what could happen for you?"

Suspicion squirmed inside and Izzy eased her hands from his. "You seem to have given this a lot of thought."

He hesitated and then lifted his hands in a gesture of surrender. "I have. Probably too much, but I mean every word. I'd love to really launch your career, Izzy."

"But why? What's in it for you?"

"I don't know. At least not yet."

"That makes no sense." She narrowed her eyes. "You're making me very uneasy, Richard. You weren't asked here to start a business relationship with me. You're here for Maya Jackson and Maya Jackson only. Templeton's my home. I have friends, fam..." *Trent.* "It's where I belong."

A flicker of irritation flashed in his eyes before he glanced at her portfolio. "Is it? These pictures tell a different story. I might be wrong, but I don't think you're happy here. Not anymore." He picked up the portfolio and handed it to her, his determined gaze boring into hers. "Maybe it's time for you to grow your career. Work on the ambition I see burning through every single thing you capture with so much verve and passion." His gaze softened. "It's your call. No pressure. Just promise me you'll think about what I'm offering."

She nodded, trepidation knotting her stomach. "I will, but I still intend to meet with Jay. I'm sure you'll agree it makes sense that I explore all my options."

"Of course. Your consideration is all I ask."

Confusion mixed with a fire for more in her life than grief, for more than the endless memories of Robbie and their times together in Templeton Cove. Wouldn't she be holding those possibilities back if she stayed here?

Richard moved to walk away and Izzy turned. "Richard?"

He faced her. "Yes?"

"Why did you come to see me this morning? It couldn't have been to talk to me about my work or you would've mentioned it over dinner the other night."

"I intended to, but the moment passed by unnoticed because I was having such a good time *not* talking business with you. However, today, I came to see you for just that reason. You're extremely talented and I'd love the opportunity to do anything I can to get your work seen by the right people. Truly. I'll see you soon."

He walked away and Izzy stared after him as he passed the security booth, waving to Mitch before continuing out onto the street.

Izzy slid her portfolio and purse onto the passenger seat of her car, shut the door and rounded the hood to the driver's side. She got into the car and gripped her keys.

In the last two days, two galleries had approached her to showcase her work. It should've been a dream come true, yet in reality, it was more of a life-affecting decision than the potential for career advancement.

She suddenly felt so unsure about something she had wanted since she was a teenager.

She started the car and as she drove across

town, her mind raced. The gallery in Templeton had been Trent's idea, which meant he believed in her work...but did he only believe in her old work? The old her?

One way or another, she had a decision to make. She either stayed in Templeton and worked with Jay Garrett, with Robbie's memory haunting her at every turn—or she moved to the city and started over. Who knew what a complete change of scenery might bring? Maybe she'd find peace and happiness where nobody expected her to be anyone but the woman she'd become.

Someone whose heart was harder and more afraid of life and living than she'd ever been before.

TRENT LIFTED HIS beer and drank, his gaze trained on the door of the Coast Inn. The bar was typically English with one difference—everyone knew everyone in Templeton and that made the Coast as welcoming as a close friend's living room. Tonight, however, Trent was not relaxed and he wasn't comfortable.

Even though Izzy had asked for this date, or whatever the hell it was, he still sensed he'd hurt her when he admitted to disliking her new pictures. She wasn't a good enough actress to hide the disappointment that had flashed in her eyes. Disappointment he'd put there, and his regret lay like a lump of lead in his gut.

He'd reacted the way he had because he hated what the shots represented. They were artistic, beautiful even, but Izzy's deep sorrow was also caught in every pixel.

Trent took another drink and gripped the glass as he placed it on the table. His job had been his refuge after Aimee died and ever since. He had no right to assume Izzy's darker projects wouldn't be hers.

He couldn't blame her if she didn't show tonight.

Her choice of the Coast as a venue was safety personified. He would've loved to take her to the Oceanside, the Cove's far superior and up-market restaurant across town, but he sensed Izzy had chosen the bar for a reason.

The meeting place and early-evening time of seven made it clear tonight was a casual thing. Nothing romantic could be anchored to it. It was a tester…maybe even a make or break between them.

Rare nerves tumbled in Trent's gut as he looked around. With dark paneling and ocean-type paraphernalia pinned and screwed to the walls, the place was decorated like the interior of a ship. Dark and light places were available for patrons to choose as they would. Which was why he'd chosen a corner table, away from the huge plasma TV and kids' video games through an archway at the back. Whatever was said tonight, he wanted to make sure he and Izzy could hear what they said to each other.

It was Friday night and the place was already filling up.

The doors swung open for a third time. No Izzy.

He'd give her the benefit of the doubt... for approximately ten more minutes. Trent scowled. Who was he kidding? He'd wait another hour if need be.

He pulled his phone from his shirt pocket. No missed calls. No texts. He scrolled through his Facebook page and resisted the temptation to tell the world he was waiting for Izzy Cooper for what he hoped would be their first official date in months. The pride that hope brought rose in his chest.

Then again, if she stood him up...

Cursing, he shut off his phone and stuffed it back in his pocket. He glanced toward the bar—and froze. That denim-covered butt could only belong to one woman.

He ran his gaze over every part of her, from the cute flats on her feet to the skinny black jeans worn with a pale peach shirt. He inhaled. She'd left her blanket of thick blond hair loose to cover her back. He'd never forget how good it felt to have her tresses lie across his chest as she slept…

She picked up the glass of red wine she'd ordered and turned. Her brow furrowed as she scanned the packed bar.

He swallowed against the longing that pulled at his chest and stood. He raised his hand. "Iz. Over here."

She turned and her face immediately broke with a wide smile. "I'm so sorry I'm late."

Relief rippled through him and he took her hand, tugging her gently forward to plant a kiss on her cheek. "It's fine. Hope a table by the window is okay?"

"It's great."

He helped her onto the high stool and she immediately eased her hand from his. "Thanks."

Disappointment tugged at him. She clearly wanted to maintain space between them. She put her purse on the table and took a sip of her drink, her gaze turned toward the window. "It's a gorgeous evening. The sunset makes Templeton look prettier than ever."

Her whimsical tone alerted Trent that something bothered her. "What's wrong? Did something happen today?"

She turned, her blue eyes instantly shadowing. "Kind of. Yes."

He raised his eyebrow in question.

She took another sip of her wine and slowly replaced it on the table before exhaling. "Richard Crawley came by my apartment."

Annoyance prickled along Trent's spine, but he fought to keep his expression impassive. "And?"

"He caught me in the parking lot just as I was on my way to the new gallery you told me about."

"You spoke to Marian?"

"Better. I spoke with Jay Garrett."

He smiled. "Straight to the source, eh?" When she didn't return his smile, Trent frowned. "So, what does Garrett's gallery have to do with Crawley?"

"He's a partial investor in another gallery in the city."

Unease whispered through Trent's gut.

"And he said if Jay wasn't interested in exhibiting my work, he would be." She sighed, picking up her glass. "Which means I would move away from the Cove. At least for a while."

"Surely you wouldn't consider—"

"As a matter of fact, I didn't say no." She met his gaze over the rim of her glass, took another sip. "And I still haven't, even though Jay didn't exactly show me the door."

"He's interested in your work?"

"Yes."

Relief should've loosened some of the tension from his shoulders, but all Trent could think about was that Izzy still considered Crawley's interest. After all this time, would it be her work that prevented any chance of them being together, rather than his?

He forced a smile and clasped her hand where it lay on the table. "So you have two galleries wanting your work. That's great."

She stared into the depths of her glass and he frowned. "Isn't it?"

When she lifted her head, her eyes were shadowed with concern. "I don't know."

"This has always been the dream, right?"

She slid her hand from his and twirled the stem of her glass. "Of course. And to have my work shown in the city is bound to be better than it being shown here in a town as small as the Cove. Plus, I can't help thinking it would do me good to get out of Templeton and leave everything that hurts so much behind. Moving to the city could be just what I need."

Trent took a long slug of his drink, his mind whirling with what to say and do as a horrible sense of loss inched into his stomach.

She stared at him. "What are you thinking?"

He took a deep breath. He could never lie to her. "I'm thinking I've haven't considered your work as something that might come between us working things out."

Her gaze held his. "Yet your work is a huge obstacle for me."

Trent closed briefly closed his eyes before opening them again. "Right."

"I'm not being obtuse, Trent. I'm telling the truth. Your work and the way Robbie died… they're too closely connected and I don't know if I'll ever be able to get past that. Don't you want me to do whatever makes me happy? A move away from here, from Robbie, could be it."

"I'd never stand in your way." He took a drink. He couldn't. If he did, what sort of man would that make him? What sort of *friend*?

"So you think I should go to the city? You agree that's where I'm the most likely to get my work recognized?"

He put his pint on the table and licked the froth from his upper lip. It was no good. He had to be honest with her. Had to be honest with what was in his heart. "I didn't say that either."

"So what are you saying?" Her cheeks flushed as her gaze searched his. "I feel so torn. I always thought I knew exactly what to do with my career. Yet here I am without any clue what to do. What if the city is the opportunity of a lifetime?"

"What if *I'm* your opportunity of a lifetime?" He squeezed his eyes shut. "I mean..." He looked at her. "Oh, Christ. Look..." He took her hand again. "I want you. You know that, but I can't offer you an exhibition. I don't have the money or the connections Jay and Crawley have, but what I do have is me. Someone who knows and cares about you. I don't want you to go. I want you to stay right here where I can see you every day. But if you want to leave..." He looked deep into her eyes. "I'm the last person who will try to stop you."

Every part of him wanted to get up, stand in front of her and kiss her—hard. So she could feel just how strongly he felt. So there could be no doubt in her mind that his feelings for her were unlikely to ever lessen or abate. Four years he'd wanted her. Four years...

He dragged his gaze from her lips and plucked two menus from the holder beside him. "Let's talk about something else. I wanted you to have a good time tonight, and this feels the opposite." She took the menu he offered her and Trent perused his, his heart beating hard. "What are you having?"

When her answer didn't come, Trent looked up.

She stared, her gaze determined and her shoulders straight. "You can't save me, Trent."

Trent stilled. “What?”

“Robbie died and then you told me about Aimee. You can’t save everybody, and if that’s what you’re trying to do for me, then that’s more reason than ever for me to get away from here.”

He shook his head and looked at the menu. The passion swirling in his blood pulsed with insult. Was he trying to save her? Was that what his frustration was really about? No. It couldn’t be. He wanted to be with her. Period. As partners. Best friends. Lovers. “I’m not trying to save you.”

“No? Then what are you doing?”

He met her steady gaze. “Trying to make you mine and me yours.”

She stared at him for a long moment before her eyes softened. “Trent, please try to understand. I can’t spend every day wondering if today is the day I lose you. I have no one who needs anything from me. I’m free to do and go where I want, and maybe that’s exactly what I should be doing instead of keeping all this anger and sadness pent up inside. My pictures could be a hit in the city. I could make more money than I’ve ever dreamed of.”

“And you think money will make you happy. It never made anyone happy. You know that.”

She put down her menu and looked past him toward the bar, her face unreadable, her eyes turned away from him.

He studied her beautiful profile. "I'd never hurt you, Iz. I know you don't need me protecting you or caring for you, but Robbie…"

"Would've wanted you to." She met his gaze, tears glinting in her eyes. "And maybe part of me wants that too, but I'm scared, Trent. Really, really scared."

He laced his fingers with hers. "And you think I'm not? I told you about Aimee to make you understand you're not alone in this and life goes on. Aimee died fourteen years ago, but I still think about her every day. She was twelve years old, I was seventeen and was meant to be looking after her but was too interested in chatting with the girl down the street to worry about what Aimee was up to in the house. The fire…" He inhaled a shaky breath. "It happened so fast, and by the time I ran back to get her out of there, flames roared from the upstairs window. I tried so hard to get to her, but the neighbors…they were pulling me back, calling 999."

She squeezed his fingers, a tear slipping over her cheek. "It wasn't your fault."

"It was and that's something I have to live

with for the rest of my life." Regret, sorrow and anguish twisted his heart and he took a breath, praying she heard him. "You'll think about Robbie every day too, but that doesn't mean you have to stop living. I want to make you happy. I want you to trust me, but if going to the city is what you think will work for you, then you should go. I just didn't want you to go not knowing how I feel about you."

She drew her hand from his and as she picked up her glass, the wine trembled. "I'll always trust you to take care of me. It's not that which makes this so hard. It's *me* I don't trust. I don't trust that I could handle losing another person. People die and people are born, and if we get into this, I have a feeling it could be something special." She took a sip of her wine. "I couldn't bear losing you. I couldn't bear losing Kate. You're all I have left. Us being together, me staying in the Cove could be a very bad decision."

"Iz—"

"If I stay here, if I try the gallery in Templeton, I'm not sure how much longer I can keep denying my feelings for you run deeper than friendship." Another tear rolled over her cheek. "But I can't stop the fear that, eventually, I'll lose you too."

Admiration and hope surged through him that she'd showed her utter vulnerability for the first time in months. This was the Izzy he'd be drawn to years ago. This was the Izzy who was soft, caring and loving, yet stronger than anyone he knew. He thought that person had gone along with Robbie, but deep down Izzy…his Izzy…was still there, struggling to find a way out.

Trent pushed to his feet and closed the space between them. With his heart pounding with the weight of her possible rejection, he looked into her eyes, slid his hands over her shoulders and moved in close.

Her beautiful eyes widened. "What are you doing?"

"I'm going to kiss you."

Even as her gaze darted around the bar, her tongue poked out to wet her bottom lip as though anticipating what came next. That was all the permission he needed.

He slid one hand to the back of her neck, under her perfect mane of silky hair, and drew her closer. With his other hand rested on her thigh, he gave a final perusal of her exquisite face before lowering his mouth to hers. Once again, her sweet taste astounded him and made him yearn for more. The electricity between them was dangerous. Hot enough to burn and powerful enough to last a lifetime.

She was rigid for a few seconds before she turned pliant, her soft moan into his mouth sexy and inviting. Whether it was the months he'd been forced to watch her grieve from afar, he had no idea, but never before had he felt so connected to anyone.

He touched her face as he kissed her, making a silent pact that if she allowed him, he'd look after her for the rest of his life.

He touched his tongue to hers and kissed her deeper, resisting the urge to pull her closer, knowing she was conscious of the people around them. The background music continued to pump from the speakers, but the patrons' voices seemed to have quieted, and all Trent was aware of was the sound of her supersexy exhalations and her tight grip on his biceps.

Slowly, she pulled back. Her cheeks pink and her eyes happy. "Well, there you go, then."

He grinned. "Yep, there you go."

She coughed and picked up a menu. "I need a burger, fries and a side order of garlic bread." She lifted her gaze to his and smiled. "I'm starving, and if you kiss me like that again, I'm going to forget to eat."

He laughed and slid back onto his seat. "Well, we don't want that, do we?"

CHAPTER NINE

IZZY EASED FARTHER back into the sofa in the far corner of her studio and let Kate do the talking. Inexplicable tension pulsed between her friend and Richard Crawley and Izzy had no idea why. They seemed to have taken an instant dislike to each other, but fortunately, Kate wouldn't have to endure him very much longer. He'd called this meeting two days before it had originally been scheduled because he'd needed to get back to the city earlier than anticipated.

As the tension between Kate and Richard mounted, Izzy was grateful for the small mercy of his early departure.

Kate continued to speak and Richard's usually cheerful persona continued to dissolve.

"So, all in all, that's where we're at." Kate closed the notepad in her lap and laid her pen on top of it. "Izzy will take the cover shot of you and the other firefighters tomorrow, and then the other firefighters' will be done one by one around the Cove or in the studio, wherever she thinks best."

He frowned. "And in the meantime, you'd like me to visit Maya and her parents in the hospital?"

Kate nodded. "Yes, but as you have been called back to work, I was going to suggest Izzy and Trent go instead."

Knowing the underlying tension in her friend's tone indicated irritation at best, out-and-out war at worst, Izzy leaned forward. "It would be good to garner as much publicity as possible for the calendar before its release. You visiting Maya, getting to know her and her parents, will interest the press…not to mention delight Maya."

He turned to Kate. "Could you give Izzy and me a moment alone?"

Izzy inwardly groaned. She didn't want a moment alone with Richard if his annoyed expression was anything to go by. The kind and interested look in his eyes before had slowly diminished ever since she hadn't readily agreed to his offer to exhibit her work.

Kate held his gaze before turning to Izzy and raising an eyebrow.

Izzy sighed. "It's fine. Why don't you put on some coffee? Richard will be leaving soon." She faced Richard, her spine rigid. "Right?"

He nodded, his mouth set in a grim line.

Kate stood and held out her hand to Richard. "Then I'll say goodbye until we next see each other."

He took her hand. "It's been a pleasure."

Tension permeated the air. Richard clearly had no idea how passionate and focused Kate was about her work. Mess with her ideas and strategies when kids or animals were involved and woe betide the target of her retaliation.

As soon as Kate disappeared into the kitchen at the back of the studio, Izzy faced Richard. "You shouldn't have done that."

"Done what?" He relaxed his shoulders, his gaze softer. "Look, cards on the table. I meant everything I said about the gallery in the city and I really hoped to have your decision before I left."

"So that's more important to you than what we can do to help Maya?"

"Of course not. Whatever you decide about the gallery, I'll still do the calendar."

"I'm glad to hear it." Izzy stood, unconvinced and completely aware her new reaction to Richard was most likely more about her than him. Wasn't she inwardly grappling for an excuse not to take him up on his offer in the city? Wasn't she just too scared to leave Templeton in order to try something new and unexplored? She held out her hand. "Look, why don't we say goodbye for now and I'll see you tomorrow for the cover shot?"

He stood and pushed his fallen hair from his brow. "Fine. When will you let me know your decision about the gallery?"

"Whenever I've decided…which isn't yet."

"I don't understand why you are biting my hand off. The city—"

"I need to be honest with you. There's every chance I'll choose to stay in Templeton. This is my home and—"

"You're making a big mistake." He shook his head. "Your pictures are too good to stay in a place as small as Templeton."

"If that's true, they will eventually find their way to the city on their own merit, regardless of where I am." She walked toward the door and opened it, turning to face him as he came closer. "In the meantime, I'd rather find out for myself whether staying in Templeton is a mistake."

"It sounds to me as though you've already made up your mind."

"I think maybe I have."

He stood opposite her and Izzy was forced to tip her head back to meet his eyes. His gaze traveled over her hair and face. "You have my card. Call me. Anytime."

She nodded. "Thank you."

With a final lingering look, he turned and left the studio. Izzy closed the door firmly behind him and released her held breath.

Kate emerged from the kitchen, holding two steaming mugs. "Has he gone?"

Izzy strode forward, taking one of the mugs from her friend. "Yes. Awkward doesn't even come close to what that farewell was like."

"Well, I'm glad he's not here anymore. The guy's a jerk. I really wish I had another celebrity lined up and I could let Crawley go." She sipped her coffee. "But I haven't, so we're stuck with him."

"What don't you like about him? You seem awfully wound up right now."

"I am. Everything about him has wound me up since he called me last night. Not to talk about Maya, or the calendar, but about you."

"Me?" Izzy narrowed her eyes. "What did he say?"

"That he thinks you are lowering yourself by staying in the Cove. That he had the ability to turn your life around." She shook her head, her gaze angry. "What gives the guy the right to think there's anything wrong with your life the way it is? He's a jackass."

Izzy inhaled a shaky breath. "A jackass who's

made my decision of whether or not to work with Jay Garrett an easy one."

Kate's eyes brightened. "You're staying?"

Izzy smiled. "I think maybe I am."

"Oh, Iz." Kate pulled her in for a hug. "I am so happy about that." She held Izzy at arm's length. "I really didn't want you to leave, but have no right to tell you how to live your life."

Izzy laughed. "You have every right...because nine times out of ten, you're spot on. About everything." Taking her hand, Izzy tugged Kate toward the sofa.

"Now, enough of our soppiness. Come and have a seat. I've something to tell you that will undoubtedly cheer you up."

Kate smiled. "Ooh, sounds interesting."

They sat side by side on the sofa and Izzy told her all about her date with Trent a few days before. "And then I said, 'Well, there you go, then.'"

Kate burst out laughing. "Wow, you really are sexy personified, aren't you?"

Izzy grinned. "Just call me Izzy the Incredible."

"That was Friday? And you've seen him every day for the last four days? God, you guys don't hold back once you finally get it together, do you?"

Immediate worry hurtled into Izzy's conscience and her smile dissolved. "Do you think it's too easy?"

Kate froze and hovered her coffee cup over the table. "What's too easy?"

"Us. Me and Trent."

"What are you talking about?" She put the cup on the table. "Nothing about you two getting together has been easy. Plus…" She wiggled her eyebrows. "You've got lots of missed time to make up for. I think it's great you've stopped fighting your feelings for him, and so should you."

"I know, but—"

"Ah, ah. No buts. Enjoy this, Iz. Please."

Izzy stared at her friend…the friend she'd come close to losing if Kate hadn't so easily forgiven Izzy's rejection of her comfort over the last few months. She inhaled as the enormousness of change she'd gone through over the last few days poked and prodded at her conscience. The happier, more hopeful feeling that now surrounded her was hard to describe or understand. It was as though Robbie had shoved Richard Crawley in front of her so Izzy could see the gargantuan mistake she could've made by leaving the Cove and turning her back on Trent.

She touched Kate's hand. "Why don't you

and I do something fun tonight? We haven't been out in ages."

"Aren't you seeing Trent?"

"He's on nights and anyway, no man will ever come between me and a good night out with my best mate."

Kate grinned. "I'm glad to hear it. We could go see a movie and finish the night off with a couple of glasses of wine at the Coast."

"Sounds good to me."

They finished their coffee and Izzy carried their empty cups into the kitchen. She placed them on the drainer and stared through the window into the small backyard. As much as she had enjoyed every moment of her and Trent's union so far, the niggling feeling that things might go wrong between them—or the unthinkable might happen—wouldn't dissipate.

If she were to lose him…a man she'd been attracted to for more years than she wanted to admit, she would never recover. Pain twisted inside her heart every time she thought of another loss, yet it quickened with excitement whenever she imagined she might be with Trent forever. Even have a family with him one day.

As the view ahead of her blurred, Kate's

footsteps sounded behind her and Izzy swiped the tears from her eyes.

"You okay?" The weight of Kate's hand fell onto Izzy's shoulder.

Izzy swilled the cups under the tap. "Sure."

"Iz…"

"Hmm?"

"What's wrong?"

"Nothing." Izzy briefly closed her eyes before turning to face Kate. She'd promised her best friend she wouldn't keep things from her ever again. Yet once again, Izzy fought to keep her fears inside. She took a deep breath. "Why me?"

Kate frowned. "Why you, what?"

"Why does the town's hottest firefighter want me? Trent is great-looking, funny and knows how to treat a lady. All I've been is horrible to him over the past few months and he still keeps coming back for more."

"Because, for Trent, it's always been you. You know that."

"Do I?" She put the last cup on the drainer and snatched a cloth from the hook beside her to dry her hands. "He's hardly being standing around pining for me. He's been dating. Admittedly, some of those relationships have lasted days rather than weeks, but still."

"Still what? This is Trent we're talking about

and now that you're slowly returning to who you were before Robbie, Trent won't be going anywhere." She widened her eyes in warning. "Unless you let him go, of course. Is that what this is about? You're not even sure you want to be with him?"

Izzy's heart swelled in her chest as certainty rushed through every cell in her body. "Oh, I'm sure."

Kate smiled. "Good, because you look happier than you have in months. Trent is good for you. Just trust that and don't think any deeper. Thinking too hard isn't all it's cracked up to be. If I thought too much about half the people I try to help, I'd be in an asylum. We have to live day by day and be grateful for the good things that happen. Those are the rules."

"You're right. Trent knows me better than most people, present company excluded. He gets my crazy and still wants me."

"Exactly. You're lucky you found your man. Maybe this time next year, I'll have found mine too."

Izzy smiled. "God bless the poor guy."

Kate grinned. "Hey, it's just going to take a certain kind of man to handle me, that's all. I'm too much woman for any bloke in Templeton, that's for sure. Anyway, enough about me. Tell me about the sex."

Izzy laughed. "There's nothing to tell. At least, not yet."

Her eyes widened. "No wonder there's so much sexual tension flying around when you two are together. What's wrong? Is it you or him?"

Izzy lifted her shoulders as though it was no big deal that neither her nor Trent had made a move toward the bedroom yet, for reasons she wasn't sure she understood. "I don't know. We'll get there when the time is right, I suppose."

Kate lifted an eyebrow. "From where I'm standing, the time is right every time I see the pair of you together. The tension is hot. H.O.T. Hot."

Izzy shook her head, tucked her arm into Kate's and steered her out of the kitchen and back to the studio seating area. "Sit. Let's concentrate on Maya Jackson instead of my sex life, shall we?"

"Fine. But don't think the subject won't come up again if you don't get on with it. A good session is just what you need."

"Give me strength." Izzy lifted her sketch pad off the table in front of them. "Right. Concentrate. Do you have the color copies of the firefighters' IDs? We'll use them to allocate their chosen month. Hopefully, one look at their picture will differentiate Mr. May from Mr. December."

Kate hauled her bag from the seat beside her and unzipped it. She grinned and pulled out a large brown envelope. "Ready?"

Izzy nodded and poised her pencil over her sketch pad. "Ready."

Kate opened the envelope and showered the copies of the firefighters' IDs onto the table. She spread them out, her eyes fiendishly bright. "It's a dirty job, but someone's got to do it."

As though drawn to Trent's picture by a tracker beam, Izzy plucked it from the lineup of twelve muscular and extraordinarily handsome men. "I know just what I have planned for this guy."

Kate grinned. "Really? What a surprise."

Izzy met Kate's gaze and they burst out laughing.

IZZY STOOD IN the studio and took another long drink from her water bottle. The group cover shot with Richard and the firefighters had been done and now Trent was the next person due to arrive at the studio. She lowered the bottle and closed her eyes. She needed to focus on raising money to help Maya, nothing else. Not why Trent hadn't made a move to get her back into bed…or how much she wanted him to. It had been months since they made love, and Izzy's desire for him burned hotter than ever.

The agony of not knowing him in every way was becoming worse than not knowing him at all, but she didn't have the confidence to make the first move.

She opened her eyes and stared toward the front window, insecurity twisting inside.

After spending so much wonderful time together, laughing and dating, Trent still seemed to be holding himself back physically and she had no idea why. Their kisses were passionate and full of yearning. He touched and caressed her but always pulled back when they could've taken that final, blissful leap.

It was as though he wanted her to be sure; that he waited for her to want him. Did he not sense how much she wanted to be with him? Or did he sense her fear of truly surrendering every part of her? Because that was exactly what she continued to do.

Once she and Trent made love again, there would be no going back. Her heart would be his, for better or worse—but she couldn't wait one more day…

A soft tap sounded on the studio door before it opened.

Trent lingered in the doorway, his gaze immediately on hers. Izzy's heartbeat quickened as he glided his study over her neck, breasts and lower until his appraisal reached her feet. Every inch of her body zinged with awareness. All six feet two inches of him filled the entrance, his wide shoulders almost brushing either side of the door frame as he stepped into the studio.

"Here I am. Reporting for duty."

She smiled and the tension eased from her shoulders. "You'd better shut the door, then." She wandered toward the tripod facing the white sheets that would provide the backdrop to Trent's partially naked body. "On second thought, you might want to lock it and lower the blinds too."

"What?"

She turned around, planted her hands on her hips and raised her eyebrows. "What I have planned for you will be for my eyes only until the calendar's released."

He grinned, his gorgeous green eyes darkening. "You're not going to scare me away, you know."

"Wouldn't dream of it."

He threw the bolt into place and turned the key in the door before walking to the picture window in front of the studio and lowering the blind with achingly slow precision. Izzy stood stock-still and resisted the urge to storm across the space between them, leap into his arms and devour his lips with hers.

He turned. "Where do you want me?"

Her gaze glided over his broad chest, strong and hard beneath the cover of a crisp, white T-shirt. *Now, there's a question.* "Lose the shirt and go into the bathroom. You need to douse your upper body in water."

His cocky smile vanished. "I need to what?"

She lifted an eyebrow and crossed her arms.

"Fine." He raised his hands in surrender. "Whatever you need."

The deep, husky and entirely masculine tone of his voice slithered over her skin and into her weakened heart. Their reunion had brought forth a new awareness, a new acceptance that life was too short to waste. Now was the time to act, to take Trent and face whatever happened next.

She inhaled and forced a wide smile. "When you're done, come and stand in the center of the sheets. I'll direct you from there."

His gaze held hers as he strolled past her, and a flutter of anticipation sent tremors through her abdomen. The sexual tension in the room was rife and he was one of the most intelligent men she'd ever met. He would know what she wanted just by looking into her eyes.

She smiled…and the hunger in his eyes told her he might just be more than a willing participant in her plans.

The rustle of clothes being discarded filled the room and Izzy returned to the table where she'd left her water. She took a drink and switched on her iPod. A 1980s rock ballad filled the room.

From the corner of her eye, she caught a flash of Trent's darkly tanned and ridiculously muscular back through the doorway as he stripped off his T-shirt in the bathroom. She strolled across the room for her camera as he pulled the bathroom door slightly closed. The muted sound of running, then splashing water, filtered from the bathroom into the studio.

Izzy concentrated on mounting a lens, desperately trying to dispel the images of what Trent was doing from running through her imagination. Her heart skipped as the shower abruptly stopped, followed by his footsteps as he reentered the studio.

She raised her head. *Oh, for the love of God...*

His black firefighter-issue trousers were tucked into steel-capped boots, red suspenders dangling, leaving his torso and chest bare. His thick, glossy hair matched the dark line running from his navel to the waistband of those stupidly sexy trousers. Izzy licked her lips as her body hummed with arousal.

Mr. April…

The idea to douse Trent in an April shower had come to her in the middle of the night. A sexily splendid idea. She'd battled with the decision to change the design over and over—but had kept to her creative plan. How the hell was she to know how much his glistening skin would turn her on?

"You want me on the sheets, right?"

"We'll start there, yes."

He grinned, his eyes dancing in such a happy and sexy way, Izzy fought to maintain every ounce of willpower not to jump him there and then. Instead, she stepped forward and put her eye to the camera, taking in more of what her mind and body had already been exposed to. Her mouth drained dry. He was beautiful. The golden-bronze sheen of his skin, the hardened ridge of his wide shoulders leading down to arms, sinewy with muscle and tendons. A body like his wasn't something a woman saw on a daily basis.

She took a few shots, before pulling back and meeting his cool green gaze. "Step toward the back a little. That's it. I need a bit of breathing space."

He smiled. "Got it."

Biting back her smile, Izzy returned to the camera, her heart beating out of control. His voice—and smile—was torture as she continued with her plan of slow seduction. The plan wasn't working in quite the way she anticipated. Trent had the benefit of being covered in water, whereas she was burning up… everywhere.

She peered back into the camera lens, mesmerized by the gorgeous sight of him. Her body yearned for his on top of hers…in hers. As much as she wanted to protect herself from further loss, further hurt, she wanted Trent. So much.

Swallowing the unexpected lump that formed in her throat, she forced a smile. "Okay, let's do this. Tip your head back as though you're enjoying the sexiest rain shower of your life. Let me see your acting skills."

The next torturous half hour passed as Trent posed and flexed under her increasingly erotic direction. She pretended she was in control of the situation, secretly hoping every direction she made would make him blanch or at least flinch. Yet the man looked as though he was enjoying every damn minute. Somehow he'd turned the tables and the whole shoot was tormenting her, not him.

"Are we done?" The low, confident rumble of his voice splintered her reverie.

She abruptly stepped back from the tripod. "Sure. That's a wrap. You did well…" She winked. "For an amateur."

He smiled. "I'll take that as a compliment."

She detached the camera from the tripod, her fingers shaking as she fought the need to run her hands over the width of his biceps, up and over the rigid plane of his shoulders to his thick neck and into his hair.

The timing had to be perfect. Romantic. Cool. Gentle.

She cleared her throat. "I'll send you copies when I'm happy with them."

"Great."

The steady approach of his heavy tread sent her heartbeat into overdrive.

He came closer and she shot a glance at the locked door of the studio. Their easy flirtations had come back tenfold, their kisses and touches simmering with a heat they both knew would reach boiling point sooner or later.

Izzy closed her eyes. She'd actually believed she could handle today.

He touched his finger to her chin, just a whisper of skin-on-skin contact as he tilted her face upward. "Hi."

She opened her eyes and her stomach knotted. "Hi."

He eased the camera from her hands and laid it carefully on her workstation. She stared at his beautiful face, and her breathing turned harried. Could she really let down her defenses and love Trent without fear of him being taken away from her one day?

His gaze ran like a soft caress over her face. "You're so sexy and talented. Just looking at you drives me insane." His gaze bored into hers, the muscles of his arms flexing and relaxing. "So I'm going to make love to you. Right now."

Her entire body weakened under the intensity of his gaze.

He eased her back until her butt pressed up against the edge of the workstation.

Her heart picked up speed as her body ached with the need to nip her teeth along one of his incredibly hard, darkly tanned shoulders.

He brushed some hair from her eyes. "I want you more than I've ever wanted anyone. You feel it, don't you? You feel the heat between us. Nothing bad is ever going to happen again. I promise."

"Don't...don't promise me that." She squeezed her eyes shut and cursed the warmth of her tears as they slipped to her cheeks.

Sobs clogged her throat as her body trembled with animalistic need to take him, own him and make him take her under, over and over again until the memories vanished and all she saw was him.

But she was still so scared to love a man who leaped into flames every day. A man who risked his life over and over in the same infernos that took her brother and his sister.

"No." She placed her hands flat on his chest. "I can't."

He gently cupped his hands to her jaw. "Look at me. See me. Please."

He ran his gaze over her face, lingering at her lips before looking deep into her eyes, begging, pleading…

The moment his lips touched hers, she was his. Her body lit with the fire she feared yet had no way of extinguishing. She clung to him, held him. She slipped her tongue eagerly into the warmth of his mouth as her skin tingled with the sensation of his hands cherishing every inch of her waist, her hips, all the way up and over her body to tangle in the hair at the nape of her neck.

"Izzy. Let me love you." He dropped his mouth to the curve of her neck and lower to her collarbone.

"Yes." The word whispered from between her lips, her body trembling with need.

He met her eyes, their dark depths seeking permission and assurance. "Do you really see me?"

She nodded. "I see only you."

He smiled and she lifted her hand to the back of his neck to bring him closer and claim his mouth once more. They took and devoured, battled and surrendered until she drew back to catch her breath.

She gave him a gentle shove backward and tugged her shirt from her jeans. *Live for now. Be happy.* The words resonated in her head and, one by one, she slipped open her buttons. The shirt brushed over her shoulders and fell to the hardwood floor. This time she saw the man, the hero, the caretaker and her very own savior. Trent wasn't everyone's firefighter and he wasn't Mr. April. He was hers.

Fingers shaking, she unhooked her bra.

CHAPTER TEN

SHE WAS BEAUTIFUL.

Trent kissed her as Izzy clung to his biceps, making him feel needed and trusted, her tongue firm and wanting in his mouth. But as desperate as he was to take her, he was all too aware of what this surrender meant to her.

He had to show her he'd take care of her, would honor her trust and love her as he'd promised.

Reluctantly, he eased his lips from hers to stare into her huge, blue eyes, now dark with desire. He had to see her love, her truth. Her cheeks flushed and her lips glistened ruby red. He inhaled the rich scent of her perfume.

She smiled, her gaze so soft with love that his heart pounded with relief, his chest hurting. Slipping his hand from hers, he bent over to unbuckle his cumbersome steel-capped boots. He glanced toward her as she kicked off her ballet flats.

Once he'd discarded his boots and socks, she held out her hand. "Come with me."

Straightening, he clasped her hand. He would've followed her to the ends of the earth. She tugged him toward a closed door at the back of the studio. His gaze roamed over her back, down to her tight, perfect ass cruelly covered in denim. She pushed open the door and flicked on a lamp on a side table. The small, neat office was bathed in a soft amber light and she turned, reaching onto her toes to gently pull his bottom lip between her teeth before clasping the nape of his neck and bringing his mouth closer.

She kissed him, her exhalation whispering softly into his mouth. The agony of waiting for her stretched Trent's patience to breaking, but still he waited. She reached for his trousers and unzipped them, her brow furrowed in concentration, her fingers busy releasing him from his boxers. He ran his hands over her shoulders; they were as smooth and perfect as the rest of her. He unsnapped her jeans.

The air hit his erection as she smoothed his boxers down his hips. With a finger to her chin, he lifted her face and hungrily kissed her again. Their patience vanished, and the careful consideration of the past few minutes evaporated into a frenzy of lustful need. He'd wanted her too long to stand on ceremony; had waited too long for her to realize he'd never hurt her as long as he breathed.

Their lips slipped apart as they discarded the final constraints of their clothing. Trent drew her into his arms, relishing the sensation of her breasts pressed firmly against his chest. She was small yet full of strength.

As he lifted her, she locked her ankles at the base of his spine and he glanced around the room as she nibbled on his neck, making him crazy. In the far end of the room, a desk sat with papers neatly stacked in one corner and a tray of memory cards in the other, leaving plenty of space in between for her sexy behind. He carried her toward the desk and lowered her on top.

She spread her legs wide, her eyes locked on his. He drank her in, taking a moment for fear of never seeing her this way again. What if she regretted the sex? What if a physical relationship ended up pushing her away from him instead of toward him?

No. He wouldn't go there.

She wanted him. He had to trust her as he wanted her to trust him.

He gently squeezed one of her breasts and she tipped her head back, arched her spine, inviting his exploration. Her eyes were hooded and her mouth open.

His body trembled. "Look at me, Iz."

Once her eyes were fully open and concentrated on his, he slid his hand over her rib cage and down to her most intimate place. He ran his fingers lightly over her before slipping two fingers deep inside. How could she exceed what he'd fantasized about almost every night since they were apart?

She groaned and writhed against his fingers as Trent hitched her closer. "Trent. Wait."

She leaned to the side and opened a drawer beside them. Fumbling inside, she withdrew a foil packet and slammed the drawer. She ripped the packet open and slowly glided her hand up and down the length of him before smoothing on the condom.

Gripping the backs of her knees, Trent yanked her forward. She gasped, her eyes shining with delight as she leaned back on her hands.

He smiled and studied her beautiful face once more before he drove deep inside her. Her obvious satisfaction burned through his body and Trent gripped her thighs, thrusting into her again. Their impatient breaths filled the air and fueled his arousal. Never before had he entered a woman and felt such a sense of belonging or connection. He wouldn't do a single thing to mess up their growing trust, to risk losing the woman he'd wanted since he first saw her four years before.

He heightened his pace as her nails cut into his forearms. She tightened around him, and her face contorted in ecstasy as she came. The sight of her, the feel of her, was too much and finally Trent tipped over the edge and straight into paradise.

Be with me, Izzy. Be mine. Always.

THE NEXT MORNING, Trent had barely bitten into his bacon sandwich when the control center call-out reverberated over the speaker system, echoing off the station walls that all units were to respond to a house fire call.

He and the rest of the crew leaped to their feet.

Rushing from the kitchen, Trent raced into the fire station courtyard toward one of the two fire trucks ordered out. He and Will jumped inside and Sam slid behind the wheel. The siren blared as they sped from the station and headed toward the given address.

Trent's blood burned with the usual rush of adrenaline whenever they were called out. Cars moved to the side and trucks mounted pavements to let them through the narrow streets and around sharp corners until they finally arrived at the emergency destination.

He was first out of the truck and didn't look back, knowing Will and Sam would be right behind him. Smoke plumed from an upstairs window and people already gathered around, their faces panic-stricken as they stared helplessly toward the burning upper level. The second fire truck came to an abrupt stop and Trent immediately turned to the fire chief to await his instructions.

Will and Sam's concern about Trent becoming distracted and making bad decisions at work resonated in Trent's head. His colleagues' observations had cut deep and he needed to prove to Will and Sam that, even though his relationship with Izzy had escalated on every level, his head would always be in the game at work. No matter what.

He shifted from one foot to the other, his focus gliding over the house and surrounding area. The need to get inside the building and attack the fire burned through him.

He turned to Chief Moyes, who darted his gaze from the house to his assembled crew. "Palmer, Paterson and Kent, I want you in protective gear and up the ladder ASAP." He yelled his instructions to Trent, Sam and Will before turning to the others standing behind them. "Marchton, Ellis and Seymour, I want you to secure the area and find out exactly who's in the house. Fall out."

"My wife's up there. She's in there. I just came home from work to..."

Trent heard the man's desperate shouts just as the husband sprinted toward the front door. Trent shoved his second arm into his fireproof jacket and grabbed the husband. He stared into the man's eyes as Will, Sam and the others rushed past them toward the house.

"Sir, you stay right here. Running in there isn't going to help your wife, or us get the fire under control and your wife safe. Do you understand?"

The man stared wide-eyed toward his burning home, his face smudged with soot. "I came home from work to get some papers. I tried to get to her—"

"I know you did, but now it's our turn. What is that room?" Trent pointed to the blazing upper floor. "A bedroom? Study?"

"A bedroom. Our bedroom. I don't know what she was doing—"

"Okay. You're going to stay right here. Got it?"

The man's jaw tightened, his gaze frantic, but he nodded. Trent returned his nod and rushed toward the house. The ladder was already positioned and Will climbed through the sheet of fog that concealed the window in an effort to get inside.

Sam followed up behind Will as Trent ran toward the open front door. A colleague behind him called out that the wife was the only person inside. A modicum of relief whispered through Trent's gut that they looked to save one life rather than multiple.

He sprinted up the stairs.

Thick gray smoke filled the landing, and flames licked around the outside of the closed bedroom door, charring its edges black. The fire was already dangerously close to spreading and smoke seeped in thicker and thicker rivers of gray from beneath the door.

There was too much risk of back draft to attempt opening the door.

He looked toward the ceiling. The wooden timbers in the roof would already be hot, ready to crack and splinter.

"Guys, what do you see in there?" Trent yelled through his mouthpiece. "Do you have the civilian?"

"Bringing her out now..." Will inhaled a long breath. "She's taken a lot of smoke. She's saying there's somebody else in the room. Sam's looking now, but it's dark as hell in here. The smell is… I don't know what started this blaze, but just don't open the door. It's burning its ass off already."

"I thought she was alone."

"I'm taking her down before we lose her."

The connection remained silent as Trent searched through the other upstairs rooms. They were empty. "All clear. Sam? Are you clear? Did you find anyone else?"

Static crackled down the connection.

"Chief, can you hear me?" Trent yelled as icy-cold fingers of dread tiptoed up his spine. Why the hell wasn't Sam answering him? He, Will and Sam worked together like a finely oiled machine, guessing each other's positions and thoughts before they came to fruition. "Chief?"

More static and then the chief's voice came through. "Loud and clear, Palmer. What do you see? We need to get the water up there right now."

"The fire is barely contained in the bedroom, sir. It's going to spread, and spread fast. Is Kent clear with the civilian?"

"He's coming to ground now. Once they're clear, we'll start dousing this thing."

"There are no other civilians?"

"No. Get yourself out here and let the others take over. All clear inside."

"The wife said there was someone else in here."

"What? Hold on."

Trent continued his search, the smoke growing denser with each passing second, trailing along the landing carpet, the flames reaching like fingers around the edge of the closed bedroom door.

"Sam? What's your position? Answer me." Trent cursed and looked to the closed bedroom door once more. He couldn't wait any longer. He needed to get inside that room. Something wasn't right. Either Sam was injured or he had his hands too full with something to concentrate on communication. Either way, Trent couldn't leave one of his best friends alone in that room. "Chief? Permission to enter the bedroom from the inside. Paterson isn't responding. Sir?"

"I'm ordering the hoses now. Get out and come clear. That's an order. The wife is with the paramedics, and the husband is adamant no one else is in the house."

"What about Sam? Is he clear?" No answer. "Sir? Is Sam clear?"

"Get out here now, Palmer. That's an order."

"Shit." Trent glanced toward the door before hurrying for the stairwell.

He'd barely taken three steps down when the bedroom door cracked open and a human fireball came screaming through the flames, collapsing onto the landing carpet and rolling back and forth. Orange, red and blue flames leaped and spread around the writhing body with a life of their own.

Trent ducked his head and scrambled back up the stairs, his gut tightening with the knowledge that the body could be Sam. He rolled the guy over and over, killing the flames. It wasn't Sam. Where was he? Trent shot another glance toward the engulfed bedroom, cursed and dragged the man by the legs through the smoke. Hefting the lifeless body onto his shoulders, Trent carried him down the stairs. "I have a second civilian, sir. Male. Have you had any response from Paterson?"

The chief came over the line. "Nothing. The water has started. Who's the man? For Christ's sake, it's not—"

"No, sir. From what's left of his jeans and shirt, it's not Paterson. I'm bringing him out now. It's bad."

Deep in Trent's gut, a knot of failure formed. The guy around his shoulders was badly burned and clearly had inhaled a lot of smoke.

His skin was charred and blackened, bright red flesh showing like craters amid flashes of pale skin, so much whiter than Sam's. As Trent emerged into the sunlight, he made for the paramedics as they rushed toward him with a gurney. He laid the man down, before leaving the paramedics to do their job. He strode toward the chief, who yelled into his handset.

"Paterson? Come in. Paterson?"

"He's still in there?" Trent glared at the chief's profile and back toward the upstairs window. "What the hell happened? Where's Kent?"

"Here."

Trent swiveled to face Will. "What happened? Where's Sam?"

Will looked past Trent to the house, his jaw tight and his gaze angry. "The guy you pulled out jumped on Sam as I was heading out the window with the wife. The last I knew, he was struggling with the guy, trying to reason with him." He wiped his hand over his soot-covered face. "Jesus Christ, why weren't we told there was more than one person up there? We need to get to Sam right now."

Trent looked toward the window. The gray smoke turned black as the remainder of the crew fought to extinguish the blaze. He couldn't lose another friend to the flames. Not now. Not ever.

"Who was the guy I just bought out? Was the wife messing around with him? The husband said there was no one else in the house." Trent turned and strode toward the man who was frantically trying to get to his wife as one paramedic worked on the woman and another fought to physically restrain the husband. Trent gripped the guy's shoulder and spun him around. "Hey. Who was in the house with your wife?"

The man froze. "What?"

"I brought a second person out. A man. Who was he?"

All the color drained from the man's face as he looked from Trent to his wife. Her face was covered with a mask, her long hair marred with soot.

The man's gaze had turned from frantic to defeated. "She must've still been seeing him."

"An affair? Your wife was having an affair?" Trent stared at the husband, his hands curling into fists. "My friend could be lying dead up there because he tried to save another man who was having sex with your wife? I don't believe this."

"Trent, knock it off." Will gripped Trent's upper arm and pull him round. "We're wasting time. Forget why the guy was up there, will you? Sam's all that matters now."

Trent stared into Will's angry eyes. "But don't you see what—"

"All I see is you flying off the handle, concentrating on the wrong thing." Will glared and moved his hand to Trent's shoulder. "Get your head in the game, Trent. Do you hear me? We need to find Sam."

Releasing him, Will ran toward the house.

Swallowing the need to shout at anything or anyone, Trent rushed after his friend, ignoring the chief's calls. Together, they entered the house just as one of the crew came down the stairs with Sam over his shoulder.

Ellis shook his head.

Trent stared in disbelief as Will's curses mixed with the screaming inside Trent's head. The vehemence of his friend's words bounced from the hallway walls. Dead. Sam was dead?

Trent numbly moved to the side as Ellis carried another of Trent's friends out into the cruel and tormenting autumn sunshine. Bile rose in Trent's throat as pain jabbed violently into his chest...another cut to lie next to the shredded mess left by Aimee's and Robbie's deaths.

Once again, fire had taken someone he loved. Once again, he hadn't been where he needed to be. If he hadn't stopped to talk to the husband, he would've been right behind Sam and Will.

He turned and walked out of the door. Spectators squinted against the sunlight as they gawped with their hands at their mouths. Firemen, paramedics and the chief blurred in Trent's red-misted vision as he fought his tears.

Clenching his jaw, he moved through the crowd to the fire truck and heaved himself inside. He gripped the steering wheel that Sam had held so many times before. Rage blistered and burned through Trent's insides and deep into his heart.

He cried out and shook the steering wheel before hitting it over and over with the heel of his hands. The job was getting inside him. Messing with his head and heart. He'd seen too much loss, pain and heartbreak over the years. Almost every call-out seemed to end in civilian injury or death.

Now they'd lost Sam.

He had nothing to offer anyone he loved. Nothing.

He'd promised Izzy the world. What the hell was he supposed to do when there was every possibility he would let her down today, tomorrow or a year from now? He had no right to love a woman who'd already lost far, far too much.

CHAPTER ELEVEN

WHEN KATE CROSSED her eyes and puckered her lips, Izzy laughed. "What's that supposed to be?"

Her friend straightened her eyes and grinned. "You. You are sooo into Trent you've been walking around with a goofy look on your face for days. It's getting pretty yuck, if I'm being honest."

"It's only been two *fabulous* weeks." Izzy playfully shoved Kate's arm and stood from her worktop, the finalized images for the calendar clutched to her chest. "And may I remind you, you were among many other people in town pushing for Trent and me to get together?"

"I know, but God, couldn't you tone down the sex a little?"

"The sex you were so keen for me to be getting on with, you mean? You make it sound as though we're doing it on Cowden Beach or over Marian's counter."

"Doesn't matter where you're doing it. Whenever I look at him or you, it's obvious you're doing it *all* the time."

"So you're jealous?" Izzy tilted her head, fighting to hold back her smile. "That's not a very nice attribute in a friend."

Kate leaned across the worktop, picked up a toy bear and hurled it in Izzy's direction. "Jealous, my ass."

Laughing, Izzy ducked and the bear hit the floor just as the phone rang on her desk.

Kate jumped down from her stool by the workstation. "I'll get it. You get on with the images. I'm so excited. I can't wait to see your ideas for the finished calendar." She snatched up the phone. "Cooper Photography. How may I help you?"

Feeling more than a little foolish about the continuing euphoria that had consumed her since she and Trent slept together again, Izzy left Kate and headed into the back office to collect some random calendar designs she'd downloaded earlier.

She held her favorite in front of her. It was simple, but to her mind, the calendar background needed to be simple when the accompanying monthly images were all the ladies would be looking at anyway. Kate popped her head around the door. "I have Jay Garrett on the phone. He wants to talk to you about the gallery."

Izzy put down the calendar images and pictures, followed Kate into the studio and picked up the phone. "Izzy Cooper speaking."

"Miss Cooper? Hi, this is Jay Garrett. Sorry to bother you at work, but I was hoping you might have some thoughts about what we discussed a few days ago."

Nerves knotted Izzy's stomach as she avoided Kate's eager gaze. Uncertainty that Templeton was the best place for her still lingered…especially when it was clear Trent was the main reason she wanted to stay rather than her career. "I'm still considering it, if I'm honest."

"Then I would be happy to discuss your reservations or anything else you'd like to ask me. Ideally, I'd love for you to run the gallery, but if you aren't interested, I do have other people to speak with."

Izzy inhaled as pressure mixed with excitement. She couldn't keep a man like Jay Garrett waiting for too long and she couldn't afford to let a chance like this slip through her fingers either. "Could I possibly ask for another day or two? I don't want to say yes and then let you down come February or March."

"I'm a hundred percent confident it won't

take long for you to be running the place perfectly. I want you to be excited about this, but two days is fine. I'm just a phone call away for any questions or concerns you might have. Okay?"

"Okay." Izzy smiled. "Thank you. I assume you'll take a commission-based cut?"

"I will, but we can negotiate the details if you decide to say yes, which I sincerely hope you do. I love this town and always try my best to support its local talent and needs. This would be a great new venture for us both. I'm sure of it."

Despite his monetary status, Izzy couldn't help being impressed by Jay's lack of ego…especially compared with Richard Crawley. But as much as possibility of leaving the Cove had preyed on her mind, she couldn't be certain she'd be making a big mistake if she entirely dismissed Richard's interest.

Closing her eyes, she pressed her thumb and forefinger into her brow. "I'll get back to you in the next couple of days. Promise."

"Great. I'll speak to you soon."

Izzy ended the call as Kate's gaze burned into the top of her head. "What's going on?"

"Jay doesn't want me to just exhibit my work He wants me to run the gallery too."

Kate's eyes widened as she sank into one of the chairs in front of the desk. "That's fantastic…isn't it?"

"I don't know. Richard Crawley is still calling me about the gallery in the city and Jay wants me here. This is crazy, right?"

"Of course not. Both of them are clearly blown away by your work, passion and experience. A man like Jay isn't going to miss taking the chance to nab you before anyone else came up with the same idea. Can't you see you're becoming hot property? First Crawley and now Jay Garrett…who, in my humble opinion, knocks Crawley right out of the park by the way."

"I don't know. Running a gallery. Is it really me?"

Kate shrugged. "You don't know until you try. You've got nothing to lose. If it's not for you, then you can give Jay fair warning and go back to working for yourself. Simple."

Izzy looked at her friend. They were polar opposites but fit so perfectly, regardless. Izzy's reserved, happy-to-work-alone ethic complemented her friend's spontaneity and smooth talking to win over charity donators, supports and backers. Kate's amazing vitality always managed to buoy Izzy's too-frequent bouts of doubt and insecurity.

"It would be an amazing opportunity, wouldn't it?"

Kate grinned. "It would."

"As for Richard, I'm really not sure I want to go to the city anymore. I thought getting away from here might be the answer in helping with my grief over Robbie, but now..." She smiled softly. "Now that I'm with Trent, this is where I want to be to *remember* Robbie."

Kate clasped Izzy's hand and squeezed. "Well, as your best...and prettiest friend... I am very glad to hear that."

"You really could use more self-confidence." Izzy winked and rose from behind her desk. "This is unbelievable. Things are starting to look a bit better, you know? I'm still working, but ready to have fun again too. I could start afresh with Trent and a gallery." Excitement spread through her at the prospect of making the gallery a place where she and the rest of the Cove would love to spend time browsing, and hopefully buying. "And I'll be exhibiting other artists' work alongside my own, so it's a win-win for everyone."

Kate came around the desk and grasped Izzy's hands. "It's a fantastic idea. You want to stay here. You love your work. It's time for you to get out of this little back alley and into the heart of the Cove, where everyone can see how talented you are."

Izzy's smile faltered as she worried her bottom lip. "Everything is still so new with Trent, though. If I commit myself to this gallery and then things go wrong between us—"

"You'll still be an artist, a gallery manager. Iz, come on, this is like a dream come true. From what you told me after you last spoke to Crawley, you aren't sure you want anything else to do with him. Your own gallery, Iz. Right here in Templeton. Imagine it."

Izzy smiled. Her own gallery. Living and working exactly where she wanted to be. The possibility escalated from a slow burn to an inferno deep in her stomach. "Do you really think it could work—" The door to her studio swung open with such force the glass shook in its frame. "My God, Leah, you frightened me half to death. What's happened? Are you okay?"

Leah Dixon, Templeton's favorite ER nurse, stumbled into the studio, her eyes glassy with tears. "I've just come off my shift and wanted to make sure you were okay."

Dread slithered like ice water through Izzy's veins as Trent rushed into her mind. "What's wrong? Is it Trent? Is he hurt?"

"No, it's…" Leah came forward and took Izzy's arm. "It's Sam. He was dead on arrival and Trent and Will are… Oh God, I've no idea what losing Sam will do to them. The three of them are—"

"Dead? Sam's dead?" Izzy snatched her arm from Leah's grasp and leaned over her desk to grab her purse. "Where's Trent now? Is he still at the hospital?" The weight of Kate's hand came down on Izzy's shoulder, but she didn't have the strength or courage to look at her friend. "Leah, where's Trent?"

"He was at the hospital when I left, but—"

"I've got to go to him." Izzy yanked her car keys from her purse, her fingers shaking. "Kate, have you still got the spare keys to the studio?"

"Yes, but—"

"Lock up for me, will you? I'll call you as soon as I can."

"Iz, wait. You can't drive like this."

Marching toward the door, Izzy flung it back on its hinges and made for her car parked outside. She unlocked the door and slid into the seat, fumbling and refumbling with her seat belt as Kate and Leah watched from the studio doorway. Finally strapped in, she started the ignition, put her phone to Speaker and dialed Trent's number. As it rang, she pulled away from the studio and tried to ignore the pain in her heart for Trent's, and Templeton's, loss.

Another good man struck down in his prime. His future and potential wiped out in a brutal swipe of fate.

TRENT STARED BLINDLY into his open sports bag as a deep sickness twisted and churned in his gut. Just as it had during the hour or so since Sam died. He and Will had followed the ambulance to the hospital, but for what reason, he had no idea.

Maybe they'd needed to hear from the professionals that Sam was really dead; needed some reassurance that there was nothing either of them could've done differently.

The doctor's confirmation of both things hadn't lessened Trent's guilt, or extinguished the horrible sense of responsibility he shouldered whenever they lost someone in a fire. Losing Sam escalated that responsibility more severely than ever.

Blinking, he clenched his jaw, shoved an extra sweater into his sports bag and whipped the zipper closed.

He needed to see his parents and comfort himself, and them, that they were okay. They were alive and safe. When they'd lost Aimee, Trent and his mum and dad made a pact to stay in touch, to regularly visit and call, but somehow over the last few months, that promise had faltered. Was that his parents' fault? No, it was entirely Trent's and his commitment and love of his job. A job that hurt as much as it brought hope.

Staying in the Cove wasn't an option. He didn't have the strength to stay here and deal with the ensuing grief that would envelop the entire community the way it had when, one by one, people learned Izzy had lost her brother.

But he couldn't leave without seeing Izzy first.

He squeezed his eyes shut. Just the thought of seeing renewed grief and pity etched in her beautiful eyes make nausea rise bitter in his throat.

Lifting his bag, he headed into the living room and grabbed his phone from the coffee table. He hovered his finger over her number. He needed some time and space but was all too aware of how that request might sound to Izzy. What kind of bastard did it make him that he was running home to the comfort of his family, when Izzy had no family, no buffer, other than him?

His front door buzzer sounded.

Trent stared at the closed door.

Izzy.

Every instinct in his body screamed of her arrival as though they were joined by thought and heart.

Swallowing, he walked to the buzzer and pressed the talk button. “Hello?”

“It’s me.” Relief shook through Izzy’s voice. “Thank God you’re here. Can I come up?”

“Sure.” He buzzed her in, opened the door and slowly walked to the settee. He sat heavily and dropped his head into hands as he waited.

Seconds later, she burst into the apartment and wrapped her arms about his shoulders, pressed a kiss to his bowed head. “I’m so sorry, Trent. So very, very sorry.”

Opening his eyes, he eased back from her grasp. “I’m fine.”

“You’re not fine.” She sat down beside him and clasped his hand. “No one can be fine after what you’ve gone through. I looked for you at the hospital and when I couldn’t find you, I came here. Leah came by the studio and told me...” She shook her head, her eyes filling with tears. “I’m so sorry.” Her gaze landed on his bag and she abruptly faced him. “Where are you going? Shall I come with you?”

His stomach knotted with guilt and the bitter taste of cowardice coated the inside of his mouth. He should be honest with her. Should tell her she’d been right all along and he wasn’t the right guy for her...that there were no guarantees with his job. He faced her. "I need to get out of town for a while. I can't be here. Not like this. Not again."

"What do you mean?"

He closed his eyes against the hurt in hers. "Losing Sam is as much as I can take right now."

"Then I'll come with you. Where are you going?"

"I want you to stay here."

She paled. "What? Why?"

"Because I need to be alone."

"Trent, listen to me." She tightened her fingers on his, her gaze sad. "Life throws bad things at us. Terrible things. For the most part, there is nothing we can do to stop or change that. I'm coming to terms with the fact that no matter what we do, how good or generous we are, there are still going to be evil and nasty things raining down on us. All we can do—"

He clenched his back teeth. "Is that what you believe? That for the rest of your life you're just going to sit back and *accept* the bad stuff?"

She shrugged. "What else can we do?"

"Once upon a time you were the most optimistic, caring and comforting person I knew. Where's that girl now, Iz?"

She slowly slipped her hand from his, her

cheeks flushed and her gaze clouded. "Gone. She's dead and gone with Robbie…with Sam."

Trent stood, irritation simmering hot and dangerous in his gut. "I think you should go."

"Trent—"

"I mean it, Iz. I can't sit here with you when you think like that. It seems to me that no matter what I say to you, what I do or try to do, you still look at the world in an entirely dark way. Maybe I'm not the person for you. Maybe you are too torn apart, too damaged by Robbie's death to ever let me in. No matter what you might have said to me, you are nowhere near ready to be with me. I love you, Iz, but I can't fix this. My role in Robbie dying was too devastating to you. I see that now."

She slowly rose from the settee, tears glinting in her eyes but her chin defiantly lifted. "I am ready to be with you, Trent. My feelings for you are real, but I'd be lying if I told you I believe life will get better. I've been told that a thousand times and it just isn't true."

"Then you need to leave. Now."

Their gazes locked and Trent fought the guilt pushing against his heart. The hurt in her eyes was deep, but he didn't look away and he didn't put his arms around her even though every part of him wanted to. They couldn't be together.

He couldn't fix her and they were better off going their separate ways.

He needed her gone before he fell apart completely.

"Fine." She snatched her purse from the settee. "I hope whoever it is you're running to gives you what you need. I'm sorry that person isn't me. Just know I'm thinking about you."

She brushed past him and when she slammed the front door, Trent flinched.

Releasing his held breath, he squeezed his eyes shut against the tears threatening to fall, before picking up his bag and slinging it over his shoulder. He walked to the window. Izzy appeared below and she marched toward her car, her hands swiping at her cheeks.

He hurt her. He'd brought her pain.

Bastard.

Snatching his keys from the table by his front door, Trent headed outside.

He got into his car and his hands shook as he gripped the wheel. He inhaled a long breath and slowly exhaled in an attempt to calm his racing heart. Feeling more in control, he shoved the car into First and pulled out of the parking lot.

The two-hour drive to his parents' was only the beginning of what he needed to grapple with the pain he'd caused Izzy and the reality that Sam had gone, but it was as good a place as any to start.

He had no right to call himself a man when he let Izzy down so badly. He had no right to even call himself a firefighter. He fought fire and constantly lost.

Getting out of Templeton was the right thing to do before people started telling him there was nothing he could've done for Sam. It was the very last thing Trent wanted, or deserved, to hear.

He drove through the center of town and out the opposite side. His parents still lived in the same town, in the same house where Trent grew up. Farther along England's southern coastline, Kingsley was a bigger and busier seaside town than Templeton. Its town center was bursting with shops, bars and restaurants that catered to thousands of tourists and holidaymakers that swept into Kingsley every summer. It was that seasonal chaos that kick-started Trent's move to Templeton four years before. He'd just turned twenty-eight and was already established as a firefighter. A fact that his parents had been proud of.

Proud, yet terrified. Aimee's death paramount in their minds.

Their constant fear had led to him eventually telling his mum and dad he was moving to Templeton. As much as he'd loved his job in Kingsley, he hankered for peace once he came off duty. That peace would never be found in his hometown.

Aimee's memory screamed from every corner of every street; cried in every room of their family home.

But now he returned for a while in the hope his childhood home would be the sanctuary he needed until he could get his head around Sam's death…and work out how to call things off with Izzy permanently.

His biggest fear of not being able to save people had come thundering back to the surface, and Izzy would be better off well away from him. He didn't need anyone to tell him how much her feelings would be hurt after his pursuit of her, but hearing that would be a damn sight better than letting her down further along the line.

Which he inevitably would.

Losing two of his friends had drawn a fat and terrifying line under that fact.

The landscape and traffic passed by in a blur as ugly thoughts and images filled Trent's head and fueled his anger at the world. When he eventually pulled into his parents' driveway, he was a mess. Just as he began to worry that coming home had been a selfish decision, or would be once his parents saw his pain, the front door opened.

His mother came out of the house with a weaved gardening basket over her arm, her wavy, light brown hair pulled back and tied in a loose ponytail at the nape of her neck. At fifty-seven, Linda Palmer looked ten years younger. She credited the fresh sea air for her youthfulness, but Trent didn't accept that. People with hearts as pure as his mother's always looked younger than people who shut their hearts to love and forgiveness.

Which meant by the time Trent turned thirty-five, he would more than likely look forty-five.

He pulled the keys from the ignition, yanked on the door handle and got out. He slammed the door and the sound raised his mother's head.

She lifted her free hand to her brow, shielding her eyes from the sun. Trent walked slowly toward her as her frown turned to a wide smile. "Oh my word, Trent. You're home. Why didn't you call first?" She rushed toward him and grabbed him into a bear hug that no woman of his mother's slim build should've been capable of. Yet, she was. All the time. "Oh, you've made my day. It's been weeks since we've seen you." She pulled back and grasped his elbows. "Let me look at you."

Maybe he should've closed his eyes or looked away, but that would have doubled his guilt for running home.

His mother's smile vanished and instant sorrow filled her dark green eyes. "No. Oh, Trent. Who? When?"

His mother's eyes turned glassy and Trent swallowed against the burning in his eyes. "Sam. Today."

"Oh no. No, no, no." She pulled him into her embrace and squeezed him. "You're home now. Everything will be all right."

Even as he closed his eyes, Trent sensed his father approach from behind his mother. He stiffened as the hand of David Palmer, the man Trent looked up to and respected more than any other, gripped his shoulder. "Let's go inside. Linda, come on now, let the boy inside."

Trent opened his eyes and met his father's concerned gaze. Silent words passed between them before his father nodded and eased Trent from his mother's grasp. "In you come, son."

His mother's quiet sob behind him tore at Trent's heart and conscience as his father slipped his arm around Trent's shoulders and steered him toward the house.

He walked into the living room ahead of his

father as his mother continued along the hallway into the kitchen to make tea. The often laughable, typically English, balm to every crisis.

His ass had barely touched the couch before his father spoke. "Who was lost this time?"

Trent held his father's solemn gaze. "Sam."

"Sam? Oh God above, I am so sorry to hear that."

"He was jumped on by a guy we had no idea was in the house. The guy's dead and so is Sam. The investigators will go in, but I doubt we'll ever really know exactly what happened in that room." He swiped his hand over his face. "If I'd left the civilian, there's a chance I could've found a way to save Sam."

"You know as well as I do you would always bring a civilian out before going back for a colleague. Did Sam die at the house?"

"Yes."

His mother came into the room and laid a tea tray on the sideboard. Her shoulders trembled as she poured the tea and Trent rose. He took the teapot from her hands and led her to the couch, pressing a kiss to her hair. "I'll do it, Mum. Sit down."

She gave a small smile and sat next to his dad.

Trent clenched his jaw as he poured the

tea. His mother hadn't known Sam particularly well, having only met him a dozen or so times when his parents visited Templeton, but he knew the tears she tried so hard to hold back would be for Sam's parents as much as their son. They'd also be for Trent. For her boy, who she silently worried about every single day.

A blaze had taken her daughter and she lived in constant fear another would one day take her son too.

With the tea poured, Trent passed a cup to each of his parents and sat in an armchair beside his mother.

She looked at him, her face pale. "Part of me wishes every day that you hadn't become a firefighter, but it never stops me from being proud of you. You do know that?"

Trent nodded and put his cup on a small table beside him. The one sip of tea he'd taken had turned his wretched stomach. God only knew how he'd get through the dinner his mother would want to feed him. He cleared his throat and eased back in his chair. "Is it okay if I stay here for a few days?"

"They've given you time off?" His mother smiled softly. "I'm pleased. Of course you can stay. The longer, the better."

Trent swallowed as thoughts of Izzy filled his mind. "I just need a few days to get my head straight and then I'll head back to Templeton. There are people…things… I need to take care of, but I just need to spend some time here first."

"I wouldn't want it any other way. It's so good to see you." His mother's eyes clouded with concern. "Can I ask who the people are you need to take care of?"

"Not people, Mum. Things. There are things I need to take care of."

"Such as?"

Trent looked from his mother to his father, whose shrewd gaze bored into Trent's with undisguised suspicion. Trent cleared his throat. "It doesn't matter. Forget I said anything."

The silence pressed down on him as his parents' watchful gazes lingered on his face.

His father stood and placed his cup on the sideboard before walking to the window. "It's going to be a nice evening." He turned, his gaze determined as he looked at Trent. "Why don't we go to the pub for a pint? We could bring back some fish and chips and save your mum from having to cook."

"Oh, David, you know I love to cook when Trent comes home."

Neither Trent nor his dad turned to look at his mother as she protested. The underlying tone to his father's voice had broached no argument. Trent exhaled a defeated breath. "Sounds good to me."

"Good." His father walked to the door. "Go and get your bags from the car and I'll freshen up a bit before we head out."

The second his father was gone, his mother pushed to her feet. "He only wants to talk to you, sweetheart. There's no need to have such a look of dread on your face."

"I don't know if I'm ready to talk. I came home to…" He shook his head and blew out a breath. "To see for myself that you were okay, I suppose."

She picked up his barely touched cup of tea. "And we are, but you know as well as I do, there's little point in avoiding a conversation with your father if that's what he wants from you." She gathered the remaining cups and placed them on the tray. "Go and get your bags. Everything will be all right. You'll see."

Trent followed his mum from the room, and as she walked into the kitchen, he stared after her, grief heavy in his heart. He'd lost another one of his friends and the woman he'd wanted for years in a single day. He wasn't sure anything would be all right ever again.

CHAPTER TWELVE

DUSK WAS FALLING as Izzy sat in her car and contemplated the front of the fire station. Her heart lay heavy in her chest, Trent's parting words echoing in her mind. Over and over she'd replayed their conversation. She closed her eyes as shame filled her. No matter how she longed for Trent to be wrong, a small part of her continued to blame him for Robbie's death and now he no longer wanted her and her miserable attitude around him.

She could hardly blame him for wanting her out of his life when he witnessed so much pain, day after day, and still managed to be the rock everyone leaned on.

Maybe she should leave for the city. Put the space Trent clearly thought they needed firmly in place. Concentrate on her career instead of her love life.

She opened her eyes. She would leave once she knew Trent was okay. After sending her parents running for the earliest departing ship months before, she wouldn't make the same mistake with Trent. She loved him, no matter how right he might be about them needing to work out their individual problems before either of them could expect to move on.

Getting out of her car, she approached the station. The courtyard was eerily devoid of firefighters and noise. She ventured deeper inside until she came to a small reception area. The woman behind the desk looked up. "Can I help you?"

Izzy forced a smile. "Yes. I was hoping to speak with the chief for a few minutes."

"Can I ask what it's concerning?"

"Trent. Trent Palmer."

The woman stared for a moment, her eyes sad. "Right. If you could wait here, I'll see if I can find him."

She strode along a corridor, stopping outside a closed door, and knocked before entering. Izzy took a deep breath and glanced around her. She shouldn't be here. Trent wouldn't want her there, but she needed to be certain that he was with someone—anyone—before she left him alone for the final time.

"Can I help you?"

Izzy turned and met the gaze of a man in his early fifties, his gray eyes somber. She took a step forward, her hand outstretched. "Izzy Cooper. I'm Trent's…girlfriend. I was hoping he might be here, but there was no one else around to ask."

"We're extremely busy, Miss Cooper."

"I appreciate that, it's just..." Words failed her as her heart pulled with hopelessness. "Do you know something? It doesn't matter. Thanks for your time."

She turned to leave.

"Miss Cooper? Why don't you step into my office?"

Briefly closing her eyes, Izzy sent up a silent thank-you before facing the fire chief. "Thank you."

She followed him into his office. It had been three hours since she stupidly let Trent go, buckling under her issues of rejection and abandonment. Now she had absolutely no idea where else to look for him.

"So, you're looking for Trent?"

The chief's question jolted Izzy from her worry. "Yes. Do you have any idea where he might be?"

"No idea at all."

Izzy tried to get a handle on her rising panic. Clearly, Trent intended to close himself off from her, but she had to know for certain he was going to be okay. She gripped the back of the chair in front of her. "I'm worried about him. I don't like to think of him alone after losing Sam today. When I spoke to him earlier, I had the distinct feeling he was running away. It's not like Trent to turn his back on the station while you're all in grief."

The fire chief frowned and sat in the chair behind his desk. "I'm sorry, but Trent has had one hell of a day. I expect he's gone somewhere where no one knows him and he can drown his sorrows in peace. He clearly wants to be alone. So if I were you—"

"You don't understand. I know what he's going through and he shouldn't be alone. No one should when they lose someone this way. I've been calling and looking for him all afternoon. Surely one of the crew knows where he is? What about Will? Is he here?"

"No, I sent him home too." The chief exhaled a heavy breath and leaned his forearms on his desk, his gaze softening. "Look, clearly you're concerned about Palmer, but take my advice and leave him be. Let him come to you. It's the only way to deal with the situation. I've hardly got a word out of anybody here all day. Just give him some space and he'll come find you when he's ready."

Sickness rolled through her stomach. Where was he? What if he'd changed his mind and realized he still needed her?

"Well, Izzy, I'm really busy, so I'm going to

have to ask you to leave. Some of the guys are outside. Maybe one of them can help you." He walked to the office door and opened it. "But bear in mind what I said. Trent might be better off being left alone for a couple of days."

Izzy stared. A couple of days? If he thought she was going to leave Trent alone with his grief for a couple of days, he'd better think again. Trent had tried again and again to be there for her when Robbie died despite her rejections. In hindsight, hadn't she relied on him being there for her? Hadn't she secretly loved him for coming back no matter how cold and callous she stupidly treated him in return? She wanted to be everything to him that he'd been to her.

She hitched her purse strap onto her shoulder and walked to the door. "Thank you for your help anyway."

"You're welcome."

The office door closed behind her and she strode through the station into the yard. Trent's chief was clearly struggling to hold things together too. His carefully controlled tone of voice and stiff body language screamed of a man doing what he could to hold his crew together in the face of tragedy. She could only admire him for that.

It was up to her to find Trent alone if need be.

As she walked toward the exit, what looked to be a skeleton team of firefighters meandered around, their expressions and gaits showing their shock and grief. The jeering and camaraderie she'd witnessed a few weeks ago had vanished, leaving behind darkness and disbelief.

Inhaling a long breath, Izzy approached three guys working on one of the four trucks lined up at the front of the station garage. "Excuse me?"

They turned and one gave a halfhearted smile. "You're Trent's girl, right? How's he doing?"

A momentary flash of pride warmed Izzy's heart at being called "Trent's girl" before it was whisked away by the reality that she had no idea how Trent was doing. "I don't know. I've looked everywhere I thought he might be, but I can't find him." She glanced around the trio of grave faces. "Would any of you know somewhere I might not have thought of?"

"Well, if you've tried the Coast and the other bars around—"

"I have and I've been back to his apartment, the Seascape..." She darted her gaze over around them, desperation sweeping painfully through her. "I've no idea where else he could be."

"You could try Will's place."

She'd considered going to Will's home but was reluctant to do so when he would be battling his own sadness. Yet where else would Trent be other than with the third person in such a tight trio of friends? He and Will would need, now more than ever, to be together to hold each other up. She sighed. "I didn't really want to disturb him if he's gone home."

"I'm sure he won't mind if he knows you're there for Trent."

Izzy nodded. "Okay. I'll go there now. Sorry to bother you after what happened today."

The firefighter nodded as the others stared, their eyes emotionless and their bodies rigid.

Turning, Izzy walked out of the station courtyard and quickly slid into her car. Gunning the engine, she exited the station and headed for Will's place. He lived in one of the cabins at the bottom of Clover Point with his wife, Helen, and their new baby boy, Oscar. Izzy gripped the steering wheel. Was it better that Sam hadn't been married and was without children? Or worse, because now he wouldn't have the chance for either?

Tears burned and she blinked them back, concentrating on her driving and negotiating what seemed an impossibly busy road.

Finally, she made it to Clover Point and

pulled into Will's graveled driveway. The last thing she wanted was to intrude on Will and Helen at a time like this, but what choice did she have if she wanted to find Trent? If he was here and drawing comfort from being with his friend, that was fine. She would leave him be.

As long as he had comfort from somewhere.

She got out of the car and approached the front door. Inhaling a strengthening breath, she lifted her hand and knocked.

Several seconds passed before the door opened and Helen, her eyes red from crying, stood on the threshold. "Oh, Izzy. Hi."

Despite only really knowing Helen from sight and occasional passing chitchat, Izzy gently touched the other woman's arm. "Hi. I know what happened today and I'm sorry. Are you okay? How's Will?"

Helen's eyes filled with tears and she shook her head. "He's upstairs. I told him to try to sleep, but I imagine he's just lying there, blaming himself."

"He and Trent would've done all they could."

"I know." She sighed. "But it's too soon for Will to accept that. He's cut to pieces. They were so close."

"I know, they all were. Trent too. I don't suppose he's been here, has he?"

Helen frowned, her eyes clouding with worry.

"No. Haven't you seen him? I thought you two were together now. Will told me last week that you'd finally—"

"We did. We are. I saw him, but he wanted to be alone and I stupidly walked away. I should've..." Izzy swallowed. "I really need to find him."

"And you thought he'd be here?" Helen's shoulders slumped and she tilted her head in sympathy. "I haven't seen him, I'm so sorry."

Izzy glanced over Helen's shoulder toward the staircase behind her. "Would you mind asking Will if he has any idea where Trent could be? I've looked everywhere I can think of. One of the firefighters at the station suggested he might be here, and now that he isn't and I don't know where else..." Her voice cracked and Izzy blinked, a tear rolling over her cheek. "I have to find him, Helen."

"Of course you do. Come in and I'll go check if Will's awake, okay?"

"Thank you."

Izzy stepped into the Kents' light and airy hallway. The wood paneling and beams along the ceiling beautifully complemented the pale cream walls and landscape paintings. Yet grief and shock cloaked everything in gray. Izzy closed her eyes, praying that Will and Trent would find a way to get over Sam's death and not let the tragedy change them the way losing Robbie had changed her.

Shutting down and shutting people out didn't help in the long term. She knew that now. The only way through the pain was to live better and harder. Embrace the love people had to offer, not refuse it.

Helen's footsteps sounded on the stairs and Izzy looked up, hope speeding her heart. "Was he awake?"

"He was. He thinks the only other place he would go if you can't find him in town is Kingsley."

Izzy frowned. "Kingsley? But that's miles away."

"It's where his parents live, where Trent grew up."

"Of course. How could I have forgotten that? Do you have their address? I've met his parents a few times, but I've never been to their house."

"When I asked Will for it, he said to tell you that it's probably for the best that you wait for Trent to come home rather than follow him to his parents'."

"Surely Will understands I need to be with Trent at a time like this?"

"I couldn't agree more, but I still think that

maybe you should listen to Will. He knows Trent better than most."

Izzy stared, sickness rolling through her. How was she supposed not to go to Trent when he would be hurting so badly? She exhaled. "Okay. Thanks, anyway."

She walked from the house, the gravel crunching beneath her feet as the door closed behind her. Now that she'd made that final leap into an intimate relationship with Trent, her feelings for him grew deeper every day. Her heart was opening in a way she'd kept under lock and key for so very long for fear of feeling any sense of loss ever again.

Yet, with Trent gone and rejecting her support, her old feelings of not being needed clutched deep inside her and it hurt deeply.

Izzy fought her tears as sadness pressed down on her, the all-too-familiar fears of abandonment and rejection rising on a nauseating wave. Her feelings were selfish, but they still hit her heart with hard and painful precision.

Getting into her car, she drove toward Kate's place in an apartment block not far from Funland, the town's fairground. She needed to see her friend, needed her advice. Should she go to Trent's parents' house or leave him be? She had no idea what result her turning up on their doorstep might bring after his brutal summary of the person she was today.

Pulling into a free parking space in the apartments' lot, Izzy got out of the car and approached the building. She pressed the buzzer to Kate's apartment.

"Hello?"

"It's me."

"Oh, thank God. I've been so worried."

"Can I come up? I need to talk to you."

"Of course."

The buzzer sounded and Izzy pushed open the glass double doors. Indecision and uncertainty had plagued her after Robbie died, but over the last few months they'd lessened to such a degree that she was sure her life was coming to resemble something close to normal.

Now it seemed they would always be there… just beneath the surface and ready to erupt whenever someone walked away from her.

THE PUB IN KINGSLEY'S town center wasn't exactly rammed to the rafters with patrons, but to Trent's current state of mind, it was far too busy and far too noisy. He took a drink of his beer, carefully avoiding his father's relentless gaze.

"I can sit here for as long as it takes, you know." His father picked up his glass. "Being out with you is the only time your mother gives me a free pass to spend the evening in the pub."

Trent placed his pint on the table. "I don't know what you want me to say. Sam's dead and I needed to be with you and Mum for a while. I thought you'd be glad."

"I am, but it's more than your grief that's brought you home. I know you better than you think I do."

Dread twisted a knot in Trent's stomach. Surely he couldn't be that transparent? "Sam's why I'm here, Dad. Nothing else."

His father lowered his drink next to Trent's. "It's more than Sam on your mind, son."

Trent's defenses slammed into place. "He died today. Aren't I entitled not to think about anything else for a few hours other than the fact that I've lost one of my closest friends?"

His father's cheeks mottled with irritation and his dark eyes hardened. "Don't raise your voice at me. That won't do either of us any good."

Trent swiped his hand over his face, further shame adding to the already sky-high pile weighing down his shoulders. "Sorry."

"Sam's death is going to be hard on you. I know that. Your mother and I will be here any time you need us. That doesn't change how well I know you."

Trent met his father's gaze. "Meaning?"

"Meaning something in Templeton has spooked you. Most likely what happened with the fire today was the catalyst that set you running in our direction. Not for the comfort we can give you, but as a means of escape. Which makes me think it's not a something, but a *someone*, and that someone doesn't know where we live. Am I getting warm?"

Trent looked to the bar. "You're wrong."

"Yeah? Then why can't you look at me?"

Trent turned as irritation simmered dangerously in the pit of his stomach.

His dad held Trent's gaze before he slowly smiled, knowledge glinting in his eyes. "What's her name? And why are you here, instead of with her?"

Trent glared. Was he a frigging plate-glass window? He opened his mouth, closed it… opened it again. "What are you talking about?"

His father leaned back and crossed his arms, his gaze unwavering.

Rare embarrassment brought heat to Trent's cheeks. He refused to discuss Izzy with his father. Not now. Not when Trent intended to finish things with her before they'd even really started. "You're wrong. I'm here to get my head straight. To have some time to come to terms with Sam dying."

His father continued to watch him.

Trent tipped his head back and closed his eyes. How was he supposed to quash his father's suspicions? He'd never been able to lie to him and he didn't want to start now. Lowering his chin, he opened his eyes and took a long drink before returning his glass to the table. He looked at his father. "Fine. It's Izzy Cooper."

His father grinned and uncrossed his arms. "I knew it. So, after all this time, you two finally worked things out, huh?" He raised his glass in a toast. "I knew the pair of you would see sense in the end." He touched his pint to Trent's, took a drink and put it back on the table. "From the few times we've seen her and how Robbie used to talk about her, I'll hedge a bet she's a beautiful girl. Inside and out. I'm pleased for you. Your mother will be too."

"There's no need to tell mum." Trent closed his eyes and Izzy's face swam cruelly behind his closed lids. He slowly opened them. "It's all off after today."

His father's smile vanished and his eyes clouded with annoyance. "What are you talking about? You've had a thing for that girl for years."

Trent fought the pain that twisted and pulled

like barbed wire in his chest. "After what happened to Sam..." He shook his head. "I can't do it to her, Dad." Trent glared, self-defense burning hot through his blood. "If by some miracle, Izzy comes to love me like I love her, I can't let her down. I promised I'd always be there for her. So that's it. It's over."

"What on God's good earth are you talking about?"

"She blames me for Robbie, okay? Even after all this time she can't accept that a falling beam killed him." Trent placed his forearms on the table and gripped his glass. He lowered his voice. "Add the fact that every day there's a chance I could be killed. She doesn't need that kind of endless worry. Not after Robbie."

"Does she get a say in that? Have you asked her?"

"I don't need to ask her. She told me so herself weeks ago, and then being the egotistical bastard I am, I wore her down until I'd convinced her otherwise."

"You wouldn't have convinced her if she wasn't ready to be convinced. Maybe I don't know Izzy like I knew Robbie, but from what you've told me about their background, they're tough. You come back here, more often than not to make sure your mother's okay, but what you've also got is somewhere safe to come when the world turns bad. Izzy doesn't have that and if she's come to see past the job, it's because she's ready to, not because of what you might or might not have said to her. If she sees you for who you are, she doesn't deserve having you bail out on her."

"And who am I? The guy who didn't have the guts to face her when the going got tough. She wanted to come with me, be with me after what happened to Sam, and I said no." Trent put down his glass. "I know what I'm talking about, Dad. Please, just understand what I'm saying."

"I'm trying, but all I've heard so far is white noise."

Trent fought to keep a rein on his temper. The longer his father looked at him, the more the pressure of indecision, the difference between doing the right thing and the selfish thing, ripped and tore at his conscience. "One day something might happen to me, and Izzy does not need that kind of pain in her life. Not again."

His father frowned as he slowly roamed his study over Trent's face as though what he'd said was complete nonsense.

"Don't you see?" Trent held his father's bemused gaze. "I can't, I won't, hurt her like that. She doesn't need a man incapable of saving people, incapable of saving her." He squeezed his eyes shut. "You know who I am. I'm the son who didn't save your daughter, my sister, for crying out loud. This isn't some unfathomable mathematical problem. It's a fact."

The silence went on for so long Trent forced his eyes open.

His father glared. "Now, you listen to me. You are my son and you're one of the bravest, strongest men I know and I'm damn proud to call you mine." His father's eyes burned with anger. "Don't dare you sit there and say you'll hurt that girl. That you didn't save our Aimee. That fire took her. Do you hear me? That one particular fire saw fit to take my baby away from you, your mother and me. Yet day in, day out, you risk your life to fight other fires to stop other people from being hurt. You're not God, son, but you are a man. A man who needs to get his ass back to that Cove and look after the woman he loves. Now, drink up before the woman *I* love comes looking for us." He drained his glass and slammed it on the table. "And I don't want to hear you say those things about yourself ever again. Do you understand?"

Trent opened his mouth to respond as barely contained anger and shock at the intensity of his father's tone burned and scorched inside.

Before he could say anything else, his father rose and stalked from the pub.

"Bloody hell." Trent drained his glass and stood before storming after his father.

His father was waiting for him outside. "Well?"

Trent met his father's glare. "You can say what you want, but I won't risk hurting Izzy any more."

"Do you want to be alone for the rest of your life? Is that it?" His father came closer, his voice a growl. "Do you? Or do you want a wife who loves you? Kiddies who love you? Cherished people who wait at home and when you walk through the front door at the end of a shift, they greet you with their hugs and kisses. Does any of that appeal to you? Yes or no?"

A hard lump lodged in Trent's throat and his chest hurt, but he defiantly held his father's glare. "Of course it does. Doesn't every man want a family?"

"Then you stay with me and your mother for two nights and two nights only. I'd say one night, but I'm not in the habit of hurting the woman I love either. You tell your mum you've been called back to Templeton on an emergency. Anything. Use your imagination."

"I need longer than two days—"

"You need nothing but that girl who's probably at her wit's end wondering what she did to make you turn away from her. I bet my ass you're hurting her now just by being here. Can't you see that? You're telling her she isn't important enough, isn't the one you need when you're hurting. What do you think that says to the woman?"

Trent stared as the truth of his father's wisdom sliced his soul. Izzy came looking for him the moment she found out about Sam. She'd most likely called him over and over since he left the Cove, but he'd turned off his phone.

His father was right. Trent might be miles away, but the words he'd spoken would be hurting her right now. He pushed his hand into his hair and held it there. "I am such an asshole."

"I wouldn't go that far, but you're being pretty damn stubborn, that's for sure." His father put his arm around Trent's shoulders and tugged him forward. "Now, let's get those fish and chips, and while we're eating you can think about what you're going to do to make things right with Izzy. It's time to face your fears, son. It's time for you to risk your heart as well as your life. You need to pass it over to someone else to take care of every now and then." His father stopped and turned Trent by the shoulders to face him. “Because that, my boy, is what love is to everyone. Love is a gift. Don’t you dare turn your back on it.”

CHAPTER THIRTEEN

IZZY LEANED HER hands on the edge of her workstation and looked at Kate. "I haven't heard a word from Trent in two days. He hasn't returned any of my messages. He has to know how worried I am, but he still doesn't want to speak to me." She shook her head as hurt squeezed her heart. "I knew this would happen."

Kate frowned. "You knew what would happen?"

"That us getting involved would end in disaster. Sam's dead and instead of coming to me, talking to me, Trent has disappeared. Doesn't that say something to you? Because it certainly does to me."

"Iz—"

"It says he'll never be able to lose another life in a fire without looking at me and remembering the way I blamed him for Robbie. I never should've done that and now he thinks I'm too weak to deal with any more pain. I couldn't look at him because of Robbie, and now that I can, he loses Sam and can't look at me."

"You're thinking into this way too much. Two days is nothing. Trent's lost one of his best friends. You know men and their need to haul off to their caves whenever there's a whiff of a crisis they can't fix. This isn't Trent rejecting you, Iz. I'm guessing he's doing all he can right now. Even if that means being alone for a while."

Izzy pushed away from the workstation and walked behind her desk, entirely aware that she was putting distance between herself and Kate's logic. If she admitted Trent's behavior was normal, didn't that make her cruel for snapping at him and telling him to go? "Rejection or not—"

"Not." Kate lowered herself into one of the visitors' chairs.

"Rejection or not, maybe me and Trent taking some time apart is a good idea. One minute I'm fighting him off, the next I can barely keep my hands off him. It's not exactly a relationship made in heaven. There's too much… I don't know…history and heat between us. When he does decide to come back, I could say something he doesn't want to hear, get needy or make everything worse for him, and that's the last thing I want to do."

"Why would you get needy? You're the least needy person I know."

"But he's changing me. He's making me need him. Making me rely on him like I did Robbie. I can't let myself be that way again, Kate. I just can't."

Kate sighed. "We're all needy in some shape or form. It's not a sign of weakness. It's what makes us human. Do you really want to be that alone? That independent? Lord knows I'd like to think I'll one day meet a man I need and rely on."

Izzy swiped at a traitorous tear as it rolled onto her cheek. "I'm so scared over how Sam died, that the Cove has lost another good man to a fire and that Trent has gone away. Why did he choose to be alone when I want to be with him so much it hurts?"

"Oh, Iz...he'll be back soon. You two have something great going and you don't want to run the risk of spoiling that by not giving him the space he's asked for. If you don't, his reaction might convince you that you're better off apart permanently. What if he sends you away again asking for more time? Your answer will be to do something rash like head off to the city and take Richard Crawley up on his offer of an exhibition. Saying goodbye to Jay Garrett's offer here."

Izzy looked down at the papers on her desk.

Kate sighed. “You’ve thought about it already, haven’t you?”

Izzy lifted her head and held her friend’s knowing gaze. It sucked how Kate knew her so well. “Why shouldn’t I? I don’t mean to sound petulant, but I really think getting away from the Cove and concentrating on my career elsewhere could be the right thing to do.”

“For who?”

“For me, of course. I’ve lived in Templeton all my life. This could be the chance to learn the be all and end all doesn’t have to be here. Maybe it’s time I explored what my life could look like without Trent being a part of it.”

Kate stared at her. Her expression dripping with skepticism and doubt.

Izzy glared. “What? Why shouldn’t I try a different avenue? Me and Trent’s lack of communication has achieved little but expose our individual fears about each other.”

“He loves you.”

Izzy huffed a laugh. “And? Who was it who said love don’t last, but cooking do?”

Kate raised her eyebrows. “Um…no one.”

Irritation seeped into Izzy’s blood. “Well, I heard it somewhere. Do you know something? You’re supposed to be my friend, and with you knowing everything I’ve been through, I would've thought you'd want me moving toward a different future."

Kate sighed and slumped her shoulders. "So this is all about business?"

"Yes. No. Maybe." Frustrated, Izzy slapped her hands on the desk, tears burning her eyes. "I'm hurt by Trent disappearing on me, and that makes me a bad and selfish person when he's just lost his friend. Because I get that, I think it might be best to leave town for a while. For me." Izzy pressed her trembling hand to her chest. "He's made it clear he doesn't need me and can stand on his own two feet. Shouldn't I at least see how I feel in the city? A few weeks ago, you were begging me to get out of the Cove and try something new. Now that I'm actually considering it, you want me to stay."

"If I thought you were doing this for the right reasons, I'd be behind the idea. Because I think you're doing it for the wrong reason, it's my job, as your friend, to try to make you see sense. Don't you want to be here when Trent gets back?"

Izzy held Kate's concerned stare, before she dropped into her chair behind the desk. "I don't know. He knows I was scared of losing him if we started anything, and now he's disappeared. I can't fall in love with him, Kate. It's too risky."

Kate stood and came around the desk. She slid her arm around Izzy's shoulders and pressed a kiss to her temple. "News flash, sister. No one, including you, allows themselves to fall in love. It just happens. Usually at the most inconvenient moment."

"Exactly. I'm protecting myself and this is just the way it has to be. I've already lost too much. I'll call Jay and tell him I've been offered another proposition and need more time. If he doesn't like it and retracts his offer, the decision is made for me."

"That's a ridiculous way to think, Iz."

Izzy opened her eyes as a stronger sense of self-worth than she'd felt in months came over her. "That's where you and I can agree to disagree. I'm thinking straighter than I have for weeks. This has to be about what I want and not about how other people fit into that. I've based every decision I've ever made on making sure I have a base, somewhere to call home. Maybe that's because our parents never gave Robbie and me any sense of stability. I don't know. But I do know it's time I grew up." She sighed. "But I won't sign any dotted lines or commit myself to anything unless it feels one hundred percent right."

"And being with Trent doesn't feel a hundred percent right?"

Izzy's heart kicked painfully. It did. It had. Now he'd gone. Disappeared.

She shrugged. "Maybe it's just great sex and there's no substance to us as a couple. If there were, he would've needed me when Sam died. I would've been the first person he thought of. God forbid anything should ever happen to you, but if it did, who would I run to?"

Kate sighed and slumped. "Trent."

"Exactly."

She slipped her hand from around Izzy's shoulders. "I'm just hurting for you, that's all. I know what reliability means to you. I know what having someone to trust means to you, but I really believe Trent's that person and more. Can't you just wait a few more days to see if he comes back?"

"No, I've made up my mind. I'm going to the city." Izzy stood and walked to the window. She stared toward the sliver of beach at the end of the narrow street. "I'll see if I can book a meeting with Richard and his gallery partner first thing tomorrow. I need to do this. If I don't, I'll never know if there's more for me outside Templeton."

"So your mind's made up?"

Izzy turned and inhaled a long breath. "Yes."

"Fine." Kate raised her hands in defeat and walked closer. "Do what you have to do. If Trent comes back to the Cove before you, shall I call you?"

"No. And tell him not to call me either. I need time to think."

"Okay. Whatever you need."

Izzy stepped forward and pulled Kate into a hug. "Thank you."

TRENT SCANNED THE CROWD of people on Cowden Beach in the hope Izzy might be among them. Over a week had passed since Sam's death, and in two days' time, he, Will and the rest of Templeton Cove would bury one of their finest men and firefighters. Trent had to believe in his heart Izzy wouldn't miss the funeral, even if she had been out of town since he returned. If she did, then he truly didn't know her at all.

Her absence had left a gaping hole in his heart...right next to the new one Sam's death had opened.

Trent tipped his beer bottle to his lips. The day he'd returned to the Cove, a futile search for Izzy had left him floundering. Instead, he'd found Kate. His pathetic pleas to speak to Izzy had gotten Kate to confirm that the day he'd come back was the day Izzy had gone to the city to find Crawley.

How could he be angry about that? He had no damn right. He'd seen how Izzy relaxed around Crawley. Had witnessed her smile and occasional laugh throughout the few days they'd shot the calendar. The guy could give her a gallery, a chance at fulfilling the career that fulfilled *her*.

He took another drink and scanned the crowded beach. But he still needed to talk to her. To find out for sure that it was over between them. People all around him jigged to the music coming from portable speakers farther along the beach, or chatted in groups as they relaxed on blankets or camping chairs. The scene would've been a happy one if his mind wasn't entirely filled with his need to see Izzy among the throng.

Trent kicked at the sand. He shouldn't have let her walk away. He shook his head. *I'm an idiot.*

"Hey, man, why so blue?"

Trent turned as Will approached. "Hey."

"What's going on? Why are you standing here on your own when—"

"When what?"

Will shrugged. "Just thought you'd be all over her the moment she came home, that's all."

Trent stopped, his beer bottle hovering at his lips.

Will smiled and tilted his head to a spot over Trent's shoulder.

He turned.

Izzy stood alongside Kate, Leah Dixon and Tanya Todd, each of them holding a glass of wine and looking relaxed. A sealed unit of four that didn't look as though any of them wanted or needed male interruption.

He faced Will and tried his hardest to maintain a cool exterior when inside, his heart danced the fandango. "Did she get back today?"

"According to Kate."

Trent glanced toward Izzy. "She looks happy. Really happy."

"Then do yourself a favor and go over there and talk to her."

"What am I supposed to say to her? I refused to take her calls and then she refused to take mine. It's been days since we've spoken to each other and she hardly looks cut up by the situation."

"I agree, but from the way she's staring at you right now, she wouldn't mind if you walked over there and spoke to her."

Trent turned. His gaze locked with Izzy's, and the rest of the people on the beach seemed to scatter left and right. Will shoved him forward and as Trent moved, Izzy did too.

When they reached each other, Trent fought

the need to reach forward, pull her into his arms and kiss her with everything he had.

Her blue gaze burned into his until her study fell to his mouth. She blinked and looked away toward the ocean. “It feels like forever since I last saw you.” The wind brushed some of her long blond hair across her face and she tucked it behind her ear. “How are you?”

“Better for seeing you.”

She faced him and smiled softly. “Ditto.”

Relief whispered through his chest and Trent relaxed his shoulders. “I shouldn’t have left the way I did. It wasn’t right and I’m sorry.”

“It’s okay. I kind of disappeared on you too, so we’re even.” She faced the ocean again. “It’s what happens next that’s important.”

He studied her profile, desperate to see her eyes. They usually revealed so much of what was inside her mind. Her voice was wistful, a little dreamy…or maybe she’d been at the beach longer than him and the wine she held wasn’t her first. No, Izzy could hold her wine better than most. Which meant her tone confirmed her sadness.

Touching his finger to her chin, Trent turned her face and looked into her eyes. “What do you want to happen next?” He slipped his hand from her face and tucked it into his jean pocket so he wouldn't act on the need to pull her into his arms. "How did things go in the city?"

"They didn't."

"But Kate said you were looking into an exhibition at Crawley's place."

"I considered it, but I knew pretty quickly that the city wasn't for me. Templeton's my home. Where I want to be."

Hope rose and lingered right above his heart. "So you're going to show your work in Templeton?"

Her eyes lit with something so close to excitement that it took his breath away. She looked so damn beautiful in the fading sun, her eyes sparkling and her smile wide. "Better."

He smiled. "What could be better than you deciding to stay here?"

"I never mentioned this to you before because I had no idea whether or not I would even do it, but… I'm going to manage the gallery."

"Manage it? Wow."

"Jay Garrett was so certain I'm the right person for the job that he was willing to wait for a decision while I was in the city. I didn't think for one minute a businessman like Jay would do that, but I was wrong and he did. I'll have the main area to exhibit my own work, but we'll also support other photographers and artists too. I'm really excited. This could be the professional opportunity I've been waiting for."

"That's fantastic. I'm happy for you."

"Thanks."

A heavy silence fell as their gazes locked. Just one step closer and she'd be in his arms, but her need for personal space was clear as she widened the distance between them and wandered a little farther along the beach.

She picked up a pebble and bounced it in her hand as though wanting to have both hands occupied. Wineglass in one, pebble in the other. The message was loud and clear. *I don't want to touch you, so don't touch me.*

Trent walked to her side. "So…"

"So…"

They both spoke at the same time and Trent smiled, praying his stretched nerves didn't show on his face. "You go."

"I was just going to say I'm glad you're back. Were you at your parents' house?"

"Yes."

"And did they…" She dropped the pebble and took a sip of her wine. "Did you get whatever it was you needed from them?"

He took a deep breath. "Yes, in more ways than you might think."

"I see."

"Do you?"

She sighed and shook her head. "No, not really. It still hurts that I wasn't the first person you looked for when Sam died." She raised her free hand to her forehead and briefly closed her eyes. "I'm sorry, I shouldn't have said that. It's none of my business what you choose to do."

"Hey." He drew her hand from her face, twined his fingers with hers and held tight. "You've got every right to say whatever you feel. I was stupid, Iz. I shouldn't have run from you and I certainly shouldn't have used words to hurt you when it was really me not knowing what to do with my grief."

Her eyes were soft with empathy, a line furrowing between her brows. "I understand, but you leaving really hurt. I can't lie about that."

"And I wouldn't want you to. I got scared of letting you down in the future. I thought it was better to let you down now, rather than later." Guilt slashed through his chest. "The last thing I wanted to do was hurt you. I was stupid to think my leaving wouldn't do that."

She pulled her hand slowly from his. "I ran too and came to the same conclusion. Albeit in a different way."

Apprehension knotted his stomach. "What do you mean?"

"We can't be together. We can be friends, but that's it." Her gaze roamed over his face, before she met his eyes. "It will be too painful for both of us. Let's just keep things how they've always been, okay?"

He clenched his jaw. "No, not okay."

"Trent, please—"

"Life's too short." He clasped her hand again, hoping to God she understood him and mentally kicking himself for walking away. "Surely we both learned that lesson after the losses we've had? We need to give us a chance."

He dipped his lips toward hers and she immediately backed away, jerking her hand from his, her eyes shiny with tears. She raised her hand like a shield. "I can't, okay? I didn't come over to speak with you for us to try again. I wanted to tell you that Kate has asked if we could go to see Maya Jackson in the hospital on Friday afternoon."

"What?" His inability to think past anything but Izzy and the fact that he'd thrown his chance to be with her away. "Kate wants us to go to the hospital?"

"Yes." She lifted her chin, her gaze determined and dry of tears. "She promised Maya she could meet one of the firefighters and me. Kate automatically chose you. Of course."

"Right. Okay. That's fine." He pushed his thumb and forefinger into his forehead, trying to think past this moment to Friday. "I'm pretty sure I'm on the night shift."

"Okay, good. I'll see you then." She took a step away and turned back. "But I'll see you at Sam's funeral first." Her chest rose as she inhaled. "I'll be there for you at the funeral. I promise."

She turned and hurried back along the beach toward Kate and their friends. Trent let her go, his heart aching. The resolve in Izzy's eyes when she'd spoken about the reasons and fears she had about them being together had been mixed with flashes of confusion, yearning and desire.

He hadn't imagined it.

Whether she knew it or not, whatever was truly in Izzy's heart was always on full display in her eyes. It was that honesty, that openness, which attracted people to her like bees to honey. It was what made people laugh and smile when she raised her camera. It was how her emotion, good or bad, poured so prevalently into her pictures.

She walked from the beach onto the promenade above before disappearing from his view. Trent drained his beer and stared at the rolling waves of the ocean. Why did everything have to be so damn hard? Was he supposed to give up his career or Izzy? His only option to choose one or the other? He loved Izzy, but he owed it to Aimee to keep fighting fire. There had to be a way to have both Izzy and his life's work.

One way or another, he'd figure it out.

CHAPTER FOURTEEN

IZZY STOOD ON the stone pathway leading into the crematorium, grateful for Kate's hand at her elbow. Cars lined the grassy areas surrounding the main building and the covered driveway where the hearse carrying Sam's coffin was parked. Izzy took a shaky breath as Sam's closest family and friends got out from the black limousine behind the hearse.

She knew only too well how they would be feeling.

Blinking hard, she cast her gaze toward the white marbled headstone in the distance that marked where Robbie's ashes were buried. The pink and white carnations she'd laid there moments before lay beside Kate's single lily. Everyone who knew him still missed him so much. Izzy swallowed the lump that gathered in her throat and turned her focus to Sam's family.

His parents were followed by Sam's younger brother and sister, and the whole family quickly embraced, silently watched and supported by others mourners waiting nearby.

Izzy swayed on her feet and breathed deep.

"Are you all right?" Kate whispered beside her, her hand tightening at Izzy's elbow. "If this is too much—"

"I'm fine." Izzy closed her eyes, her heart aching for Sam's family. "It's just so unfair."

"I know. Let's join the queue and follow the family inside. The sooner we get you a seat, the quicker you can sit down. You don't look well."

Dipping their heads, Izzy and Kate followed Sam's coffin inside behind the family. The crematorium wasn't very big, and as more and more mourners entered, the space quickly filled. She and Kate found a seat and Izzy looked around. Every Cove resident she knew, and a few she didn't, was there, softly mumbling words of comfort to each other or dabbing their eyes with tissues.

The picture was so reminiscent of Robbie's funeral that grief weighed heavy on her heart and shoulders. She opened her clutch, took out a handkerchief and balled it tightly in her hands as she stared at the back of Sam's mum's bowed head. She could only imagine the pain and self-control Andrea battled.

A scuffle beside Izzy was quickly accompanied by the scent of pine and musk. She lifted her head, and her gaze locked with Trent's. He seemed to hesitate before he sat beside her and covered her hands with one of his. "How you doing?"

She smiled softly. "Shouldn't I be asking *you* that?"

"I'm okay." He blew out a heavy breath. "Although being here, like this, makes me realize a small part of me has been denying Sam's gone. It's good to have closure, but right now I feel as though the fire happened this morning. I can see and hear everything all over again." He looked at her, his eyes bright with unshed tears. "I can see and hear everything the day Robbie was killed too."

Izzy nodded and a tear rolled over her cheek. "The pain never goes away, but…" She looked toward Sam's parents. "After today, his mum and dad will be able to grieve him properly. The funeral is the most painful day because you know you have to keep going. You have to put one foot in front of the other and try not to sink into the floor the way you want to."

As music filtered from the speakers at the front of the room, the murmurs abated until only the occasional whimper or wail carried through the oppressive space. Grateful for Trent on one side of her and Kate the other, Izzy pulled back her shoulders and forced her gaze to Sam's coffin as the vicar started to speak.

"Welcome, ladies and gentlemen, to this special service to honor the life and work of Sam Paterson, a devoted son, friend and firefighter. As much as loved ones linger over the death of beloved parents, friends, neighbors and, unfortunately, children, a funeral is a time to start to celebrate the life that has passed. It is a time to see, embrace and support the people who loved Sam as they gather together in their grief to bid a final farewell as he begins his journey beside God. We weep, we ask why..." The vicar paused and concentrated his gaze on Sam's parents, his face solemn and his eyes sad. "We often want to be angry at the world and all the sadness it bestows on us." He looked out into the congregation. "But we must try to believe in God and the tests he gives us, knowing we will fight to find happiness again even if the pain never fully subsides."

Izzy ignored her tears as they rolled over her cheeks, and clung tighter to Trent's hand. He squeezed her fingers and she turned to look at his handsome, tight-jawed profile. Would he be next? Would he be the next man in Templeton to die? Pain tore through her at the hurt that they hadn't worked out; that at a time when they should've turned to each other, they'd turned away.

As her desire to be with him rose traitorously inside her, Izzy faced front and swallowed her feelings, pushing them far away along with her regret for what they'd lost together and individually.

Trent losing his sister had made his family and their home more important to him than ever, a place he could always return to without having to give a reason or explanation. Robbie's death and her parents' subsequent departure didn't mean they hurt any less than Trent's mum and dad, but their leaving meant Izzy was now afraid to truly believe in, or lean on, anybody. Why hadn't she accepted her parents' pleas to let them in? Why hadn't she done more to realize their suffering could only be worse than hers? To lose a child…

Her tears gathered, stinging her eyes.

She would call her mum and dad the minute she returned home. There were still so many apologies she had to make to the people she'd pushed away.

The vicar's speech had been a clear message to the importance of looking forward, not back. Slowly, she'd gained the sight to imagine the possibility of a brighter future, that she had much to be thankful for and one day, Izzy hoped, Sam's loved ones would manage the same. She had to believe that, or there would be no point in any of them carrying on.

After a sad and difficult service, Sam's coffin disappeared behind a red velvet curtain and his favorite dance track played as they exited the building—loud and strangely appropriate when Izzy thought of Sam. The small ripple of laughter lessened the heavy sorrow.

With her hand still in Trent's, they slowly walked outside into a small courtyard where everyone was gathered to read the cards tucked into bouquet after bouquet of flowers. Bursts of vivid color stood against the rain-soaked concrete like a beacon of hope and prosperity.

Standing back, Izzy stared as Jay and his wife, Detective Inspector Garrett, their arms around each other's waist, slowly led the line of mourners as they stepped forward to pay their respects. Marian and George Cohen followed. Then came Chris and Angela Forrester with their young daughter who solemnly carried a single white rose that she placed next to one of the bouquets. Behind them, Tanya Todd walked arm in arm with her sister, Sasha, who must've have come back to the Cove especially for the funeral.

As more and more residents gathered, Izzy looked at Trent. "We live in a wonderful town."

His chest rose as he inhaled. "I wouldn't want to live anywhere else. Not anymore. Templeton is home to me now."

"Me too." She gazed across the space at the Walker family gathered together in the far corner, their arms embracing and their lips pressing kisses to each other's cheeks. "Bianca must be finding this incredibly hard. I can't believe how well she's coped with losing Robbie. She's amazing. I wish I had half of her strength."

"You do. She's no more amazing than you, Iz."

"Even though I was Rob's sister, Bianca was engaged to him. Her whole future changed in the blink of an eye. I mourn the loss of a brother. She mourns the man she wanted to spend the rest of her life with."

"Pain can't be measured. People feel what they feel."

"I suppose."

They stood in companionable silence for a few seconds before he eased his hand from hers. "I have to get back to the station. I'm on duty."

Izzy frowned. "Haven't you been given the day off? Surely you want to go to the wake?"

He stared toward the flowers. "I volunteered. A lot of us did. I think working is the easier option. I'm pretty sure Sam would've done the same if it was one of us who died rather than him."

She touched her fingers to his chin and when he met her gaze, she looked deep into his eyes. "I'm so proud of you."

His gaze softened. "Ditto."

As his focus drifted to her mouth, the tension shifted and Izzy took her hands from his face and fought her longing to place her head against his chest. "Are you still okay to go to see Maya at the hospital with me tomorrow?"

He lifted his gaze to hers. "Sure. I'll pick you up from the studio?"

She nodded.

"Okay. Then I'll see you around two." He seemed to hesitate before he dipped his head and pressed a firm, lingering kiss to her forehead. "Take care."

She kept her eyes closed as he walked away, and only when she could no longer hear his footsteps did she opened her eyes and let the tears fall for Sam, Robbie, Aimee and all those who missed them.

SPOTTING TRENT AS he pulled up outside the studio, Izzy snatched her purse from her desk, along with a teddy bear and the wrapped and framed picture she'd taken especially for Maya. She hitched her purse strap onto her shoulder and took a deep breath. She'd been looking out for Trent for the last twenty minutes to ensure that she caught him arriving, thus barring any chance for him to get out of the car and come into the studio.

After their quiet exchange at the funeral yesterday, she had to maintain a distance between them. Her attraction to him was still rife...and she suspected his to her was too.

The same as Trent's parents' place was his sanctuary, the studio was hers and she no longer wanted him to breach it. His presence inside these four walls would only mess with her fortitude that he belonged in her life as a friend—not a lover or a lost-and-found piece of the puzzle that made everything in her life make sense.

Striding toward the door, she opened it and raised her hand in a breezy wave before turning to lock the studio door and gather her senses.

With the door locked, checked and rechecked, she ran out of stalling options and dropped her keys into her bag. Pulling back her shoulders, Izzy walked confidently to the curb and opened the passenger door of his car. She plastered on a smile as she struggled to slide into the car with her arms full. "Hey."

His smile was wide and bright, his dark

green eyes sparkling and surprisingly happy. "Hey. Do you want me to put those in the backseat for you?"

"I'm fine."

"Are you sure?"

"Of course. I've really been looking forward to today." She reached for her seat belt, thankful for the excuse to break eye contact as she pulled it over her shoulder and locked it. "It will be good to get to know Maya."

"Absolutely. We'll do our best to make sure she has something to smile about today, at least."

Izzy managed to get comfortable and arrange everything neatly on her lap. She glanced at Trent from the corner of her eye. He looked in his side mirror and pulled away, driving along the street to join the main road. He was dressed in his uniform trousers, navy T-shirt and red suspenders...and looked ridiculously edible. Her stomach knotted. How was she supposed to act like she hadn't slept with the man when he looked the way he did?

She tried and failed not to glance at his hands and bared forearms; tried and failed not to sneak another peek at his profile. She frowned. Did he too have the inability to stop smiling?

She forced her clenched teeth apart and her

lips down. The ache in her cheeks screamed their relief. "So, how are you?"

"Not too bad." He continued to stare ahead. "You?"

"Not bad." Excruciating awkwardness filled the car, and Izzy slumped. "This is silly. I know you must be hurting. Sam's funeral was hard. Really hard."

His smile wavered. "It was, but it's done and now we need to wait for the good memories to overtake the bad ones. It happens. Just takes time."

She stared at the passing shops, bars and cafés and tried to remember how beautiful and colorful the Cove was and that it didn't always feel as gray as it did right now. She exhaled a shaky breath. "That's true. Slowly, my memories of Robbie are changing." She glanced at him. "The light at the end of the tunnel has grown from a pinprick to the width of a thumbnail, so I'm grateful for that at least."

He briefly squeezed her hand before returning his to the steering wheel. "You know where I am, Iz. Anytime."

She swallowed. "Thanks."

As much as she wished it weren't true, over and over, she'd wished Trent hadn't left Templeton and gone to his parents. That single action had succeeded in stirring up all her old insecurities. Their short time together was like a flash of bright pink through a black-and-white photograph. A snippet of sunshine through the darkness and now everything had dimmed once more. Yet here she was, side by side with him…and most likely would be over and over again in the future.

Templeton wasn't the place to be if a person intended to live her life alone. Practically everyone knew everyone else. The likelihood was, eventually, she'd claw her way back from her true feelings for Trent and escape the horrible heaviness in her chest that had been there for days. Before that happened, though, she had to find a way to handle seeing him when she was out and about. It was impossible to avoid anyone in the Cove forever.

She looked to the side window. Sam's funeral had been torture. Not just for Trent, but for the entire community. Shocked expressions and tear-streaked faces had dominated the small crematorium, the mood somber and damn near heartbreaking.

The curious, sometimes triumphant looks that had been sent in her and Trent's direction proved people had pretty much bet on their reunion. Yet neither she nor Trent acknowledged people's interest.

He cleared his throat. “Any more news with the gallery?”

Izzy sat a little straighter and faced front, grateful for the topic choice. “Not yet. It will be a couple of weeks before things are settled and then I guess it will be a case of me and Jay working out the details of how we’ll run the gallery. I’m looking forward to working with him. He’s a really nice guy.”

“Well, if you need a model in the future, you know where I am.”

He tipped her a wink and Izzy smiled. “Fancy this modeling thing now, do you?”

“I certainly had a good time with the last photographer who took my picture. Worth asking if she wants to photograph me again.”

“Very funny.” Her stomach knotted with memories of that day and how it had ended with her and Trent on her office desk. Heat warmed her cheeks and other places. “Maybe a slot will come free in her diary one day.”

“Maybe it will.”

Izzy turned to the window. Why were they flirting? Then again, maybe this was just Trent being Trent. He’d flirted with her since the day Robbie introduced them four years ago. Hell, he’d flirted with plenty of girls in between too.

Flirting was Trent’s coping mechanism. She knew that better than most of the girls who’d fallen for his charms before her. She'd just been stupid enough to be caught too eventually.

The journey to the specialist children's hospital was over an hour's drive, but they managed small talk for half of it before tense silence hovered heavy enough for Izzy to turn on the radio.

At last, they pulled into the hospital parking lot.

As soon as Trent cut the engine, Izzy snapped off her seat belt and struggled from the car. She stared at the hospital's facade, and the bitter taste of grief coated her throat. The last time she was at a hospital, she'd followed the ambulance carrying Robbie… Little did she know her brother was already dead.

"You okay?"

Trent's voice beside her made her jump and she turned. He'd put on his fireproof jacket and held his hat in one hand and a huge soft panda in the other. She swallowed against her weakening heart. That was *so* not playing fair. She looked to the hospital again. "Not really. You?"

When no answer came, Izzy turned.

The concern in his eyes deepened and he put the bear and his hat in one hand and stole his other arm around her shoulders. "No. I feel as though I've spent far too much time in hospitals over the years, but I'm determined to make today about Maya and what she needs."

He stared ahead, his jaw tight.

Unable to bear his suffering over Sam, she cupped her hand to his jaw, guiding his face to hers. "It has to get better eventually."

His gaze melted from anger to fierce determination as he reached up and drew her hand from his face. "Let's hope so because I don't remember ever feeling as crappy as I do right now."

"Trent—"

"Come on, let's get inside." He stepped toward the hospital and spoke over his shoulder. "One day at a time. That's what Sam always advised and I think it's about time I started listening to him."

Pushing away her helplessness, Izzy followed Trent through the sliding doors into the hospital. As he spoke with the receptionist, Izzy joined him.

Trent smiled at the older woman. "Great. Thanks for your help." He faced Izzy. "Maya's on the pediatric oncology floor. Paddington Bear ward. Her mum's with her and they're expecting us."

"Great." She nodded and drew in a breath. "Let's go."

They took the elevator and by the time the

neon digits showed level two, Trent had taken hold of her hand. She glanced at him, her heart a mess of gratitude and fear. Gratitude he was there with her, making her strong once again, and fear that if she leaned on him, she'd forget how important it was that she stand alone.

He continued to stare at the floor numbers as they rose. Izzy forced her shoulders down and held his hand a little tighter.

The elevator pinged at the fourth floor and, hand in hand, they walked along the corridor until they found the Paddington Bear ward and Maya Jackson's room. Izzy looked at Trent and he winked with an encouraging smile.

She returned his smile, gently knocked on the door and pushed it open.

Maya Jackson was awake and nodding at something her mother said from the brown plastic seat beside Maya's bed. The little girl's dark gaze flitted to the door, and her pretty face lit with a grin. Izzy instantly fell in love. Even without her hair and the tube coming from her nose, Maya Jackson was one of the most beautiful little girls Izzy had ever seen. Her huge eyes shone with happiness despite the horrible disease she fought, her smile wide, revealing perfect pearly white teeth.

Her mother stood and held out her hand. "You must be Izzy. Hi, Kerri Jackson."

Izzy shook Kerri's hand, whose strained smile did little to alleviate the clear exhaustion etched on her face. "Nice to meet you. Thanks so much for letting us meet Maya today."

"It's my pleasure. She's so excited to meet a real-life photographer and firefighter." She held her hand out to Trent. "Trent, isn't it?"

"It is. Nice to meet you."

Izzy looked to Maya. "And you must be Maya. Hi, sweetheart." Izzy stepped toward the bed and held out her gifts. "Here, these are for you."

"Thank you." The little girl's gaze ran over Izzy's face, her smile wider than the sun. "You take pictures."

"I do, and I'm hoping the pictures I've taken of Templeton's firefighters will raise lots of money to help you get out of this hospital and back home."

Maya looked to Trent, her eyes wide. "Are you a real firefighter?"

"Yep." He came around the bed to Maya's other side and whipped out the huge stuffed panda from behind his back. "And this is our mascot, Toby. Do you think you could look after him for a while?"

"Sure." She giggled. "He's a funny mascot."

"Well, we're funny firefighters." Trent crossed his eyes and pulled a face that set Maya giggling louder.

Kerri laughed behind Izzy and she laughed too. She stared at Trent, her heart dangerously close to a complete and irrevocable meltdown. The man was a walking, talking hero, however she tried to look at him. She was hard-pressed to find a single fault, and if she were anyone else, she'd hold on to him and never let him go.

But she wasn't anyone else and neither of them deserved another loss in their lives. It was better this way. Wasn't it?

Turning away from him, Izzy focused on Maya. "Why don't you open the present I bought you?"

"Okay." Maya moved the bear Izzy had bought her and tucked him safely beside Toby under her bedsheets. "What's his name?"

"Robbie." Izzy smiled as Trent's gaze burned into her temple. "He likes being with you already. I bet you two become fast friends."

"We will. Toby too."

"Absolutely."

Kerri touched Izzy's arm. "How are things going with the calendar? Are you done?"

Izzy faced her as Trent took a seat on the edge of Maya's bed. Their laughter and chatter warmed the room as Izzy spoke to Kerri. "We're all done and the calendars are with the printers." She smiled. "It's going to fly off the shelves, I'm sure of it."

The worry in the devoted mother's eyes didn't lessen as she sneaked a peak at Maya.

Izzy took Kerri's hand and urged her to the corner of the room. "How is Maya? Is there anything else we can do to help?"

Tears shone in Kerri's eyes as she stared at her daughter. "She's doing amazingly well. In fact, the doctors have said things are looking more and more encouraging."

"That's great news." Izzy followed Kerri's gaze as Trent plopped his hat on Toby's head, setting Maya off into another glorious fit of giggles. "She's a brave girl. You must be incredibly proud of her."

"I am. She's my inspiration."

The door opened and a young nurse in a pale green uniform covered with tiny printed zebras entered, pushing a wheelchair. "Hi, Maya. It's time to go and see the doctor. Shall we ask your visitors if they mind waiting here for you?"

Maya's smile vanished and her wide eyes snapped between the nurse, Trent and Izzy. "I don't want to go now. I'll go later."

Kerri stepped forward and grasped Maya's

hand where it lay limply on the bed. "It's okay, darling. Izzy and Trent won't mind waiting." She looked at Izzy and Trent in turn. "Will you?"

"Not a problem at all. I'd love to chat with you more."

"I need to stay here and make sure Toby doesn't start eating your grapes."

Trent and Izzy looked at each other as their words tumbled over each other.

Maya giggled and sat back so the nurse could see to the tubes and switches and get Maya transferred to the wheelchair. Izzy stood back as the little girl cooperated so fluidly with her mother and the nurse that it was tragically clear just how regular the routine had become.

Once seated in the chair, Maya beamed and waved as she was wheeled from the room with Kerri following.

The door brushed closed behind them and Trent sat heavily on the bed, staring at Maya's pillow, the dent from her small head still hauntingly visible.

Izzy blinked back the burning in her eyes and picked up Maya's unwrapped second gift. It was a photograph Izzy had taken of Cowden Beach, Maya's favorite place to play. The shot was taken at sunset, and the oranges and pinks were shown off in a driftwood frame she'd found in the toy cum trinket shop in town. As Maya had been a budding photographer before she became ill, Izzy hoped the picture inspired the little girl to fight to get better and see the world was still a beautiful place.

She smoothed her finger over the picture. "She's going to fight this cancer and win, you know."

"God, I hope so."

Izzy came around the bed and sat beside Trent. "She will. Just you watch."

His gaze roamed over her face, lingered at her lips before he met her eyes. "We need to stop this, Iz."

She stiffened. "Stop what?"

"Messing about. I want you and you want me. I look at that little girl, I look at Sam… Robbie. If we don't start fighting everything that frightens the hell out of us, all the illness and death is for nothing. We're living right now. Look at Bianca. You were right yesterday when you said she isn't hiding away or avoiding everything that might go wrong through the rest of what I hope is her really long life."

Izzy inhaled and dropped her head onto his shoulder. She admired Bianca so much. Her brother's fiancée had somehow found the strength to take each day as it came, accepted the love of the Cove to pull her through. Izzy closed her eyes. All she'd done was shun people and hide.

She lifted her head and met Trent's sincere gaze. Her heart swelled with the love and attraction she desperately wanted to contain, but the fight was so hard. She loved him. What was she really running away from when everyone on the planet faced the risk of loss every day too?

Lacing his fingers with hers, she looked down at their joined hands. "Bianca and Robbie were beautiful to watch together. I know Scott still feels responsible because the explosion happened at his garage. Bianca being his sister must make it pretty tough on him." She sighed. "Who would've thought that sassy, confident Bianca and loving, happy-go-lucky Robbie, one of the most unlikely unions to ever grace the Cove's shores, would work so perfectly?" An unexpected sob lodged in Izzy's throat. "And now Bianca's trying so hard to move on and not stay in the same place doing nothing."

"She's got a strong family around her."

Izzy met his eyes, her own burning with tears. "But I haven't, Trent, and it's hard for me to be brave on my own."

He softly kissed her cheek. "You're not alone."

She leaned into his unwavering strength,

moved her arms around his body and held on tight. "It's not just my endless fear of losing you in a fire holding me back from us trying again, you know."

"Then what? You need to explain this to me. I'm going crazy not being with you."

She straightened. "You are?"

"Of course I am. How could you think otherwise?"

"You seemed so happy in the car...you flirted with me."

He shrugged, a soft smile curving his lips. "Why wouldn't I? Look at you."

She playfully shoved him, suddenly feeling vulnerable under the undeniable admiration in his eyes. "See? It's that. I don't want you to change and you will. It's inevitable." She stood and crossed her arms in a bid to calm her traitorous, hopeful heart. She faced him. "How are you supposed to fit into my nice, quiet, orderly life when you live on such a potent mix of danger and excitement?"

He huffed a laugh. "A potent mix of danger and excitement? Come on, Iz. It's a job. Do you really think it's those two things that make me face fire every day?"

"Firefighting isn't just a job to you. You started fighting fire for Aimee, but you've continued for years since you lost her. You've saved hundreds of lives, Trent. Your job is a need in you now. A passion. I don't want to be the one who takes that away. If you changed anything about you for me, you wouldn't be the man I lo…admire so much."

He stood and came toward her, his green eyes darkening with the unmistakable desire she had no way of deflecting. Every single time he looked at her that way, it weakened her.

She took a step back. "Stay there and just think about what I said for a moment."

He came closer and slowly unwrapped her arms and dropped a kiss to her jaw, lower to the sensitive curve of her neck. His breath whispered across her skin. "I want you to change me, Iz. You'll make me better and I'll do the same for you."

"But how will my worry for you ever change? It's only going to get worse."

"You'll get used to it." He smiled. "Especially when I come home from every shift safe and sound."

"But the closer we get, the deeper we fall in love… Please, Trent, try to understand. How am I supposed to move past the fact that you could die every time you're called out?"

"I don't know, but you have to find a way. This thing between us is too good to throw away on ifs and maybes. Don't you think?"

He straightened and brushed his lips across hers. "How about you talk to some of the other girlfriends and wives of the crew? You know Will's wife, Helen, right? Go see her. Talk to her and ask how she manages every day." He smiled, softly. "If you weren't worried for me, you'd be different than all the other loved ones who worry about the crew and then I'd be thinking something wasn't right. This fear isn't irrational, Iz. It's understandable." He kissed her forehead. "Even more so in your case."

"I don't know."

"Look at me."

Exhaling a shaky breath, Izzy dragged her gaze from a spot on the opposite wall to his beautiful, loving and penetrable stare.

"We're going to give this everything we've got, okay? We're going to make it work." He leaned in and lifted her hair away from her neck to nip and kiss at the sensitive area below her ear. "Agreed?"

Her knees trembled and her core pulled. To fight him was only possible if she didn't allow him close enough to touch her. If she didn't maintain that space…

She coughed and rested her hands on his shoulders as if to push him away and she would have…if some invisible force hadn't tipped her head to allow him better access to her neck. "Have you noticed we're in a hospital?" She sighed. "In a room where a little girl is fighting for her life?"

"Yep, that's why I'm asking you right here, right now. Are we together or not?" He moved his mouth to hers and moved his tongue gently, seductively over hers. "Are we going to start living? Yes or no?"

"Yes," she murmured into his mouth, reclaimed his tongue with hers. "We're going to start living."

"Ahem."

They jumped apart.

Izzy brought her hand to her swollen lips. Kerri Jackson stared in disbelief, her mouth open. The pediatric nurse's eyebrows were raised almost to her hairline, but she looked suspiciously as though she fought a smile. As for Maya…the girl looked happy enough to burst. "Are you guys girlfriend-boyfriend? Cool."

Mortification ran over Izzy in a wave of heat as she opened and closed her mouth. But nothing filtered through her embarrassment to her brain.

Trent left her standing against the wall and dropped to his haunches in front of Maya. "Cool? Really?"

Maya grinned. "Uh-huh."

"Are you sure? Because if you want me to kick Izzy to the curb and wait for you to grow up, I don't mind."

Maya blushed bright red and as the nurse and Kerri both laughed and leaned over the wheelchair to swat Trent, Izzy grinned and joined in the assault from behind. Maya's shrieks of delight bounced off the wall and straight into Izzy's rapidly filling pool of happiness.

CHAPTER FIFTEEN

TRENT STARED AT Izzy across their sea-view table at the Oceanside and fell a little deeper. It had been a week since their visit with Maya at the hospital, and the connection between them had grown stronger every day. She was sexy, funny, clever and ambitious…and the combination turned him on more than he thought possible. Yet now, as she inched toward trusting him and allowing him to see inside her heart and mind, deeper layers slowly revealed themselves, making him want her more than ever to become someone permanent in his life.

Sure, he'd known for years how attracted he was to her, but now the atmosphere between them was tangible…to the other residents of the Cove too, if the suggestive comments they'd received from a handful of their peer group was anything to go by.

"Stop staring at me." Izzy picked up her wine and brought it to her lips, her happy gaze on his. "I don't even want to know what you're thinking, because whatever it is, I'm sure it isn't suitable for public conversation."

He smiled and lifted his eyebrows. "Shall we skip the meal and head home, then? Eating's overrated anyway."

"A girl needs to eat if she plans on using her energy reserves."

Her blue eyes shone like Bristol glass under the candlelight. The quip on Trent's tongue vanished when her stockinged toes ran up and under the hem of his jeans to tease his calf.

She grinned. "Don't you agree?"

He picked up his wineglass and drank deep, his gaze on hers. "You're a bad, bad girl, Izzy Cooper." He lowered his glass. "But I like it."

She laughed and, regrettably, pulled her foot away. "You need to behave. We can't spend every evening in bed."

"Why not?"

"Because...because..." Her cheeks flushed. "Stop looking at me like that. Just because, okay?" She narrowed her eyes. "Eat and stop talking."

Smiling, Trent picked up his knife and fork. He loved teasing her, loved being with her and, most of all, wondered how the hell he'd lived all those months without making love to her.

He cut into his steak and speared some potato. "So, did you have coffee with Helen today?"

"I did." Her voice quieted. "We went to Marian's."

Trent looked up, bothered by the caution in her tone. "And?"

She put down her knife and fork and lifted her glass. "And I'm not sure our conversation changed anything. I'm still just as scared for you." She took a mouthful of wine, her gaze sad. "For us."

"Will and Helen have been married a long time, Iz. Together even longer. It might be that Helen's just grown used to the job, that's all."

"You're wrong." She returned her glass to the table and shifted forward in her seat, her beautiful eyes wide with worry. "She says the longer she's with him, the more she worries. When they were single, the fact that Will was a firefighter excited Helen. Then they got married and she slowly grew used to starting to look at the clock every five minutes from just before the end of his shift until she heard his key in the front door." She closed her eyes. "And now that they have a baby..."

Trent fought his unease. Was he kidding himself that the job ever got easier for a firefighter's loved ones? Was he lying to Izzy for his own selfish desires? He put down his cutlery and took her hands. "Listen to me. You're right. Helen's right. My job's dangerous and I'm wrong to keep telling you not to worry about what might happen, but I know we've got a chance at some real happiness here. Aren't you willing to give us a try *despite* what might or might not happen?"

"It's fire, Trent." She slipped her hands from his and drew them into her lap, her eyes blazing with frustration. "Ignoring its dangers isn't normal to me in any shape or form. Mum and dad taught Robbie and me to live life as we wanted, to embrace our dreams and passions, not let outside influences hold us back." She shook her head. "But now, with Robbie gone, fire is my nemesis. The one thing that continues to burn deep inside me. This isn't the same as me being with you without knowledge of what devastating loss fire can cause."

Fear of her retreating again engulfed him. He wanted to be with her so damn much. "But you're here tonight despite speaking with Helen. There must be something you see in us that you want."

A small smile lifted the corners of her mouth. "It's not what I see. It's *who* I see. You. You're a pain in the ass with your sexy smile, gorgeous green eyes and body like iron."

Trent grinned, relief pumping through him like lifesaving oxygen. "Well, thank God for that."

Trent's mind turned to the idea he'd had earlier. An idea that could well send Izzy running for the hills, but something that felt important and clear in his growing feelings for her. He leaned forward. "I have an idea that will get us out of bed for a few days."

She raised her eyebrows. "And you want that why?"

He smiled. "It was you who said we can't spend every evening between the sheets, remember?"

She picked up her fork and frowned. "Did I? I must have lost a piece of my brain for a moment."

Trent took a long, steadying breath and then said what was on his mind before he lost his courage. "How about we go away for the weekend?"

"Where?" She put some pasta in her mouth and chewed, her beautiful eyes wide with interest.

He had no idea why, or how, the rash idea burst into his mind, but now that it was there, Trent knew it was a good one. "I want you to spend the weekend with me at my parents'."

She coughed, put down her fork and reached

for her water. Trent turned to his food and pretended the suggestion was no big deal. The truth was, he'd never brought *any* woman home to meet his parents. Ever. This was a deal of gargantuan proportions. He forced his gaze to Izzy's. Judging by the terror in her gaze and the red blotches on her upper chest and throat, she entirely agreed with him about the magnitude of his suggestion.

She leaned forward, her hand splayed on the tablecloth. "They know about us?"

He shrugged, feigning nonchalance. "Sure. I told them after we visited Maya. They're really pleased about it too."

"But they don't know me like they knew Robbie. How can they know enough about me to be pleased?"

He gripped her fingers and stared into her eyes, willing her to believe just how wonderful a woman she was. "You make me happy. You make me want to enjoy more than just my work. That's all they need to know. They have a great place near the beach." He released her hand and took a mouthful of wine. "You'll feel at home in no time."

"Feel at home? Trent, this isn't something to joke about. Meeting parents is..."

"Meeting parents is what?" He put down his

glass as worry of what she was about to say gripped his chest. “Iz?”

She exhaled. “I don’t know if I’m ready for that.”

Disappointment flooded through him, and Trent sat a little straighter in his seat. If she had to set the pace to feel comfortable, then he would concede to that. No problem. “Okay, no pressure. It was just an idea.”

The surrounding chatter and classical music coming from concealed speakers seemed to hitch up a notch. Every scrape of a chair across the terra-cotta floor tiles resounded louder than before, and each chink of a glass filtered to Trent’s ears on high frequency.

“Trent?”

He met her gaze.

“I’m sorry.”

“It’s okay. Maybe you’re right. Maybe it is too soon.”

“No, that’s not what I mean.” Her gaze softened. “I mean, I’m sorry for saying that. What I should’ve said is it sounds like a great idea. When do you want to go?”

“Are you sure?” Tentative hope rose in his chest.

“I am.” She smiled and relaxed her shoulders. “I’d love to meet your parents. You asking just took me by surprise, that’s all. Plus,

I know for a fact that you don't make a habit of taking the women you date home to meet your mum and dad." Her gaze softened further. "And you look so heartbreakingly gorgeous when a girl says no to your plans. How am I supposed to resist?"

Laughing, he took her hand and pulled her forward. He kissed her and tightened his grip on her hand to prevent her from moving back in her seat. "It's not very wise to mess with the emotions of a six-foot-two fireman, especially one as well built as I am, you know."

She lifted an eyebrow. "No? What are you going to do? Tell me what's what?"

This woman needed a lesson…one he'd give her the minute they got back to his apartment. "Absolutely."

She grinned. "I was hoping you'd say that."

He released her and they sank back into their seats, the sexual tension between them humming across the table. How soon could they eat their meals and get back to his place?

He forked another slice of his steak. "You know something? It was what my dad said after I told him I was seeing you that made me see sense and come back to the Cove as quickly as I could."

"What did he say?"

Her cautious gaze belied her nervousness,

her returned unease that Trent wanted so desperately to vanquish. He had to stop running at full speed. Just because he was 100 percent certain Izzy was the woman for him, it was going to take longer for Izzy to believe the same.

He cleared his throat. “He knew pretty soon after I’d arrived that it wasn’t just Sam’s death I was running away from. Dad took one look at me and somehow knew I was running away from a person too. He’d already guessed that person was you.”

She frowned. “But how long ago did you tell him we were involved?”

“Apparently, he’s known for years how much I liked you, but never said anything to me or Mum. He said he chose to wait for the inevitable to happen.” Trent smiled, hoping to make her smile too. “He told me love is a gift and that I shouldn’t turn my back on it. Didn’t take me long to realize he was right, so I got back in my car and came home. To you.”

She picked up her wine before turning away from him to stare across the restaurant.

Trent studied her profile. “Iz?”

When she turned, tears shone in her eyes. “Your dad sounds like a good man.” She smiled. "It's no surprise his son turned out to be such a great guy too."

Trent smiled and lowered his shoulders. "He is, and I'll spend the rest of my life trying to build a life as good, honest and well meaning as he has. He and Mum will love you, Iz. They'll be happy for us."

Her chest rose as she inhaled a shaky breath. "We can go this weekend if you like."

"You sure?"

"Yes. Definitely."

"Great." Trent winked and nodded to her plate. "Now eat up so we can get out of here. I don't think I can wait much longer to get you home and in my bed where you belong."

She laughed and returned to her food.

Trent stared at her bowed head. She might have agreed to visit his parents, but her uncertainty showed in the stiffness of her shoulders and the blush at her cheeks. He didn't need to ask Izzy to know what she thought. He knew her well enough to know that mentioning his parents had only served to remind her of the absence of her own.

He pushed his fork into some potato as determination to show Izzy that family didn't always equate to those a person was joined to by blood. One way or another, he would show her that love, comfort and trust were sometimes found in the most unlikely people, in the most unlikely of places. She was an amazing woman. One whom any man would be lucky to have on his arm and anyone would be lucky to have in their life.

The biggest challenge would be getting Izzy to realize how special she was when everyone she ever loved had left her…some in the most horrible, life-altering way.

IZZY SLIPPED THE straps of her silk camisole over her shoulders and stared down at Trent as he lay on his back beneath her. His green gaze shone dark with desire and his jaw was clenched tight as he hungrily watched her discard her final piece of clothing.

Sweet liberation whispered through her and she embraced it willingly. She loved Trent… maybe from the first day she saw him. And now—finally—they were together.

Smiling softly, she reached toward her bedside cabinet and picked up the foil-packed condom. She ripped it open, holding his gaze as she smoothed the protection onto him with purposely slow precision, her body tingling with anticipation and arousal. His obvious lust for her, his love, turned her on more than he could ever imagine.

Her surrender scared the hell out of her, but she would not deny or fight it anymore. Wasted time was behind them and determination to enjoy the months and, hopefully, years ahead with this kind, strong and sensitive man who'd waited so patiently for her was paramount in her heart and soul. Now that she'd relinquished her defenscs, all that remained was her prayer that Trent would stay with her. Always.

Leaning over him, she inhaled the spicy scent of his aftershave as she pressed her lips to his neck, higher to his stubbled jaw and slowly across his chin to claim his mouth. A sigh escaped her lips as he gently gripped her bottom, holding her still against him as she tried to shimmy a little closer to her goal. Their tongues tangled and their lips crushed as heat and want grew.

Their love singed every part of her, its power as uplifting as it was frightening.

"I need you inside me." She whispered into his mouth. "Now."

"Patience."

She quivered. He slid his hand between her legs, his fingers moving achingly lower until they reached her core. He teased her until Izzy was forced to draw back from his kiss and bite her lips together to stop from crying out in frustration. The man knew exactly how to touch and torment.

"Trent, please." She dropped her mouth open as he continued to rub and caress her, her orgasm inching so very, very close. "I want you so much."

Just when she thought she would tip over the edge, he moved both his hands to her waist and glided her forward. She gratefully rose to her knees and, with her gaze on his, guided him inside. She savored every ounce of the love that glistened so beautifully in his eyes.

She smiled softly and moved slowly, searching for his rhythm and hers until they joined in perfect, unbelievable unison as they had done every single time they made love.

His jaw tightened. "I love you, Iz. So much."

"I love you too."

Their gazes locked and their teeth clenched as they sought the blessed climax that hovered so pleasurably out of reach.

"Come for me, Iz. Let me see you."

His words edged her closer, his eyes growing darker with every forward motion. Then she was there. Izzy flung her head back as her orgasm burst through her core and spread through her body, swelling her heart with the profound and passionate love she had for Trent and everything he was.

His hands gripped her waist as he groaned and his pleasure shuddered through her body. She opened her eyes and tried to catch her breath.

He squeezed his eyes shut, his jaw tight, before collapsing against the pillows. Slowly, his eyes fluttered open and he exhaled. "What did I do to deserve you?"

She smiled. "I'm feeling pretty lucky myself, you know."

He shook his head. "You've got to be the sexiest woman in the whole damn world."

Joy and satisfaction swept through her and Izzy grinned before shifting away to fall to the bed beside him. "Well, if I am, it's you who makes me that way." She blew out a breath and flung her arm heavily across his chest. "Never in my life has sex been this…hot, good, amazing."

He turned his head and kissed her. "We belong together, Iz. Always."

Her heart stuttered at the undisguised love in his eyes, and she lifted her hand to glide her fingers over his cheek to his jaw. "Thank God you waited for me to see that."

His somber gaze brightened as if she'd handed him all the money in the world. They kissed again before she laid her head on his chest. But even with his steady heartbeat in her ear, her smile slowly dissolved as thoughts of the trip to his parents' place tiptoed back into her mind. As much as she wanted to go, she couldn't quash the fear the visit evoked.

She had not seen her parents since Robbie's funeral six months before. They'd exchanged emails, the odd phone call, but they hadn't come home. Not even for a single day.

She'd spoken to them by telephone after Sam's funeral, wanting to hear their voices even if she couldn't see their faces. She'd even swallowed her misplaced pride and asked them to consider coming home for a visit. Her mum had promised to get back to her soon with a date.

That had been days ago and still her phone remained ominously silent.

Tears burned and Izzy closed her eyes.

Hadn't they sensed how desperately she wanted to make up for her cold treatment of them in the past?

"What are you thinking about, Iz?"

She opened her eyes and swiped at the tears on her cheeks. "Mum and Dad."

"Something wrong?"

Shifting onto her side, she stared into Trent's concerned gaze and forced a soft smile. "It's nothing. I just miss them sometimes, that all."

He frowned. "It's because I asked you to

meet my parents, isn't it? If you've changed your mind, it's okay. I understand. I don't want you to do anything you aren't ready for."

"I want to meet them. Honestly." She ran her nails over the hardened muscles of his pecs. "It's not that it's *your* parents. It's just that they're parents, period. You'd think by now meeting other families, seeing into their lives and how different they are from mine wouldn't bother me." She met his gaze. "But it does, and I can't lie about how much Mum and Dad's continuous absence often hurts too."

He cupped his hand to her jaw, his thumb gently sweeping back and forth across her cheek. "My parents are fantastic, Iz. You'll be in their company for five minutes and feel comfortable, I promise. I really hope when we leave them, you won't come away looking at what you don't have, but come back to the Cove feeling as though you've gained something. They'll look after you like they look after me. I guarantee it."

She looked at his chest as shame washed over her. "Maybe I shouldn't linger in my own wants when both our parents have lost a child. My mum and dad might not be here, but at least they're alive." She forced her gaze to his. "I'm sorry."

"Hey." He kissed her firmly on the mouth.

"Don't be sorry for your feelings. I'll never judge what you feel, because that's what makes you who you are. And for the record, I've yet to find a single aspect of you I don't like. Our parents lost Aimee and Robbie and day by day they're learning to live with their memories. That's all they can do. My parents keep Aimee alive in their hearts through loving and helping others. Maybe your parents do the same with Robbie in a different way. All I know for sure is Aimee was a caring, loving girl. She wouldn't have wanted Mum and Dad to be unhappy and she wouldn't have wanted me to be unhappy. You come home with me and you'll get that. You really will."

She stared into his eyes and a little more of her reservation and fear dissolved. "I love you, Trent."

He grinned, his eyes shining as he winked. "I love you too. Everything's going to be great. I promise. We'll leave for Kingsley tomorrow night so Mum will have a chance to make up the spare room." He grimaced. "I'll be in my old room. Guaranteed. Mum and Dad are all for free will, but they won't think it proper or right for us to sleep together under their roof. Their principles are just another reason why I love them."

She wiggled her eyebrows. "Then we'd better make up for our enforced nocturnal separation now, hadn't we?"

"Absolutely."

She screeched as he leaned over and pinned her beneath him, her body instantly responding with desire and glorious anticipation for round two…or was it three?

CHAPTER SIXTEEN

IZZY PRESSED HER hand to the nerves dancing in her stomach as she got out of Trent's car and stared at the front of his parents' home. Even though the small bungalow was situated high on a hill above Kingsley's seafront, providing fantastic views of the beach and ocean, with the holiday season over and everyone back to school and work, the drive through the town center had filled Izzy with the eerie sense of a ghost town.

Silently admonishing her irrational trepidation, she took a deep breath and joined Trent at the back of the car.

He opened the trunk and set her weekend bag on the ground before pulling out his sports bag. He closed the trunk and faced her, his gaze happy. "Are you ready for this? Mum will give you all of ten seconds to say hello before she's got the kettle on and asking you a million and one questions."

"Don't say that. I'm nervous enough as it is." She glanced toward the house. "The last time

I saw your parents I was your friend's sister. Nothing more."

He took her elbows and stared deep into her eyes before brushing his lips across hers. "First of all, they're going to love you. Second, my parents are happy if I'm happy."

"So your mum isn't going to think I'm the woman who's going to take you away from her? Isn't that what mums usually feel about their sons' new girlfriends?"

"Maybe." He dropped his hands from her elbows and picked up their bags, his gaze thoughtful as he considered her questions. "In fact, I would make sure you do all you can to show off your culinary and darning skills, in case she worries you won't look after me properly."

"I can't cook, you know that...and what the hell is darning?"

He grinned and pressed a kiss to her temple. "I'm kidding. Come on."

"Trent, wait." She grasped his elbow, her gaze toward the house. "How much have you told them about me?"

He frowned. "What do you mean?"

"They know how Robbie died, right?"

"Of course."

Izzy looked toward the house again. "Do they know how I feel about your job?"

"I haven't said anything about that." He kissed her quickly on the mouth. "Because I'm hoping it's something we can get through."

"But what if it isn't? Bringing me here like this, maybe it was the wrong thing to do when we've only been back together a couple of weeks. They might get the wrong idea."

"The wrong idea?" His gaze turned wary. "As in they shouldn't get their hopes up we're the real deal? That you're already thinking we won't last?"

"I didn't say that." Her cheeks grew warm. "All I'm saying is—"

He squeezed her hand. "Listen. Everything's going to be fine. I'll intercept any awkward questions, okay? I want you to relax and enjoy yourself."

He turned and walked up the short pathway to the front door. Izzy stared after him. She should've chosen a better moment to voice her concerns. This weekend was important to them both, and now wasn't the time to linger over her doubts that refused to be silenced.

She followed Trent along the pathway to where he was waiting for her at the front door and forced a smile.

He visibly relaxed and pushed his key in the door. "Ready?"

Drawing on every ounce of strength that had

gotten her through some of the toughest times in her life, Izzy gave a curt nod. "Ready."

He grinned and pushed open the door. "Mum? Dad? We're here."

Footsteps slapped against stone as Trent's mum emerged from a door at the end of the hallway. She hastily wiped her hands on a towel, before flinging it onto her shoulder and coming forward with her arms outstretched. "Look at you. Home again. I need to mark the calendar." She pulled him into a hug and closed her eyes.

The floorboards at the top of the stairs creaked, and Trent's father descended. He was tall and handsome, possibly a few years older than his wife. Izzy smiled. It was kind of nice to have confirmation from whom Trent got his looks.

His dad smiled as she met his assessing gaze. "Izzy, it's a pleasure to see you again. David Palmer." He took her hand as he came to stand beside her. "And the woman holding Trent so tight he's in danger of exploding is Linda, my wife and Trent's mum. Linda? Maybe you'd like to say hello to Izzy?"

Linda released Trent and came toward Izzy with a warm and welcoming smile. "Izzy, hi. I'm so sorry. I just love having my boy home." She pulled Izzy into an embrace and pressed a kiss to her cheek. “Welcome. I hope you’re hungry. I’ve made mashed potatoes, Trent’s favorite pork and apple sausages with our very own homegrown peas.”

“That sounds fantastic. Thank you. I hope you didn’t go to much trouble.”

“Not at all. Now.” She let go of Izzy’s hand and faced Trent, her brow furrowed. “Be a gentleman and take Izzy’s bag up to Aimee’s room. Your bedroom is already made up, as always.” She lifted an eyebrow, her gaze stern. “Okay?”

Trent turned and pulled an “I told you” face at Izzy and she bit back a smile, grateful the teasing gesture banished the awareness she was to sleep in the same room Trent’s passed sister once had. It felt strangely like an honor.

“Izzy?”

She blinked and faced Linda, her eyes alight with warmth. “Come with me, my love, and we’ll have a nice cup of tea. David has the patio heater on so we can sit outside.”

“Great.”

She clasped Izzy’s elbow and looked to Trent. “Upstairs, Trent. Don’t keep Izzy waiting. I suspect the poor girl is parched.”

Trent rolled his eyes at Izzy behind his mother’s back as she steered Izzy toward the door from where she’d emerged from a few minutes before. The kitchen was big and homely with cream-painted walls and beech-wood cabinets. Gorgeous dusky pink curtains were pulled back at the window above the earthenware sink, and a matching set hung at the French doors that led to a softly lit patio beyond.

"Take a seat while I pour the tea." Linda gestured toward the small dining table. "The boys won't be long and we can take our tea outside to enjoy the last of the sun. Did you have a good journey here?"

Izzy sat and placed the strap of her purse over the back of the chair. "We did. We left late enough to miss the rush-hour traffic, but early enough to miss people coming out for the night."

"Good thinking."

No matter how she longed to feel differently, the family-oriented air of Trent's childhood home tightened her chest with a deep longing to see her parents again. The bungalow was as foreign to her as a spaceship on Mars. She had no idea how to act. If she didn't make one slipup after another while she was there, it would be a miracle.

Insecurity and doubt pushed like a lead weight against her rib cage.

Trent's parents were caring, happy and inviting despite their daughter being so cruelly stolen from them. Whereas, after Izzy's pushing, her mum and dad had fled the pressure and grief of Robbie's death and Izzy's depression. Even though parents and daughter reached an uneasy peace that resulted in Izzy giving them permission to leave, she hadn't meant any of the scathing words she'd said.

And now Mr. and Mrs. Palmer's warmth and kindness only further illuminated how horrible and unreceptive Izzy had been to her parents, friends and other residents at the Cove during the months following Robbie's death. Would she ever be capable of the same kind of authentic happiness Trent's parents seemed to have?

Or would her punishment be the inability to ever have a trusting and fulfilling relationship?

Blinking, Izzy turned her attention to the door as Trent and his father entered the kitchen. Both men met her gaze and she smiled at their identical and gentle scrutiny. "Hi."

"Hi, yourself." Trent came toward her, winked and squeezed her hand before he sat on the seat beside her. "Mum looking after you? Not frightening you too much? She can be a bit of a tyrant sometimes."

"Excuse me, Trent Reginald Palmer." His mother glared. "Don't you dare taint my good name in front of Izzy. Whatever will she think of me?"

Trent laughed and Izzy did too before she turned to Trent and mouthed, "Reginald. Nice." He narrowed his eyes in playful warning and Izzy grinned.

"Okay, you two, let's have this tea outside before we get stuck into dinner. Once those sausages are cooking, I won't want to wait." Trent's dad chuckled as he took the loaded tea tray from his wife and headed through the open patio doors. "The seat nearest the heater is my wife's before anyone thinks to grab it."

"Oh, David. Don't be such a fusspot."

Trent's mum followed her husband outside as Izzy and Trent rose from the table. Izzy lifted her bag from the chair and Trent slipped his arm around her waist. "You okay?"

"Sure. Your parents are lovely."

He ran his gaze over her face before looking carefully into her eyes. "You look terrified. What are you thinking?"

She considered telling a white lie to appease him, but no part of her wanted to start this potentially beautiful relationship with a lie…even a white one. She exhaled a shaky breath and glanced toward the open doors where Linda poured the tea while her husband chattered. Izzy faced Trent. He stood so close she had to tip her head back to meet his eyes. The spicy scent of him drifted over her, giving her courage. "It's… Oh God, how do I say this?"

"Talk to me. I want you to be happy here."

"That's just it."

He frowned. "What?"

She inhaled. "You came here—"

"Iz, I explained that—"

"And now that I've met your parents I'm not surprised." She pressed a hand to his chest and smiled in an effort to allay the worry in his eyes. "But I can't help being afraid that I'll never be the refuge to you that your parents are. They are so amazingly happy, kind and welcoming despite…"

"Despite Aimee?"

She nodded and glanced toward the patio doors and smiled when Trent's parents snapped their heads around to face the view rather than the kitchen. "I feel so bad about how I behaved after Robbie died, and I can't help worrying I'll become that person again in the future. What if I'm not enough for you when you have this wonderful home to come back to whenever you feel the need? I've never had a home like this and I'm not sure I ever will."

He kissed her, before swiping some fallen hair from her eyes. "Maybe not, but if we work out, you'll be a part of *my* family, so stop worrying and just enjoy our time here. Okay?"

As he took her hand and led her outside, Izzy tried to silence his "if we work out" as it resounded in her head. She swallowed. Did she need to put the brakes on their intimacy or risk out-and-out heartbreak? If the "if" was still there for Trent, it meant neither of them was as invested in them as they should be. Trent wasn't her and didn't have the same innate loneliness she suffered. Was she leaning on him too hard, too fast?

He was her rock, as he was for Will and Sam. It was Trent's strength and sense of protection that had attracted and repelled her like a yo-yo all these years. It was why she'd avoided him for so long. Now that she was in his parents' home and they were together, she had no idea how she would be without him by her side. She took a deep breath. It was time to drag back a little of her self-protection before any damage seeped through and left her more afraid of heartbreak than ever before.

TRENT WALKED DOWN his parents' stairs, the taste of Izzy's lips branded on his like a tattoo. Having her sleep in Aimee's bedroom was as surreal as it was satisfying. To have her visit with him at his parents' place was something he hadn't imagined, let alone believed might one day happen. The conversation had flowed through tea and gradually turned to out-and-out laughter through dinner. His parents' faces when they looked at Izzy gave Trent all the confidence he needed to believe she was the woman for him.

He walked into the kitchen.

His mother sat at the table, a glass of red wine in her hand as she flicked through a magazine. A soft smile curved her lips as she hummed along to the music coming from the digital radio on the counter.

God, he loved her. She bore the weight of her losses and the joy of her gains as they came. She didn't falter, doubt or wreak vengeance. No matter how hard the blow. His smile faltered. On the other hand, her son often struggled to stay above water. What if he was someone destined to let people down? What if he continued to fail to save lives? Izzy's fears about his job were slowly becoming his own. He now worried about making promises…especially to Izzy as she joined the people who trusted him.

He walked toward the bottle of red wine by the sink. "Mind if I join you?"

"Of course not." His mother closed the magazine and smiled. "Has Izzy gone to bed?"

"Yeah. She says she's tired."

"She *says* she's tired?" She raised an eyebrow. “That sounds suspiciously like you don’t believe her.”

Trent lowered himself into the seat opposite his mother and took a sip of his wine. “I just want her to enjoy her time here, that’s all.”

“And you don’t think she is? She seems happy to me.”

“She is… I think. I’m probably worrying unnecessarily.” He took another drink and dismissed his melancholy with a wave. “So, why are you sitting here on your own? Where’s Dad?”

“Watching a documentary that involves lions tearing apart bison. I’d rather sit out here, thank you very much. So, why do you think that beautiful and lovely lady upstairs isn’t enjoying herself?”

Trent shifted back in his seat. “Can’t we just talk about lions instead?”

“No.”

He exhaled and leaned his forearms on the table. “It’s complicated.”

“I can do complicated. Complicated is my middle name. Hit me with it.”

“When Robbie died in that garage fire, Izzy changed. She pushed me and anyone else who wanted to be there for her as far away as possible.”

“That’s called a coping mechanism, Trent.

We all have our different ways of dealing with things. You run away. Izzy turns away."

"I don't run away."

"Then what do you call coming back home a few weeks ago?" She tilted her head to the side, her gaze soft and full of love. "Of course I want you to run here rather than somewhere else where you'll be alone. What I don't understand is why Izzy's way of dealing with her problems is bothering you so much. From what I've seen, she's doing admirably. Sure, there's an element of sadness hanging over her. One that might always be there, but judging from her ability to laugh and joke with me and your father the way she did, she's going to be just fine." She took a sip of her wine, her gaze on his. "I think the real problem here is you, not Izzy."

"How do you do it, Mum?" He shook his head, admiration for the woman sitting in front of him yanking on his heart. "How do you go on after losing Aimee?"

Her cheeks flushed and she looked into the depths of her glass. "One day at a time. That's all any parent who loses a child can do." She looked up, unshed tears glazing her eyes as she squeezed his hand where it lay on the table. "It's all anyone can do who loses someone they love deeply. I think whatever's going on inside that big heart of yours is there because you're afraid of loving someone the way you did Aimee. No matter how much you might *think* you want to be with Izzy, you owe it to her to be honest about what's going on in here." She pressed her hand to his chest. "If you can't be in the relationship one hundred percent, you should get out now. It's not fair to either of you."

"It's not that." He picked up his glass. "The more she tells me she's afraid of things ending badly between us, the more afraid I am of letting her down when she needs me most. It's nothing to do with how I feel about her. Her smiling and laughing is great, but I'm not convinced it's real. Not yet."

"You know, I did the same pretending as Izzy possibly is now, but each day my laughter and smiling comes a little easier. She'll get there in her own time. It isn't up to you to carry her along. Believe me, your father tried the same with me and it doesn't work." She sighed. "The problem with strong, hardworking and caring men like you and your father is you think you owe the world everything to make up for what you view as a hanging offense but is actually just a mistake. Do you blame yourself for her brother? Is that what this is about?"

"No...not really." He drew in a long breath and exhaled. "I suppose I still hate that Izzy is hurting so much and at one time she pointed her pain and blame at me, but that's not the case anymore. She's apologized for that."

"Then what is it?"

Trent held his mother's gaze as his mind scrambled with thoughts and his gut writhed with uncertainty. "I think about Aimee and Robbie every day. And now I'll think about Sam too. I don't want to keep beating myself up about every life I didn't save, but how can I not? It's the truth of the job."

"Then maybe it's time you gave it up."

Trent stilled. As much as his job was getting to him, he couldn't ever imagine not doing it. Sure, he thought about quitting now and then, but the thought never lasted any amount of time. Firefighting was a massive part of him. It was what made him who he was. He sometimes wondered if he'd ever walk away before he was forced to retire...or was dead. He loved his work as much as he sometimes loathed it. Fire was his nemesis...his enemy...his lifeline. He couldn't imagine executing as much energy or passion into anything else.

His mother's gaze hardened. "God knows, I'd be celebrating if you walked away from firefighting, but I think they'll have to push you out the door before you'll go."

"There's no way I can give up my work."

"Then what are you going to give up? Because if you want this to work out with Izzy, or any other woman for that matter, you're going to have to surrender something. I suggest you get rid of the guilt, inability and fear you've got slithering through your blood like poison because Izzy could be your anecdote, Trent. Don't throw her away."

"I've got no intention of throwing her away."

"I've seen you grieving, I've seen you angry at the entire world, but this self-loathing is different and that means it must be your relationship with Izzy that's put it there. Maybe she's not the woman you thought she'd be? Maybe you had an idyllic fantasy in your head of saving the girl when she's perfectly capable of saving herself in her own time?"

His mother's summary cut a little too close to the bone. Hadn't Izzy made the same suggestion to him? He clenched his jaw. "It's not that."

"Then what?"

"I worry she isn't ready for what I want to give her, or even if I'm capable of giving her what she wants. As much as I understand her fears, fighting fire gives me purpose. I want

Izzy, of course I do, but I'm not sure she'll want me in the long term if I continue to fight fire and will inevitably lose some days."

"That's her choice to make. Not yours. It might be that Izzy isn't the right girl for you, but either way, you owe it to her to be honest."

"I pursued her, Mum. I wanted her and now that I've got her..." He shook his head and drained his glass. "I don't know what's wrong me. How could I want her so badly and then worry she isn't right for me?"

A noise behind him made Trent turn.

Izzy stood in the doorway, her beautiful face free of makeup and pale but for the two spots of color high on her cheeks. She cleared her throat and lifted the empty glass in her hand. "Um, I just came down to refill my water."

His mother stood, the legs of her chair screeching across the terra-cotta tiles in her haste. "Of course. Here, let me."

Trent rose to his feet and reached for Izzy's arm as she made to walk past him. "Iz..."

She stepped away from his grasp, her gaze icy cold.

He dropped his hand as his heart picked up speed. "Let me explain."

His mother came toward them and held the water out to Izzy. "Here you go. Why don't you two sit down? I'm just off to bed."

Heavy silence filled the kitchen as his mother clearly tried her hardest to appear casual as she returned her magazine to the rack, emptied her half-drunk wine into the sink and made for the door. "Sleep tight, my loves. See you in the morning."

Trent watched her leave, Izzy's gaze burning into his temple from where she stood across the kitchen. Once he heard the telltale creak of his mother's footsteps on the stairs, he turned. "Come and sit down. Please."

Her gaze hovered on his, her shoulders high. "I heard what you said."

"I know and that's why we need to talk." He pulled out the seat beside him. "Sit. Please."

She hesitated before coming forward. As she placed her glass on the table, the water trembled. "I don't know what you want me to say."

"Then I'll talk first and you can say whatever you feel once I'm done. Deal?"

She nodded and took a sip of her water.

Trent inhaled a long breath, his heart a mess of love and loss that he didn't understand but knew he had to verbalize or risk his reservations causing a chasm between them. He cleared his throat. "When I said I don't know if you're the right girl for me, I really meant that I'm scared I'll never be the right man for you. It doesn't matter how much I might love you, if you can't get over how Robbie died. I fight fire and I love my job…most of the time. If every time you look at me you worry I'll end up dead, I worry how we'll go the distance. I love you so much, but…"

"I get what you're saying."

He stared into her beautiful eyes. "And?"

"And I think I've still got a lot to work on, but I'm trying, Trent."

He swiped his hand over his face, guilt he might have further hurt her searing his chest. "I know you are."

"Then what else would you have me do?" She blinked and her eyes shone with unshed tears, but her gaze determined. "Right now I'm giving you my best. If that's not enough for you, I don't know what else I can do. I'm here. Now. At your parents' home. Doesn't that show you how serious I am about being with you…how much I love you?"

"Yes, but—"

"I told you weeks ago that you were my safety net for Robbie dying. That if I didn't blame you, or at least someone, then I had to accept all the pain and hurt that comes with acknowledging that an accident, a twist of fate, killed him. That there was nothing anyone could've done."

"But that's the truth, Iz. There was nothing."

She closed her eyes. "I'm slowly accepting that, but it's still..." She opened her eyes. "So damn hard."

"Iz—"

She abruptly stood. "I think we've still got a lot to think about. Both of us." She lifted her glass from the table. "I'm going to bed. We'll talk more in the morning."

Feeling like crap, Trent let her go as she walked to the door without a backward glance. If he knew her at all, they wouldn't talk in the morning. She'd shut down and shut him out. He swiped his hand back and forth over his jaw...and maybe it would be less painful for them both if he let her. No matter how much they might want to be together, their worries about their relationship failing wound through them, bounding their insecurities in a tight, unwanted noose.

CHAPTER SEVENTEEN

AT SEVEN THIRTY the following morning, the taxi drew to a stop outside Izzy's studio. She stepped out onto the pavement and paid the driver before walking to the door at the side of the studio that led to her upstairs apartment.

After her conversation with Trent, coming home to Templeton had been the right decision.

She had hesitated outside his closed bedroom door at his parents' place but hadn't felt strong enough to resist any words he might have spoken to convince her to stay. So instead, she'd fled…in exactly the same way she was so hurt by when he'd gone home rather than come to her. Maybe that was a failure on her part, but whether or not that was true, what else was left for them to discuss? Until she came to terms with the fact that Robbie's death was an accident and the chances of Trent surviving his firefighting career were good, those two obstacles would always lie between them like immovable boulders.

Tossing her keys onto a small table by the

door, she hung her jacket on the end of the banister and put her overnight bag on the stairs.

She'd have no choice but to talk to Trent when he returned to the Cove, but for now she just needed to be home. Her loneliness might hurt, but maybe she was better off alone.

She and Trent had tried and failed too many times. It was clear they weren't meant for each other. They'd each suffered too much loss, too much hurt. Their insecurities were testament to that, and if he hadn't already, Trent would soon reach the same conclusion.

Slipping off her boots, Izzy tilted her neck side to side in an effort to release some of the tension from her body. Her hastily written parting note to his mum and dad had thanked them for their warm and welcoming hospitality, but she'd kept to herself that as much as she appreciated their kindness, being part of such a closely connected family had been suffocating. A step too far.

She slowly exhaled.

Her entire body ached from the hours she'd tossed and turned until dawn in Aimee's bed. She'd battled over and over whether to stay and speak with Trent in the morning, but in the end she couldn't take another minute in a house that frightened her as much as it secretly delighted her. The deep family feel of the place, its closeness, had ultimately threatened claustrophobia…yet made her yearn to have the same sort of family one day.

Sighing, Izzy strolled toward the kitchen and that was when she heard the voices behind the closed door. Voices so alien in her apartment, yet so deeply familiar, her heart beat fast with undoubtedly misplaced hope that maybe, this time, her parents were back in the Cove for good.

She halted as her hand turned clammy on the door handle.

Her parents' pathetically muffled whispers and giggles seeped into Izzy's stomach, making her nauseated. She pressed her hand to her racing heart. How long had they been here? She could've been away for days, even weeks, as far as they knew.

Why had they come back now?

When she'd let down her defenses and opened her heart to Trent and his parents? She might have asked her own parents to visit, but now her mum and dad's presence could remind her all over again of what she didn't have on a permanent basis and just how dangerous it was to love someone as much as she loved them.

Taking a slow, strengthening breath, Izzy lifted her chin, pushed the kitchen door open and flicked on the light.

"Surprise!" Her mum and dad's joined exclamation bounced from the tiled walls, ratcheting Izzy's trepidation to boiling point.

"What are you doing here?" Even though the joy immediately fell from her parents' faces, Izzy stood a little straighter and forced her nonchalance higher. "I've been out of town. I could've been gone for days as far as you knew."

"We came back yesterday, sweetheart." Her mother took a step closer, hesitation clear in her gaze. "Kate told us you were away, so we're staying in the guest room. You don't mind, do you?"

"Yes, Mum. I do mind. Couldn't you have called? Emailed? Anything to let me know your plans."

"We wanted to surprise you." She smiled. "When we saw the taxi pull up, we switched off all the lights—"

"Well, you achieved your objective. I'm surprised." She brushed past them toward the small dining table and put down her purse. She could not allow their unannounced return to get to her. Not now. Not when she'd made the decision she was better off alone. Now that she understood the intelligence, the practicality, of keeping her emotions in check and showing the world she was just fine on her own. It shouldn't matter that she could see nothing but love in her parents' eyes, but it did.

She swallowed the threatening lump welling in her throat. "How did you get into my apartment?"

"We have a key, remember? You gave it to us when we left for our last job." Her mother came forward, her arms outstretched. "Aren't you surprised to see us? Aren't you happy?"

Izzy stiffened as her mother's arms came around her, her carefully painted lips pressing a kiss to each of Izzy's cheeks. She eased from her mother's embrace and looked at her dad, who had strolled across the kitchen to fill the kettle at the sink. "It's good to see you, sweetheart. You look well."

Izzy stared at each of them as disbelief and irritation swirled inside her. "So this is it? After all the horrible things I said to you the last time you went away, you forgive me? We start over?"

Her mother smiled, tears shining in her eyes. "Of course we forgive you. We love you. When we got your call, I thought my heart would burst with relief. You sounded happier, more sure of yourself...you sounded like our Izzy."

Tears burned Izzy's eyes as love swelled inside her. She slumped her shoulders. "Maybe I should've come away with you."

"We did ask you, sweetheart. Lots of times. We even cleared it with the people in charge on the ship." She cupped her hands to Izzy's jaw. "But that's all in the past. It's so wonderful to see you. Our tenants are leaving today, so your father and I will move back into the house. Don't you want—"

"You're staying?" Izzy's heart stumbled with pathetic hope as she lifted her face from her mother's gentle grasp.

"Yes. At least for a while."

Unable to cope with her parents' looks of happy expectation, Izzy turned away and pretended to busy herself by searching the fridge. They could still leave whenever they were ready. The scraping of chair legs across the floor broke the ensuing silence. She briefly closed her eyes, took a deep breath and turned.

Her parents looked at her from their seats at the table.

Izzy trembled. Why did she have to be so weak? Now she faced them, her strength had abandoned her and she suddenly longed to rush forward and have them pull her into their arms, tell her everything was going to be okay. But nothing was okay.

She slammed the fridge door, walked to the counter and pulled three mugs from the hooks beneath the counters. "How long is a while?"

"We don't know. A few months...maybe a year."

A year. A whole year. Izzy silently cursed the joy and relief she didn't want to feel as it spread through her. "Why now? What's happened?"

Her mother glanced at her father and Izzy followed her gaze. Her father cleared his throat. "We were wrong to leave, but we didn't know what else to do to help you...help ourselves. When Rob died you shut down completely. He was your world and you made it clear that no one, including us, could be what you needed. We were equally as devastated as you, Iz. We just didn't have the strength to stay here and ease your suffering when you didn't want our comfort. We're sorry."

Izzy closed her eyes. How could she deny her father spoke the truth? She had shut her parents out the same way she had everyone else in the Cove. Quick, decisive and determined, she had turned to her work for some semblance of strength, rather than lean on any human being who could be taken away from her or leave her life of his or her own accord.

She exhaled a heavy breath and opened her eyes. "You're right. I'm sorry. I shouldn't have treated you that way. You'd lost a child and all I could think about was how I felt." She slumped her shoulders and looked at each of her parents in turn. "Maybe I had no right to be angry at you for leaving, but it hurt. It really, really hurt."

Her dad shook his head, his eyes dark with sadness. "I know, sweetheart. He was our boy. Our son."

Her mother stood. "We really thought you didn't want us here."

"I was selfish. I realize that now. I've slowly started to move on and I hope you have too." She turned back to finish making the tea, her hand trembling as she picked up the kettle. "I'm different now. Robbie, you..." *Trent.* "The pain changed me. I'm not the same person I was when you left. I've gotten used to looking out for myself, and to be honest, it scares me that you're back if you're only going to leave again."

She placed two of the mugs on the table. "And you will leave. Templeton isn't the place you want to spend the rest of your lives, but I do. I think you want something the Cove will never give you, but for me, it gives me everything. I love the ocean, the people and the community. Maybe I separated myself from all that for a while, but I'm trying my best to crawl back. I don't think I need anyone else to help me to do that. Not anymore."

Her mother frowned, confusion shadowing her gaze as she looked from Izzy to her husband and back again. "But everyone needs someone. Even you. These guards you've put up aren't protecting you, they're hurting you. Do you really think your father and I would've left if we thought you were going to push everyone else away too? We thought you were pushing us away because we're your parents. That you were striking out at the people you knew would always love you, no matter what."

Izzy's heart beat faster and she swiped at the tear that dared to fall. "Maybe I was, but once I started pushing people away, it became easier and easier until I couldn't stop. And now..." Her voice cracked and she looked to the ceiling, blinking back her tears. "I think it might be better that way until I can figure out a way to believe I won't eventually lose everyone I love." She dropped her chin and looked at her mother. "When you left last time, it was so much worse than all the others. Back then it was okay because I had my brother. When you left after Rob died..." She exhaled a shaky breath and embraced her emerging courage as it ignited inside her. "It felt as if you didn't care about either of us, and eventually I believed that. Now that you're back, I'm not entirely sure what you want from me, or even if I can give it."

Her mother came toward her and this time Izzy didn't stop her. Exhaustion and a strange sense of having purged the darkness came down upon her. She sank into her mother's embrace and closed her eyes as she inhaled her familiar perfume, unexpectedly grateful for her mother's arms around her.

"We want absolutely nothing from you that you aren't willing to give," her mother whispered. "My hope is you love us as we love you, but if you don't, that still won't stop us from loving you. Not ever."

Pain and guilt slashed at Izzy's heart and she pulled back. "I do love you…and you, Dad." She looked at each of them. "I'm just scared of weakening, scared of trusting anyone. Including you."

"We're all scared, sweetheart." Her dad smiled softly. "And I'm sorry your mother and I made you feel so alone."

Her mother squeezed Izzy's hand. "Has this fear of weakening got anything to do with your relationship with Trent Palmer?"

Izzy stilled. "What?"

Concern darkened her mother's gaze. "I was shocked when Marian told us earlier that you were seeing so much of him. He's a firefighter, Izzy. And he was there when Robbie died. I don't think being with someone who risks life and limb every day is going to be good for you."

"I agree." Izzy slipped her hand from her mother's and brushed past her parents to stare out the window. The sun slowly filtered across the grass in her garden, brightening the patio and barren flowerpots. "And it's about time he and I accepted that."

"I didn't mean for you *not* to see him. I'm just saying—"

"Believe me, Mum. It's better for everyone if I don't."

TRENT GRIPPED THE steering wheel as he crawled along the Cove's promenade toward Izzy's studio, every car in front of him stretching his patience. "Come on, damn it. Come on."

When his parents had found Aimee's bed empty and neatly made, they'd assumed Izzy had popped out to the shops or for a walk. In fact, his mum and dad had waited a full hour before coming the conclusion that maybe, just maybe, she'd left Kingsley altogether. They had woken Trent at nine, which was God only knew how long after Izzy's nocturnal exit.

The traffic crawled forward and he pressed the speed dial on his docked phone for the twentieth time. Izzy's number rang and then switched to voice mail.

"Iz, it's me. Will you call me back? We can't leave things as they are. I love you. There was no need for you to leave. We're okay. We'll always be okay. Please, just call me back."

He disconnected the call and forced his focus onto the street.

When his phone rang, his heart jumped and he accepted the call. "Iz? Look, everything we said last night can be sorted out. We can—"

"Trent, it's the chief."

Heat rose in Trent's face and he coughed. "Chief. What can I do for you?"

"Are you back in town?"

"Just got here. I'm heading toward Autumn Parade. What's up?"

"I need you to turn around and head for Heather Lane. There's a warehouse fire on the trading estate and I'm down two officers. Gosford's in charge because I'm stuck at the office dealing with an arson investigation. The fire's a big one. I need all hands on deck."

Trent inwardly cursed. "Sure, no problem." Talking with Izzy would have to wait awhile longer. "I'm in the car, so I'll head straight over."

"Great. Spare gear will be on board one of the trucks, as usual. Look after yourself out there. I've told the others and now I'm telling you. There won't be any more firefighters lost from my house. Do you understand?"

"Yes, sir."

The line went dead and Trent checked his mirror before turning the car around to head off in the opposite direction. Flashes of Sam's smoke-blackened face as he'd been wheeled through the hospital filled Trent's mind, and adrenaline surged through him. He pressed harder on the accelerator. He had to get to that warehouse and support his colleagues.

There won't be any more firefighters lost from my house.

He glared ahead. *Damn right, there won't be.*

It wasn't long before Trent followed the mass of gray smoke swirling toward the clouds. Then he smelled the burning. He rounded the final bend that took him through the tall iron gates at the entrance to the trading estate. Following the trail of the smoke through the maze of roads housing the many warehouses and temporary construction offices, he soon drove onto the warehouse's courtyard.

Turning off the engine, he snapped off his seat belt and leaped from the car, taking in the sight ahead of him as he jogged toward one of the three attending fire trucks. The warehouse blazed totally out of control. God only knew how long it would take the crew to get the fire contained. Smoke billowed and swarmed from the doors and lower windows, the blistering, snapping flames six or seven feet high.

Climbing through the side door of one of the trucks, Trent pulled out a stored set of protective clothing and a helmet. With his focus on the warehouse, he quickly dressed as heat reached out and seared his face.

He buckled his helmet and ran toward Jack Gosford, who clutched a handset as he watched the warehouse, concentration and concern etched on his face.

"Gosford?"

His crewmate turned, and relief shot into his gaze. "Palmer. Thank Christ you're here. I wasn't sure the chief would track you down. We've already got an extra crew helping out from across town and another on its way from Clandown."

Trent looked toward the burning building. "Who's in there?"

"Ellis, Chamberlain, Smith and Kent. I've got everyone else on the hoses. We estimate at least half a dozen civilians are still inside."

Trent stared toward the building, every part of him desperate to get inside and help, fully aware the last of his best friends was inside along with members of the public. "Where do you want me?"

Gosford narrowed his eyes and darted his study over the front of the warehouse, and then to the crowd of workers huddled a few feet away. "Just hold tight while I find the company's fire officer. I want to do another check of how many civilians are unaccounted for. Wait here."

Impatience hummed through Trent's body, making him want to run for the building, regardless of protocol…but Sam's words about Trent's need to act so urgently haunted him. If Trent failed to follow procedure and another firefighter lost his life, he'd only have himself to blame.

"Palmer."

Trent turned as Gosford jogged toward him. "The fire officer is certain there are now only four employees unaccounted for. We've already brought two out alive. I want the minimum number of crew inside until we get this thing contained. You're on water."

Trent nodded and sprinted toward one of the heavy hoses.

The team worked for the next hour fighting the fire's flames as they licked the building from inside, crawling and reaching to the outer walls. Time and again as Trent worked, his mind turned to Izzy and a horrible foreboding stole through him as hot as the fire he fought.

Deep inside, a demon curled and bit at his conscience. She had run home because she was scared of his job, not him. It was fire that scarred and maimed their chance of lasting happiness. How could he ever convince her he would be safe while he continued to fight fire? His mother had said she too would be thankful when he quit the job.

Was that it? Would he have to surrender his passion in order to be with Izzy?

Sweat trickled down his temples and he refocused on the job, but no matter how hard he and his colleagues tried to contain the fire, it continued to viciously burn. All the civilians had been brought out alive, but it was still too soon for celebration.

Trent squinted toward the burning building. Something about the fire wasn't right. They should be gaining notable ground by now, but instead, the flames continued to reach higher. An accelerant of some description must be accountable for the relentlessness.

He looked around for Gosford. If the fire was still in command of the fighters, more of them needed to get inside and ascertain what was going on behind the building's redbrick walls. He spotted Gosford's white helmet and Trent passed the manning of his hose to one of his colleagues.

He jogged toward Gosford, who stood closer to the warehouse, the fire cracking and spitting at full volume.

Once Trent reached Gosford's side, he cupped his hands around his mouth. "Let me get in there. I'll take McCarthy with me. I think we need to investigate the south side of the building. I'm pretty confident there's something back there causing this thing to snap and snarl like this."

Gosford ran his hand up and down his jaw, his gaze trained past Trent to the burning building. "I was going to order you to do that in another ten minutes or so. What's your gut telling you?"

"That I need to get in there. Right now. Do I have permission to enter?"

Gosford nodded, his gaze as hot as the blaze. "Go. Take McCarthy with you. Scan the area and get your asses back out here with a report. No trying anything without my say-so. Understood?"

Trent gave a curt nod and broke into a

sprint before Gosford changed his mind. Trent scanned the gathered and perspiring firefighters, looking for McCarthy. He spotted him and ran forward, slapping his trusted colleague on the shoulder. "We've got permission to enter. Something's not right. I want you to come with me to check it out. I've got a really bad feeling about this one."

McCarthy swiped the back of his hand across his forehead. "I'm right behind you, buddy. Let's go."

Trent shouted out their departure to his colleagues before leading the way. After he and McCarthy had located the easiest and safest way to enter, Trent assessed the situation inside the first room.

The entire area was lit by a sea of moving red, orange and yellow. Every flame danced and surged. The temperature approached boiling. Trent squinted through his mask and lowered his mouth to the radio. "This way. Follow me."

The perpetual unease that had gripped him outside veered up a notch as Trent bent low and followed his instincts. He stole from the room and into a corridor.

Boom!

The force of the explosion hit him in the

chest and he was thrown backward. Something hard hit the back of his head and spine.

A loud *crack* reverberated in his head…and everything turned black.

CHAPTER EIGHTEEN

IZZY COLLAPSED ONTO her sofa, her favorite dinner of nachos layered with thick cheese, sour cream, guacamole and salsa on the side, duly positioned in pride of place on her lap. Putting her soda on the side table, she reached for the remote and flicked on the TV, purposefully ignoring her phone beside her.

Trent had given up calling and texting her almost two hours after she left his parents' house. As much as Izzy told herself his surrender didn't matter, that their split was for the best for both of them, her heart continued to take its merry time catching up with her brain.

She popped a nacho into her mouth and tried to concentrate on the ending credits of a soap as they raced up the TV screen. Yet, just as it had all day, her mind drifted back to Trent and their time together. Tears burned and the happy, laughing family of the advertisement on-screen blurred. Izzy angrily swiped at her tears with the heel of her hand.

Goddamn it. Forget him. Forget everything.

Her apartment buzzer reverberated through the room and she froze, her mind racing. Was it Trent? If it was, what would she say to him? Should she even answer the buzzer or just pretend to be out partying, instead of gorging on a calorie-loaded comfort food feast for one?

"Oh, hell." She slid the nacho bowl onto the side table and stood just as the buzzer sounded a second time, hitching her irritation nicely into place. Being annoyed with Trent was a far safer place to start a conversation from.

Taking a deep breath, Izzy tilted her chin and headed for the door. She pressed the button. "Who is it?"

"It's Mum. Can we come up? Your dad's brought your favorite chocolate pecan pie from Marian's as a bribe…and as an apology for us letting ourselves into your apartment earlier. We're truly sorry, sweetheart. We shouldn't have surprised you that way."

As disappointment that it wasn't Trent at the door swept over her, Izzy forced a smile. "I've already forgiven you. You know that. Use your key and come on up. The pecan pie sealed the deal."

She headed back to the sofa. As she sat, Izzy pulled the huge bowl of nachos into her lap. Happy they were still warm enough to be edible, she devoured another two chips in quick succession.

"My disgusting consumption is the first thing that can go on my 'why Trent is no good for me' list," she murmured, and picked up the remote. She flicked through the channels to the find the local news, knowing it would be the first thing her father would do once he entered the apartment.

The jangle of a key sounded in her lock and her mother walked into the apartment, followed by Izzy's father, who wore a sheepish expression. Izzy smiled, guessing he took credit for their permitted entrance by way of pie.

Izzy shook her head, fondness for him swelling her heart. "Put the pie on the kitchen counter, Dad. We'll have it with some tea later."

His face dropped. "Don't you want any now?"

She lifted the nacho bowl. "Currently have something else going on."

Her father saluted his understanding and disappeared into the kitchen.

Her mother sat beside Izzy on the sofa. "You look tired, sweetheart. Have you worked with Kate all day?"

"I have, but it was worth the tiredness."

"Oh?"

Fighting the regret that it wouldn't be Trent who first heard about her day, but her mother, Izzy dragged up some enthusiasm. "We spent the whole day calling up as many businesses as possible in Templeton and beyond, asking them to stock the calendars I told you about."

"Did you get much success?" Her mother stole a nacho and put in her mouth. "You were so cruel to tell me about the semiclad firefighters and then rush off this morning without showing me the proofs. I've felt bereft all day."

Izzy smiled. "As soon as I've finished *my* nachos, I'll go grab you a copy."

"Good."

They turned to the TV and Izzy blindly watched the advertisements, her mind wandering to the most significant call she'd received that day. She glanced at her mother as she slipped off her high-heeled shoes and settled more comfortably into the sofa. Should she tell her parents about the phone call or keep it to herself awhile longer?

Sometimes it became unnervingly clear how much she held back from her mum and dad after having learned to deal with so much alone.

Izzy swallowed her trepidation. While they were here, she would embrace their presence and confidence until they disappeared again.

Who knew? Maybe sharing in their daughter's life would encourage them to stay. She cleared her throat. "I also had a phone call from Jay Garrett this afternoon."

Her mother's smile dissolved and her hand stopped midway toward a second dive into the nachos. "Jay Garrett? Why were you speaking to him? Is something wrong?"

"No. Why should anything be wrong?"

Her mother sniffed. "No one makes as much money as his father did, and now Jay does, without being up to no good."

"That's not true and you know it. The Garretts have never done anything but good for this town."

"That's a matter of opinion, darling. You are clearly too young to remember the real Jay Garrett."

Gripping the nacho bowl tighter, Izzy struggled to hold on to her patience. "Well, as far as I know, Jay's a good man with a lovely wife, and neither of them has ever done anything to upset—"

"Ah, but he didn't always have the detective inspector by his side to keep him in line, did he?"

Izzy's patience snapped. "Why do you have to have such a negative view of everything and everyone in the Cove? Just because you like to travel around the world at every opportunity, some of us think Templeton is pretty perfect."

"Really? Even with Robbie being killed here?"

The room chilled.

"Why would you say something like that?" Izzy fought her anger. "Do you know what? Forget I said anything."

"I didn't mean to upset you. All I'm saying—"

"Mum, I really don't want to argue with you about this. In fact, I'd really appreciate it if you and Dad would show me some support while you're here."

Her father entered the room and took a seat in one of the armchairs on either side of the sofa.

Her mother faced him. "Frank? Izzy had a call from Jay Garrett this afternoon." She raised her eyebrows. "What do you think of that?"

Izzy lifted her chin, determined to own what had happened between her and Jay this afternoon. Why should she need or care for her parents' approval about her decisions? They'd made it clear over the years that their children were free to do as they pleased...usually without any parental input or guidance.

She reached forward and picked up her soda from the table and drank, easing her dry throat. "If you must know, Jay called me to set up a meeting with his lawyers, and mine, so we can go over my new working contract."

"Working contract?" Her dad frowned. "Izzy, the best thing for an artist is to be freelance surely? I thought you were doing well with your work. Why would you commit to something that will inevitably suffocate your creativity?"

"This will not suffocate my creativity. In fact—"

"We've always encouraged you and your brother to follow your dreams." Her mother frowned. "Why would you give away your talent as though it is worth so little?"

"If you let me explain." She looked at her parents in turn. "Jay wants me to run a new art gallery in town. My work will take up most of the space, while other local artists utilize the rest. He doesn't want to suffocate my creativity. He's positively encouraging it. Not just mine, but others' too."

Her parents exchanged a skeptical look. Izzy waited. The protective walls she'd built had slowly lowered over the last few weeks, but with her parents' doubt so clearly etched on their faces, those walls threatened to reerect themselves pretty quickly. She fought back with all her might. She didn't want to be the person her parents' words and actions had made her in the past. She wanted to be the person Trent made her. Even if his job and their individual insecurities meant they couldn't be together.

"Oh. Well, that changes everything." Her mother smiled and her shoulders relaxed. "Doesn't it, Frank?"

Her father continued to stare at Izzy, his eyes narrowed. "And Garrett will take a cut of the profits?"

Izzy sighed. "Of course. It's business, but Jay has already said how much he admires my work and hasn't put any limitations or instructions on me. He also believes I'm the best person to judge what other work to show at the gallery. I'm really excited about this. Can't you find it in yourselves to be excited for me too?" Despite their negativity, Izzy smiled and embraced the positive energy that burned inside her. "It's the first time I've even considered anything so public since Robbie died. The time feels right to move forward and try something new."

Her mother delved once again into the nacho bowl. "Then we're very happy for you. Aren't we, Frank?"

"Sure. Good luck with it, darling." He leaned forward and snatched out a nacho, put it in his mouth.

Knowing their less than enthusiastic acceptance was the best she could hope for, Izzy released her held breath. "Right, then." Feigning annoyance, she faked a glare at them in turn and moved the nachos out of their reach. "You do know these are mine, right?" They both frowned, clearly misunderstanding her humor. Izzy sighed. "Do you know what? Go crazy. I'll eat the entirety of the pecan pie instead."

She put the bowl on the table in front of them and her mother and father dove in, completely unconcerned by their daughter's sarcasm.

Her dad's gaze darkened with disquiet once more. "I always thought you'd end up in New York or London, any one of the world's huge cities. I still think you're too talented to stay in the Cove, Iz. I know you love it here, but—"

"But nothing, Dad. Templeton is my home and, most likely, always will be. You know, most of the people who come to live here never leave. You and Mum are the exception. Don't you see that?"

He held her gaze before raising his hands. "Fine. Your life. Your choice."

"Thank you." Izzy turned to her mother. "And thank you, Mum."

"For what?"

"For being at least a little pleased for me. It means a lot."

"Oh, sweetheart. If this is what you want—"

"Hey, wouldn't Trent be involved in that?" Her dad waved his hand toward the TV. "Wow, that's a big one."

Izzy rose to her feet, her parents falling into silence beside her.

Icy-cold fingers tiptoed up Izzy's spine as she stared at the TV screen, her previous whisper of happiness vanishing as terror rose and clenched like a fist in her chest.

"The explosion happened while several firefighters were inside the warehouse fighting the blaze. It is also believed that there may have been up to four civilians inside as well. Channel 4 news has been told that all the firefighters at the scene have been accounted for and are at Templeton General being treated for any injuries sustained. Nothing has yet been confirmed regarding the civilians, but that may be due to their families—"

Izzy snapped her gaze to the pale, shocked faces of her parents. "So Trent's okay, right? The newsreader said all the firefighters have been accounted for? Trent's okay. He must be."

They stared at her, their gazes full of fear.

Izzy trembled. “Right?”

Her mother and father only continued to stare at her, their mouths open and their eyes filled with worry.

Shaking off her paralysis, she reached for her phone. The sharp, painful knot in her stomach that had occurred when Robbie died wound its warning once more. She dialed Trent’s number, but the call went straight to voice mail. She numbly redialed…and dialed a third time.

The phone slipped from her hand to the carpet. What if Trent was dead? She closed her eyes. No. She wouldn’t go there. He would be okay. It didn’t matter that her heart raced, her body forewarning her of the pain that could once more rip her wide-open.

“Izzy, listen to me.” Her mother pushed to her feet, her arm outstretched. “You’ll hear soon enough if anything has happened to—”

“I can’t sit here and hope some mention is made of him on TV. I have to know for sure, Mum.”

Ignoring her parents as they both stood in front of her, Izzy snatched up the phone from the floor and dialed Trent’s number again. “Trent, please pick up. Please.”

The phone continued to ominously ring and just as his voice mail kicked in, Izzy ended the call. She couldn't stand to listen to his voice mail message again. Nothing would be enough now other than to hear his voice directly as he took her into his arms and kissed away her tears.

If he had gone to the hospital, would he have been discharged and gone back to his parents' place in Kingsley?

Tears filled her eyes. She had no idea where he would be. Not anymore.

This was her fault. She'd chosen to walk away from him…from them.

It didn't matter that her mother had agreed Izzy being with Trent was a bad idea; that she'd said the same thing over and over to herself. If he'd died in that explosion, if he was no longer on this planet, she would surely die too.

Walking across the room, Izzy purposely put space between her and her parents just as they had done to her and Robbie so many times before. She didn't need them right now, but she did need Kate.

She dialed her friend's number.

Kate picked up on the first ring. "I just saw it on TV. I'm on my way over right now. We'll find him, Iz. We'll find him alive, okay?"

Izzy nodded, words catching like barbed wire in her throat.

"Iz? Are you there? If you can hear me, say yes."

Izzy swallowed against her arid tongue. "I can hear you. Hurry, Kate. Please."

"I'll be there in ten minutes."

The line went dead and Izzy somehow managed to move her feet toward her bedroom. In a zombielike state, she stripped off her pajamas and pulled on jeans and a shirt. Even though her mother and father were only in the next room, Izzy couldn't talk to them. It was almost as if her body had shut down while her brain battled the trauma inside.

If Trent loved her at all, he wouldn't have gone into that building without knowing it was safe. He wouldn't have put her through what she was going through now. If he loved her, he would've waited, ensured that the building wasn't going to rise and engulf him like what the vile pictures that had flashed on the TV screen seemed to imply. He knew her fear, knew that her heart couldn't take the blow of him dying.

She always known she wasn't strong enough for a relationship with a firefighter. Why had she given in to her feelings for Trent and taken him into her bed and heart?

She vehemently shook her head as a painful sob caught in her throat. Trent didn't need to be with her. He needed to be with a strong woman, a brave woman. Not a woman likely to have a breakdown every time he was called out.

If she could just see him one more time, look into his beautiful green eyes and see his gorgeous smile, then she would let him go. Yes, she would…she really would.

TRENT FOUGHT AGAINST the weight of his eyelids, willing them to open, but his efforts were useless. Every inch of his body ached or throbbed with pain. He'd tried countless times to lift his arm, but the thing weighed two hundred bloody kilos. How the hell was he supposed to call Izzy to let her know he was okay if he couldn't even open his eyes or lift his useless arm?

The murmur of subdued voices drifted over him and he battled again to pry open his eyelids. They opened a sliver before drifting closed again.

More murmurs.

Who were the owners of those voices and why were there people in his bedroom?

Maybe he'd have more luck using his voice than his body.

He opened his mouth and slid his arid tongue over his even drier lips. "Hello?" The word barely came out a whisper. He swallowed and filled his lungs, pushing every ounce of strength—which wasn't much—into a second attempt. "Hello?"

"Trent? Mate? You awake?"

Will. Thank God. Trent nodded...or at least managed to twitch. "Yeah, man. I'm awake. Just waiting for my eyes to realize it."

"Christ, you gave us one hell of a scare, bud." Will blew out a breath. "First of all, we all thought we'd lost... Do you know something? It doesn't matter what we thought. You're awake and that's the best damn thing I've seen or heard for the last three days."

Three days?

Trent finally won the eyelid battle...albeit they flickered like they were plugged into a loose electrical socket. "What are you doing in my bedroom and why have I been lying here for three days?"

"Your bedroom? No, man, you're in the hospital."

"The hospital?" Trent's eyes fully opened. "Oh man. Did I pass out? What about McCarthy? Is he okay?"

"Right here, Palmer."

Trent flicked his gaze to the other side of the bed. "Hey. How are you doing?"

"A lot better than you, my friend." McCarthy smiled and uncrossed his arms. "There was no need for you to take the full brunt of that explosion, you know. It would've been a lot fairer if we'd split it fifty-fifty."

"Funny. I'd laugh if I had the strength." Trent attempted a smile. "Have either of you spoken to Izzy?" He looked at each of the men in turn. "Is she okay?"

Will frowned. "Don't go worrying about Izzy. You should be thinking about yourself for a while. You had a close call. Another couple of feet closer to that blast and you'd be dead."

"What caused it? Do you know?"

"The whole place is under investigation, but so far, the unofficial summary is that the fire was caused by a spark in the computer server. The fire suppression system malfunctioned... apparently. But there was enough flammable material in that warehouse to light the entire trading estate. As to what caused the actual explosion, the investigation team still isn't entirely sure."

Trent closed his eyes. "Well, they'd better catch whoever started that thing." He fought to open his eyes again. "Were any lives lost? Did you get to the civilians in time?"

McCarthy stepped forward. "Everyone got out alive. You were the one and only casualty. Thank God, you weren't the one and only fatality. It's great to see you awake, Palmer. I'm going to head back to the station. The chief will want to know you're awake. I'll track down a doctor on my way out and send him in here. Catch up with you guys later."

Trent waited until McCarthy left the room before he tried to sit up a little, but it was hopeless. "Goddamn it." He clenched his teeth against the screaming pain that ripped through his ribs. "I need to call Izzy, Will. I need to speak to her."

"Will you just relax?"

"Relax? The last time I spoke to her we were damn close to breaking up. Again. She left without giving me a chance to explain it doesn't matter what we discussed, I still want her. Izzy will always be the right girl for me. I have to speak to her."

Will smiled and shook his head.

Trent glared. "What are you smiling about? I'm serious."

"I'm trying not to laugh at you getting all bent out of shape…not that you're in particularly good shape right now."

"Look, I know we're good mates and everything, but I swear to God if you don't—"

"Izzy left about ten minutes ago when McCarthy and I practically shoehorned her out the room. She's been at your bedside more or less every minute, night and day. She's here in the hospital, mate. I sent her to the cafeteria to get some coffee. She looks as though she's having as much trouble keeping her eyes open as you are."

"She's here?" Trent grinned and his cheekbones screamed their indignation. "Well, go get her."

The door opened and Trent's heart immediately swept into overdrive. He inwardly cursed his battered body and stared at Izzy's sheet of perfect, long blond hair as it flowed like moving water down her spine. She walked in backward, a loaded coffee carrier wobbling precariously in her hands. She turned and smiled at Will. "Coffee as ordered."

She glanced in Trent's direction and did a double take. "Oh my God. You're awake."

Will lunged forward and grabbed the tray from her hands. "I've got this."

Smiling, Izzy came to Trent's side and he stared into the gorgeous blue eyes he hadn't seen in far too long. "Hi."

"Hi." She grinned, her eyes shining beneath unshed tears and her cheeks flushed pink. Her smile faltered, and she frowned. "Don't ever do that to me again."

He smiled. "I can't promise—"

"No, you promise me, Trent Palmer. You promise me right now."

The woman he loved looked absolutely terrified and it was he who'd put her through that. He wiped his smile. "I'm okay, Iz. I'm awake and as far as I can tell I just have a few bumps and bruises."

"Did the doctor see you?" She glanced at Will. "Has he been checked over?"

"Iz, look at me." Trent spoke as firmly as a man with a throat like sandpaper could. "I'm going to be fine. I promise."

"Oh, Trent." Tears slipped over her cheeks and she leaned over him to press a soft kiss to his forehead, to his cheek and, as light as a whisper, to his lips. "You're awake."

Will cleared his throat. "Well, I'm clearly surplus to requirements here, so I'll head off. It's good to have you back with us, buddy. Take care of him, Iz. If I see the doctor, I'll try to stall him for a few minutes and give you two lovebirds a bit of time alone, shall I?"

Trent smiled, his gaze locked on Izzy's. "Good idea, man. See you soon, okay?"

"You got it."

The door closed behind Will, and Trent met Izzy's beautiful but concerned gaze. Her study roamed his face. "Do you hurt?"

"A little."

She shook her head. "I was terrified, Trent." She inhaled. "I'm so glad you're okay, but listen to me. I can't—"

"Don't say it, Iz. Don't say you can't handle this. You're so much stronger than you give yourself credit for. Just think about how strong we're going to be together. Won't you allow yourself to do that? For me."

She squeezed her eyes shut. "I'm sorry. Please don't hate me. I love you, and..." She opened her eyes. "Being with you, spending time with you, has finally released me from the grief-ridden, self-imposed prison I was in, but this...this risk and danger...it's too much."

"I'm not letting you go, Iz. Not again."

He tried to move, but the searing pain through his ribs made his breath catch painfully in his lungs. He snapped his teeth together to trap his yell inside.

"Trent, don't move. Please. The last thing I want is to upset you when you're in so much pain, but it would be worse to lie—"

"Enough." He glared at her as frustration rolled through him on an irritated blend of helplessness and confusion. "Why fight what we have? We need to straighten this out between us once and for all, because we can't keep going on like this. I love you. Why can't that be enough?"

She stilled, the blush at her cheeks darkening as she stepped away from the bed. "You really don't know why love isn't enough for me?"

Trent searched his brain for some clue to what she was thinking and feeling, but nothing came forward, only the damn force of the headache currently drilling through his temples.

She pulled back her shoulders. "My parents love me, Trent. Robbie loved me. It isn't your love that has me backing away, it's the probability that you are one day going to be killed. It would be bad enough losing you as a friend, but as a lover? A husband? The father of my children?" She shook her head, tears rolling over her cheeks. "There's nothing to straighten out. You've had doubts for the same reasons."

"It's not that I doubt us."

"You've said *if* we work out. You told your mum you sometimes doubt I'm the right girl for you. Don't you think those thoughts are equally as important as my fear of you dying? We're too different. Too mismatched. Sure, we might be in love and have great, explosive, fantastic sex, but that *isn't* enough. Not by a long shot."

Trent swallowed against the pain burning around his heart that had nothing to do with his injuries. He couldn't deny her summary of what the last few weeks had been like for them. He couldn't take back his words or fears because they were still very much in the back of his mind. Yet still he couldn't shake his love for her. Not even a tiny bit of it.

He coughed. "Well, for one, I can't see how great sex isn't something worth holding on to." He wiggled his eyebrows in a futile attempt to banish her anger and make her smile. "Can you?"

"I'm not joking, Trent." The crack in her voice sent a splinter through his heart. She shook her head. "I can't keep doing this with you."

She moved away from the bed and picked up her purse from a chair in the corner of the room.

Come back to me, Iz. Don't leave me when I can't chase after you.

Her shoulders rose and then fell as she exhaled heavily into the silence. Seconds ticked by until, finally, she returned to the bed. She leaned over him and her soft, floral scent washed through his senses, making him inwardly curse to high heaven and back.

Gently, she kissed him on the mouth and stepped back. "I've wanted to be with you for so long, but held back for fear of certain heartbreak. Either from you being hurt in a fire, or the moment you realize how much I hanker for a quiet, family life, and instead, you walk away in pursuit of the next dose of danger or excitement."

He clenched his jaw. "I don't need danger or excitement anywhere else, because being with you gives me enough of both. I love you, Iz." He ran his gaze over her face as certainty of what had to happen, what needed to be sacrificed came upon him with ball-kicking clarity. "I want to be with you, and if that means—"

"Don't. Don't you dare say it." She squeezed her eyes shut. "I won't be the woman who took away your spontaneity, your job, your world." She opened her eyes and they shone with tears. "If you change any of those things for me, I'll end up hating myself and you'd eventually hate me too. That's something I could never live with."

"You're wrong." His frustration turned to anger. "Do you really love me, Iz? Forget everything you just said and answer the question. Do you love me?"

She stared, her gaze so soft he didn't need to hear her answer, but *she* did. She needed to hear it and own it.

"I love you, Trent." She inhaled a shaky breath and released it. "I think I have since the first day I saw you."

Hope and relief swelled inside him. “Good. So, if you want to leave the hospital, then go, but know this. The minute I’m out of this bed is the minute I come find you.”

She dipped her chin before turning and heading for the door. She paused with her hand on the handle. “Do you know what makes you even more of a stubborn pain in the ass?”

“What?”

She faced him. “That you know full well I’ll be back here every damn day until you’re able to walk out of here on your own.”

Trent smiled as the door whispered softly closed behind her.

CHAPTER NINETEEN

TRENT FOLLOWED—OR HOBBLED—out of the Coast Inn behind Izzy. A week had passed since he was released from the hospital and he could finally move without his cracked ribs yanking the breath from his body. November would soon become December, and along with the Christmas decorations that had begun to spring up all over town, so had his determination that eventually he and Izzy would find their way.

The only obstacle left to overcome was Izzy herself.

She turned to look at him in the dark parking lot, the chilly breeze causing her to tug her scarf over her jaw. "How are you feeling?"

Trent stared at her. She was his girl. His woman. His everything. The question was, would he ever be everything to her? "I'm all right."

She lifted an eyebrow. "Only all right? We've had a good day, haven't we?"

He smiled and took a step closer, every part

of him wanting to put his arms around her and pull her in close. He refrained or risked losing her completely. He had no real certainty she didn't still feel the same way she did when he'd been lying in the hospital. "It's been great. Never in a million years did I think I could convince you to stick by me all day."

She smiled, her blue eyes glistening in the lights coming through the bar windows. "Well, a day of me taking photos is pretty hard to resist. First on Clover Point, then the beach, Marian's and now here. The whole day has been great. Truly. Plus, the time I've been able to spend with my mum and dad straightening things out, of course. I've finally stopped beating myself up about the way I treated them. They love me and I love them. That's all I need. No more looking back."

He smiled. "You're happy, aren't you?"

She nodded. "I am. They're onboard about the gallery and they're sticking around for the foreseeable. It feels good to have them share in my life again. Fingers crossed..." She sighed. "They'll come to see the Cove for the fabulous place it is and stick around even longer than I dare to hope for."

"I'm happy for you, Iz. Really."

He cast his gaze over her face, committing her happy expression and dancing eyes to memory because after what he said next, Lord only knew when they'd get to talk this way again. "There's something I want to say. Something I tried to say at the hospital but you cut me off."

The light in her eyes dimmed and her smile faltered. "Trent, we've had a great day. Please don't spoil—"

"I'm not spoiling it. I'm hoping what I say will finish it perfectly." He shoved his hands in his pockets to stop from touching her and looked into the distance. "I love the Cove too, Iz." He shifted his gaze to hers. "I want to live here forever. Build my home here…my family."

She looked to her feet for a moment before lifting her eyes to his. "Me too."

He smiled, tentative hope speeding his heart. "Then I want you to hear me out, okay?"

The skin at her throat shifted as she swallowed. She opened her mouth as if to speak before snapping it shut and nodding.

Trent took a deep breath and fought the urge to at least take her hand. "I love you, Iz. I think I always will. So because of that love, I've decided to give up the firefighting. I've had a good run and done all I can to atone for what happened to Aimee. I'm tired. I don't want to do it anymore. I want to spend more time with family, friends…you."

"Trent…"

"Please. Let me finish. I need to say this and then I'll give you the space you've asked for."

It was difficult to tell in the semidarkness, and with her wrapped up in a coat and scarf, but he was certain she'd stilled as her face paled. Almost as if space from him was the last thing she really wanted. His heart kicked with longing for her, but neither of them could go on this way. It was make-or-break time.

He exhaled a shaky breath. "The explosion shocked me in a million different ways. I came too close to dying to ignore the signs. So I plan to quit the brigade as a crew member but, if they still want me, I'll stay on as a volunteer and train new candidates in between. It's what I want."

"But…" She gently took his hand. "Firefighting is your life. It's who you are."

"No. It's who I became after Aimee died. Believe it or not, I wanted to be a swimmer, a lifeguard, up until then."

She looked deep into his eyes, her gaze steady. "As long as you're saving somebody, right?"

He clenched his jaw. *You can't save me, Trent.* Her previous words to him echoed in his mind. "This isn't about saving people. It's about saving myself from a broken heart. I want to be with you, but until you truly believe it's for no other reason than the fact that I love you, I'm not going to bother you anymore. Do you still love me, Iz?"

"What?"

"It's a simple question. Yes or no?"

She eased her hand from his and crossed her arms, glancing toward the bar. "There's nothing simple about that question."

"Then take some time to think about it."

"I don't need any time." She faced him. "I love you. I have for four long years, but that doesn't mean I believe you're giving up firefighting for yourself, rather than for me."

"Fine. Then come find me when you do. I'll be waiting…however long."

"But—"

"No buts, Iz. This is the way it is."

He dropped his gaze to her mouth for one painful second, before leaning forward and brushing a soft kiss to her cheek. Briefly closing his eyes, he nodded before turning and walking away, his heart heavy with the sorrow he saw in her eyes and the horrible certainty in his heart that the woman he loved was so far from healing that she would never, ever be his to care for.

IZZY LIFTED ONE of her more recent photographs from the box on the gallery floor and held it aloft. She squinted, trying to see the image through a critical eye, rather than her own, which told her it was one of her best shots ever. Trent smiled back at her from the photograph, his brilliant green eyes happy and finally free of the bruising and red veins caused by the explosion. She fought her smile, but it was fruitless. He was and, she feared, always would be the most handsome, kind and caring man she'd ever met.

His white teeth gleamed, his strong forearms veined and wide as they rested on the top of one of the stiles leading from Clover Point down the incline toward Cowden Beach. The grass blew behind him, sending the shimmers of silver at their tips skimming along the surface to meet with the ocean's horizon in the distance.

He looked so wonderfully content.

Now Christmas was right around the corner and the sparkling lights and carols in every shop were layering sadness around Izzy's heart like the bricks of an igloo.

She so wanted to be with him, but the fear of fully loving him still scraped at her heart. She couldn't believe that he quit the fire brigade. In her heart of hearts she still feared he had done that for her, rather than himself.

Blinking back tears, Izzy carried the large framed picture of Trent toward one of the three white walls she intended to keep free to showcase her work.

She and Trent were in a state of separated limbo she'd instigated with her unerring inability to trust he wouldn't eventually leave her in some way. It didn't matter how many times she'd insisted he move on, forget her, he refused to do so while she was incapable of believing his gargantuan decision about his future. She wanted to. So much.

Izzy stared around the space that was now hers to do with what she wanted and smiled softly. Telling Richard Crawley she had decided to stay in Templeton was absolutely the right thing to do. Being in the Cove, the place she loved more than any other, and being able to manage an art gallery. A truly empty canvas to do with as she pleased.

Through her meetings with Jay this week, she'd discovered a flare for business she would never have explored if she had chosen the city over Templeton.

Moving across the gallery, she stared at three of her photographs she'd lined up against the wall, ready for hanging. All three shots were of the same panoramic view of Templeton's promenade. However, the first was taken before Robbie died, the second after and the third she'd taken just before her and Trent's final separation.

It would be impossible for anyone to look at the three pictures together and not see how the photographer's work had begun, changed and twisted through a darker period and then evolved into something entirely new today.

There could be little argument that the third was the brightest of the three. The images were physical evidence that she was happier with Trent than she had ever been in her life. What sort of person did that make her when her beloved brother lay dead? She pressed her hand to her stomach and turned away from the photographs.

The front door opened and the under floor sensor announced the visitor's arrival. Izzy turned.

Kerri Jackson came through the door pushing Maya in her wheelchair, the little girl's gorgeous face lit with happiness and a Santa hat on her head. "Hi, Izzy."

"Maya. How wonderful to see you." Izzy grinned, her melancholy thoughts vanishing as her heart swelled with fondness for this amazing, brave and beautiful little girl. "What are you doing here?"

"We came to see you. All my numbers added up, which means I can get out of the hospital for a little while with Mummy."

Izzy fought tears that held the possibility of a tsunami and snapped her gaze to Kerri. "Wow, that's fabulous news. How are you?"

"All the better for tracking you down." Kerri smiled. "All we need now is to find Trent and Maya will stop holding me captive."

Izzy stilled, her forced smile aching her cheekbones. "Trent?"

"Uh-huh." Maya sat forward in her chair and stretched her neck toward the back of the gallery. "Is he in the back somewhere? Mummy promised we could all go to the bakery by the beach. She wants tea and scones and I want tea and chocolate cake, but I'm not going unless you and Trent come too."

"He's…um…he's…" Izzy's cheeks burned and her stomach knotted with a horrible despair. "He's not here right now. I suspect he's working."

"At the station?" Maya's eyes widened with excitement. "Could we go see him?" She tipped her head toward Kerri. "Can we? Please?"

Kerri shifted her focus to Izzy, her brow furrowed. "Everything's okay between you and Trent, isn't it?"

"Sure." Izzy's cheeks burned hotter and she turned to walk behind her desk. Her saying Trent could be at work was a big fat lie. She had no idea where he'd be. Not anymore.

How was she supposed to face disappointing Maya by telling her about their separation? Clearly, the little girl viewed Izzy and Trent as the next William and Kate.

Izzy shuffled some papers on her desk. "I haven't seen him today, that's all."

"Call him."

Izzy looked up. "I really don't think..."

Her words trailed off. Maya's excited grin was so wide the tube across her face pushed upward to crinkle the skin around her eyes. She was so wonderful. Izzy's heart melted a little more.

"Please, Izzy. Trent likes me. He'll be happy I've come to see him."

Izzy exhaled and slumped. How on earth could she resist such a claim when what Maya said was 100 percent true? She raised her hands in surrender. "Okay, I'll call him right now. Why don't you and your mummy play with some of those toys over there in the corner? That's what I use when I photograph children to make them smile."

"Are they sick?"

Izzy's heart twisted. "Not always. No."

"Then they should always smile." Maya shrugged. "Come on, Mummy."

Izzy stared after Maya and Kerri as they headed toward the toys. Her heart beat faster as Maya pointed at and then clutched one soft toy after another her mother passed to her.

Life was cruel. Short. Unpredictable. Yet there were people like Maya, Trent, Bianca—Robbie's fiancée—and Trent's parents who didn't live in fear every day after losing so much. Instead, they pushed forward, faced their battles and strove to build better, bigger and happier lives.

Izzy swallowed as guilt and failure bore down on her. Was she really so weak that she'd never take another risk with her feelings for as long as she lived? Did she really want to be alone when there could be years of laughter and joy between the hard times?

She dragged her gaze from Maya and Kerri and pulled her phone from her jeans pocket. Her throat dried as adrenaline pumped through her. She dialed Trent's number.

He picked up on the second ring. "Iz? Hi."

Izzy closed her eyes. There was no mistaking the hope in his voice. "Hi. How are you?"

"All the better for hearing from you."

"Are you busy?" She grimaced. There was so much more she needed to say to him, so much more she had to confess and apologize for. "Only I've just had some visitors wander into the gallery."

"Visitors? I'm intrigued."

She smiled at the teasing in his voice. "Why don't you meet us at Marian's in twenty minutes?"

"Sure, if you can be trusted that I'm actually going to like these people."

"Oh, you'll like them."

"As much as I like you?"

Her stomach flip-flopped and she smiled. "Maybe."

"Right. Well, I'll see you soon, then."

"If you arrive before us, I have an order for tea and scones for two, tea and chocolate cake for one and whatever you fancy."

"Oh, you know what I fancy. See you soon, Iz."

The line went dead and Izzy ended the call before pressing the phone to her chest. She slowly exhaled in an effort to slow her racing heart. All these weeks had passed…could he still want to be with her?

Maya and Kerri laughed as they guided the toy bears and dolls through the air like airplanes, Maya screaming engine noises as loud as she could. The adoration, hope and love that shone in Kerri's gaze as she watched her daughter was undeniable, and the moment caught like a hook in Izzy's chest.

Right there. That was her lesson. Love. Everyone, everywhere, deserved love. No matter how short, how long, how deep or fragile. Everyone needed to give and receive love.

She released her held breath and planted on a smile. "So, who's ready for tea and chocolate cake?"

Maya stopped midroar and snapped her gaze to Izzy's, her eyes bright. "Is Trent coming?"

Izzy smiled, falling a little deeper in love. "He is. We'll meet him at Marian's, okay?"

"Okay." She held the toys toward Kerri. "Quick, Mummy. Trent's coming."

Laughing, Kerri took the toys and pressed a lingering kiss to the top of her daughter's head before carrying them back to their box. As she did, she looked at Izzy and mouthed a thank-you.

Izzy nodded and smiled as she tried to ignore the knot of nerves in her stomach. It was now or never for her and Trent. She just prayed she wasn't too late.

FIFTEEN MINUTES AFTER Izzy's call, Trent stood in line at Marian's counter. Every two seconds, he swung his gaze to the front window. He tapped his foot against the tiles. Izzy hadn't sounded that happy in so long. The habitual worry she'd held in her voice had gone and she'd even teased him…something that seemed impossible when he'd last seen her.

Oh, they'd laughed and talked then, but flirtation and teasing had been out of bounds. Any trying on his part was shot down by the wariness in Izzy's eyes.

"What can I get you, handsome?"

Marian's voice cut through his contemplation and Trent turned. He smiled. "Well, I'll have a mug of your finest ground coffee, if you don't mind."

"Coming right up." She frowned, her gaze darting over his face. "How are you feeling?"

"A darn sight better than I did a few weeks ago."

"Hmm, and what about the injuries I can't see?"

Trent swallowed and slid his gaze from Marian's toward the suddenly fascinating coffee machine behind her. "What do you mean?"

Silence.

He flicked his gaze back to hers. She stared at him, her brows raised and her eyes expectant. "Well?"

"Everything's fine. A-okay. Just fantastic."

Her usually sparkling brown eyes lost their shine as she narrowed them to slits. "Do you really want to go there? Or do you just want to be nice and cut to the chase? Where's Izzy these days?"

Trent briefly closed his eyes before opening them again. Everyone in the entire town knew only too well how dangerous it was to hold back with Marian. Give it up or else wait for her to torture the information out of you with the skullduggery of a Bond villain. Her methods were quick, sharp and, nine times out of ten, something all of her victims needed in order to reach their goals.

As much as everyone knew this about her, it didn't make it any less stressful when you were inside her radar.

"Fine." He leaned forward and gripped the counter. "Izzy's meeting me here any minute now."

"And?" She held his gaze, her focus resembling a cat bearing down on a mouse. "What then?"

"What do you mean?"

"Are you going to let her walk away again? What will this be? The third or fourth time?"

Ouch. He straightened. "Do you know something? It doesn't matter how much you think you're going to wear me down—"

The doorbell above the front door reverberated like the bell in a boxing match.

Marian snapped her gaze to the door, a huge smile brightening her face. Trent didn't need to turn around to know Izzy had entered.

Yet he did turn.

He sent up a silent thank-you to God that her gaze was turned away, allowing him a few seconds to look at her as she held the door open for Kerri and Maya Jackson to enter.

Izzy was dressed casually in dark blue skinny jeans that clung to her ass like a second skin. Trent followed the length of her legs down to the brown knee-high, high-heeled boots on her feet...and promptly swallowed his growl of lust as it rose in his throat. The whole ensemble was topped off with an open snow-white jacket and V-neck sweater that lifted to reveal an inch of flat stomach as she leaned over Maya's wheelchair to tickle the girl's chin.

The woman was cruel to come into the bakery looking so much more edible than anything Marian could whip up in her kitchen.

"Trent!"

He snapped his gaze to Maya and grinned. "Hey, it's my girlfriend. Why have you been holding out on me so long, huh?"

She giggled and Trent strolled toward them, pointedly winking at Izzy and hoping she understood the question was for her, not Maya. The answering blush at her cheeks and the way she moved so quickly to shut the door told him she'd received the message loud and clear.

Smiling, he nodded to Kerri Jackson before dropping to his haunches in front of Maya. "What are you doing out of the hospital? Did you escape? Hold everyone up at gunpoint? Tie up the nurses?"

Maya screamed with laughter and held out her arms. For a moment, Trent wasn't sure what the gesture meant, but a second look into her eyes had him standing up and leaning into her embrace and carefully wrapping his arms around Maya's too-thin body. Tears burned beneath his closed eyes as he cursed the world's problems and challenges.

Only when Maya released him did he stand back. "So, this is our very first date, right? What do you want? I can buy you everything on the menu."

She laughed and Trent took the wheelchair handles from Kerri and pushed Maya to the counter. For all his teasing with Maya, every nerve in his body was stretched with apprehension and hope. Izzy had called and asked him here, but was it purely for Maya, and despite the smile in Izzy's voice over the telephone, had anything really changed?

He reapproached the counter. "Marian, may I introduce Maya Jackson? The only girl for whom the entire Templeton firefighting crew was willing to pose and preen for a calendar."

"Well, hello there, lovely lady." Marian beamed, her brown eyes shining brighter than ever, her smile wide. "How are you?"

"Good, thank you. Trent wants to be my boyfriend, but I think Izzy loves him best."

Trent stilled…at least his body did. His heart danced the fandango.

Marian grinned and looked at Trent. "Smart cookie, isn't she?"

"One of the smartest." He cleared his throat. "How about a pot of tea and some scones for the ladies? And what would you like, Maya?"

"I want tea with the ladies too, but with cake, please. Chocolate cake."

Marian laughed. "I like a girl who knows what she wants. Why don't you join your mummy and Izzy over there in the corner and I'll bring everything to you in just a minute?"

Trent met Marian's knowing and laughing gaze before he turned and steered Maya toward the booth where Izzy and Kerri Jackson were quietly chatting.

The next hour passed with smiling laughter and Maya's steady stream of chatter, the perfect buffer to the tension emanating between him and Izzy. Every now and then, Trent purposely held her gaze until she looked away, her cheeks red and her eyes heartbreakingly happy. Deep in his heart, Trent hoped she was there because she wanted to be with him, but he daren't consider it until he heard confirmation from Izzy.

"Why don't we leave Trent and Izzy to finish their tea?" Kerri Jackson rose from the table, her gaze soft on Maya's. "We'll see if we can get some hot chocolate from the hut on the beach."

"Yay!" Maya slapped her hands on the arms of her chair. "Can I have cream?"

Trent smiled and slid his gaze to Izzy. Her gaze locked with his, and this time it was him who looked away. Her eyes were dark with desire and misted with a hint of promise.

Was this it? No more turning back or separation?

Maya and Kerri waved and left the bakery, calling out a goodbye to Marian as they reached the door. Trent watched them go, his heart pounding. Once the door closed behind them, he took a deep breath and faced Izzy.

"Hi." Her eyes were full of a quiet determination, a sense of self-assurance he hadn't seen for a long, long time.

He smiled. "Hi."

"So, I guess we need to get some things straightened out."

"I guess we do."

She moved forward to place her forearms on the table between them. She laced her fingers, and when he looked at her hands, the knuckles were white. Inhaling, he took a chance and reached out to cover her fingers with his own.

He waited as relief she didn't pull away pushed at his chest.

"Trent?"

"What?"

"I believe you."

His heart turned over. There it was. The one thing he'd ask her to say to him when she was ready to believe his love was never going to change, that he'd given up firefighting for himself rather than her…that she was ready to be with him. Forever. No doubts. No turning away. For either of them.

Shifting closer, he smoothed his hands up and down her forearms, looking deep into her eyes. "I believe in you too."

"I want to be with you. Always."

"Ditto."

Her smile faltered and a little of the light faded from her eyes. "But I only want you to give up firefighting if you're sure it's what you—"

"I already have."

The light reappeared in her eyes. "You have?"

He smiled. "Yes. With or without you, the explosion was a sign. I'm out, Iz. I don't want it anymore. I want you. I want a wedding. I want kids..." His stomach knotted. Was he saying too much? "What do you want?"

She grinned, tears glazing her eyes. "The same. Every single part of what you just said. I want it all."

Trent smiled, reveling in the quiet, fantastically beautiful sound of her laughter. Still holding one of her hands, he stood and came around the table to slide into her side of the booth. She inched toward him as he sat. Using his free hand, he brushed some of her hair from her eyes and took in the full beauty of a face he would never tire of watching.

"Do you want to go to bed?"

She laughed. "My word, you are so romantic."

He wiggled his eyebrows. "I know. That's why you love me."

Leaning in, he covered her mouth with his and she slid her hands onto his shoulders, pulling him closer. Their tongues tangled and he kissed her deeper, harder, letting every ounce of his love and admiration for her pour into her as he felt hers pour into him.

Neither of them moved away, stopped or even faltered in their kiss. Not even as the whole bakery burst into wolf whistles and applause.

* * * * *

Be sure to check out the other books in the TEMPLETON COVE STORIES *miniseries by Rachel Brimble*

FINDING JUSTICE
A MAN LIKE HIM
WHAT BELONGS TO HER
CHRISTMAS AT THE COVE
HER HOMETOWN REDEMPTION

All available now from Harlequin Superromance.

And look for the next Templeton Cove story, coming in 2017!